Bernard Capes (1854–1918) was a prolific Victorian author who published more than 40 books—romances, ghost stories, poetry and history—and won awards in England and America. He is best remembered as an accomplished writer of horror stories in the vein of M. R. James, and has the distinction of writing the first detective novel commissioned by Collins—*The Skeleton Key*, published in 1919, whose enormous success (eight different editions in ten years) paved the way for a century of successful crime fiction. It was his only crime book, as Capes died in the influenza epidemic on 2 November 1918 before *The Skeleton Key* was published. A plaque commemorating his life is in Winchester Cathedral, near where he lived.

By the same author

The Black Reaper

BERNARD CAPES

The Mystery of the Skeleton Key

WITH INTRODUCTIONS BY

G. K. CHESTERTON

AND HUGH LAMB

COLLINS
CRIME
CLUB

COLLINS CRIME CLUB

An imprint of HarperCollins*Publishers*
1 London Bridge Street
London SE1 9GF

available from the British Library

ISBN 978-0-00-833727-8

Printed and bound in Great Britain by CPI Group (UK) Ltd,
Croydon CRO 4YY

This book is produced from independently certified FSC™ paper
to ensure responsible forest management.

For more information visit: www.harpercollins.co.uk/green

INTRODUCTION

All authors, especially fiction writers, have to tread at some time on the edge of the dark slope that leads to obscurity. Some are unlucky enough to miss their step while still alive; many more slide down after their death. Such an unfortunate was Bernard Capes, who published 40 books (in 20 years) but passed into the shadows within three years of dying. He deserved better.

Bernard Edward Joseph Capes was born in London on 30 August 1854, a nephew of John Moore Capes, a prominent figure in the Oxford Movement. He was educated at Beaumont College and raised as a Catholic, though he later gave that up and followed no religion. His elder sister, Harriet Capes (1849–1936) was to become a noted translator and writer of children's books.

Capes had a string of unsuccessful jobs: A promised Army commission failed to materialise; he spent an unhappy time in a tea-broker's office; he studied art at the Slade School but, despite a lifelong enjoyment of painting and illustrating, it did not result in a career.

Things picked up for him in 1888 when he went to work for the publishers Eglington and Co., where he succeeded Clement Scott as editor of the magazine *The Theatre*.

At this point in his career, he made his first attempts at novel writing, publishing two under the pseudonym 'Bevis Cane': *The Haunted Tower* (1888) and *The Missing Man* (1889), the latter published by Eglington. They did not do well enough for him to use the 'Bevis Cane' name again.

Eglington and Co. went out of business in 1892 and Capes was up against it. Among his various ventures was a failed attempt at, of all things, breeding rabbits.

At last, aged 43, Capes found his true vocation. In 1897 he entered a competition for new authors organised by the *Chicago Record*. Capes came second with his novel *The Mill of Silence*, published in Chicago the same year.

He entered the competition again in 1898 when the *Chicago Record* repeated it. Capes hit the jackpot. His entry, *The Lake of Wine*—a long, macabre historical thriller about a fabulous ruby bearing the name of the book's title—won the competition. It was published that year and Capes was a full-time writer from then on.

And write he did. Out flooded short stories, articles, newspaper editorials, reviews and novels, including two more in 1898.

Bernard Capes married Rosalie Amos and they moved to Winchester, where he spent the rest of his life. They had three children. His son Renalt became a writer late in life, and his grandson Ian Burns carries on the Capes writing tradition as the author of the children's book *Scratcher*.

With nearly 40 books already to his name from a variety publishers, Capes' historical adventure, *Where England Sets Her Feet*, was published by William Collins Sons & Co. in April 1918, with a second book, *The Skeleton Key*, already under contract. The significance of this new 'criminal romance' to the 100-year-old publishing house was yet to be realised. Modestly publicised as '*a story dealing with crime committed in the grounds of a country house, and the subsequent efforts of a clever young detective to discover its perpetrator*', it coincided with a burgeoning post-war fashion for detective fiction. Within a few months of its publication in the spring of 1919, a flood of unsolicited crime-story manuscripts poured into the Scottish publishers' Pall Mall office, and Collins acted quickly to capitalise on this new-found demand for detective stories.

Sadly, Capes himself never knew of *The Skeleton Key*'s success, for he was struck down by the influenza epidemic that swept Europe at the end of World War I. A short illness was followed by heart failure and he died in Winchester on 1 November 1918. He was 64 and had enjoyed only 20 years of writing.

His widow organised a plaque for him in Winchester Cathedral, among the likes of Izaak Walton and Jane Austen. It can still be seen, next to the entrance to the crypt.

Capes wrote historical adventures and romances, mystery novels, crime stories and many fine short stories, a lot of them dark and sinister tales (he was quite fond of werewolves). As a great fan of Wagner, he wrote a novel, *The Romance of Lohengrin*, published in 1905. At his memorial service in the cathedral in 1919, the organist played Wagner in his honour.

Published shortly after Capes' death, complete with a hastily commissioned introduction by G. K. Chesterton that added to its notoriety, *The Skeleton Key* had already been reissued six times when, ten years later, Sir Godfrey Collins launched the company's first dedicated crime imprint, The Detective Story Club—'for detective connoisseurs'—a mixture of genre classics and cheap reprints. It was only natural that Capes' book should be one of the launch titles for the new list, and so in July 1929 it appeared in its eighth edition alongside five other titles, priced only sixpence, with a dramatic jacket painting and an extended title intended to increase further the book's popularity: *The Mystery of the Skeleton Key*.

By 1930, the 'Golden Age' of crime fiction was well underway, and Bernard Capes' novel began to disappear as more and more inventive detective stories appeared on the market. In his 1972 book, *Bloody Murder*, Julian Symons called *The Skeleton Key* 'a neglected *tour de force*', but it's only now, more than 40 years later, that Capes' landmark novel has found its way back into print.

The story introduces the detective Baron Le Sage, who unravels a rather complicated murder. Le Sage is in the line of Robert Barr's detective Eugene Valmont (who had appeared in 1906), and Agatha Christie's Hercule Poirot (who was yet to be created), with a touch of Dr Fell, and is one of Capes' most interesting creations. As one character remarks, 'Chess is the Baron's business.' He might have appeared again if Capes had survived longer. It's good to see him, and Bernard Capes, back at work again.

HUGH LAMB
February 2015

CONTENTS

INTRODUCTION

To introduce the last book by the late Bernard Capes is a sad sort of honour in more ways than one; for not only was his death untimely and unexpected, but he had a mind of that fertile type which must always leave behind it, with the finished life, a sense of unfinished labour. From the first his prose had a strong element of poetry, which an appreciative reader could feel even more, perhaps, when it refined a frankly modern and even melodramatic theme, like that of this mystery story, than when it gave dignity, as in *Our Lady of Darkness*, to more tragic or more historic things. It may seem a paradox to say that he was insufficiently appreciated because he did popular things well. But it is true to say that he always gave a touch of distinction to a detective story or a tale of adventure; and so gave it where it was not valued, because it was not expected. In a sense, in this department of his work at least, he carried on the tradition of the artistic conscience of Stevenson; the technical liberality of writing a penny-dreadful so as to make it worth a pound. In his short stories, as in his historical studies, he did indeed permit himself to be poetic in a more direct and serious fashion; but in his touch upon such tales as this the same truth may be traced. It is a good general rule that a poet can be known not only in his poems, but in the very titles of his poems. In the case of many works of Bernard Capes, *The Lake of Wine*, for instance, the title is itself a poem. And that case would alone illustrate what I mean about a certain transforming individual magic, with which he touched the mere melodrama of mere modernity. Numberless novels of crime have been concerned with a lost or stolen jewel; and *The Lake of Wine* was merely the name of a ruby. Yet even the name is original, exactly in the detail that is hardly ever original. Hundreds of such precious stones have been scattered through sensational fiction; and hundreds of them have been called 'The Sun of the Sultan' or 'The Eye of Vishnu' or 'The Star of Bengal'. But even in such a trifle as the choice of the title, an indescribable and individual fancy is felt; a sub-conscious dream of some sea like a sunset, red as blood and intoxicant as wine. This is but a small example; but the same element clings, as if unconsciously, to the course of the same story. Many another eighteenth century hero has ridden on a long road to a lonely house; but Bernard Capes, by something fine and personal in the treatment, does succeed in suggesting that at least along that particular road, to that particular house, no man had ever ridden before. We might put this truth flippantly, and therefore falsely, by saying he put superior work into inferior works. I should not admit the distinction; for I deny that there is necessarily anything inferior in sensationalism, when it can really awaken sensations. But the truer way of stating it would perhaps be this; that to a type of work which generally is, for him or anybody else, a work of invention, he always added at least one touch of imagination

The detective or mystery tale, in which this last book is an experiment, involves in itself a problem for the artist, as odd as any of the problems which it puts to the policeman. A detective story might well be in a special sense a spiritual tragedy; since it is a story in which even the moral sympathies may be in doubt. A police romance is almost the only romance in which the hero may turn out to be the villain, or the villain to be the hero. We know that Mr Osbaldistone's business has not been betrayed by his son Frank, though possibly by his nephew Rashleigh. We are quite sure that Colonel Newcome's company has not been conspired against by his son Clive, though possibly by his nephew Barnes. But there is a stage in a story like *The Moonstone*, when we are meant to suspect Franklin Blake the hero, as he is suspected by Rachel Verinder the heroine; there is a stage in Mr Bentley's *Trent's Last Case* when the figure of Mr Marlowe is as sinister as the figure of Mr Manderson. The obvious result of this technical trick is to make it impossible, or at least unfair, to comment, not only on the plot, but even on the characters; since each of the characters should be an unknown quantity. The Italians say that translation is treason; and here at least is a case where criticism is treason. I have too great a love or lust for the *roman policier* to spoil sport in so unsportsmanlike a fashion; but I cannot forbear to comment on the ingenious inspiration by which in this story, one of the characters contrives to remain really an unknown quantity, by a trick of verbal evasion, which he himself defends, half convincingly, as a scruple of verbal veracity. That is the quality of Bernard Capes' romances that remains in my own memory; a quality, as it were, too subtle for its own subject. Men may well go back to find the poems thus embedded in his prose.

G. K. Chesterton

Mrs Bernard Capes wishes to express her gratitude to Mr Chesterton for his appreciative introduction to her husband's last work, and to Mr A. K. Cook for his invaluable assistance in preparing it for the press.

Winchester.

CHAPTER I

MY FIRST MEETING WITH THE BARON

(From the late Mr Bickerdike's 'Apologia', found in manuscript)

SOME few years ago, in the month of September, I happened to be kicking my heels in Paris, awaiting the arrival there of my friend Hugo Kennett. We had both been due from the south, I from Vaucluse and Kennett from the Riviera, and the arrangement had been that we should meet together for a week in the capital before returning home. *Enfants perdus!* Kennett was never anything but unpunctual, and he failed to turn up to time, or anywhere near it, at the rendezvous. I was a trifle hipped, as I had come to the end of my circular notes, and had rather looked to him to help me through with a passing difficulty; but there was nothing for it but to wait philosophically on, and to get, pending his appearance, what enjoyment I could out of life. It was not very much. The Parisian may be a saving man, but Paris is no city to save in. It is surprising how dull an empty purse can make it. It had come to this after two days, either that I must shift my quarters from the Ritz into cheaper lodgings, or abandon my engagement altogether and go back alone.

One afternoon, aimless and thirsty, I turned into the Café l'Univers in the Place du Palais Royal, and sat down at one of the little tables under the awning where was a vacant chair. This is a busy spot, upon which many streets converge, and one may rest there idly and study an infinite variety of human types. There was a man seated not far from me, against the glass side of the verandah whose occupation caught my attention. He was making very rapidly in a minute-book pencil notes of all the conspicuous ladies' hats that passed him. It was extraordinary to observe the speed and fidelity with which he secured his transcripts. A few, apparently random, sweeps of the pencil in his thin nervous fingers, and there, in the flitting of a figure, was some unconscious head ravished of its most individual idea. It reminded me of the 'wig-snatching' of the eighteenth century; yet I could not but admire the dexterity of the thief, as, sitting behind him, I followed his skilful movements.

'A clever dog that, sir,' said a throaty voice beside me.

It came from a near neighbour, whom I had not much observed until now—a large-faced, clean-shaved gentleman of a very full body and a comfortable complacent expression. He was dressed in a baggy light-grey suit, wore a loose Panama hat on his head, and smelt, pleasantly and cleanly, of snuff. On the table before him stood a tumbler of grenadine and soda stuffed with lumps of ice, and with a couple of straws sticking from it.

'Most,' I answered. 'What would you take him to be?'

'Eh?' said the stranger. 'Without prejudice, now, a milliner's pander—will that do?'

I thought it an admissible term, and said so, adding, 'or a fashion-plate artist?'

'Surely,' replied the stranger. 'A distinction without a difference, is it not?'

No more was said for the moment, while I sat covertly studying the speaker. He reminded me a little of the portraits of Thiers, only without the spectacles. A placid, well-nourished benevolence had been his prominent feature, were it not somehow for the qualification of the eyes. Those were as perpetually alert, busy, observant, as the rest was seemingly supine. They appeared to 'peck' for interests among the moving throng, as a hen pecks for scattered grain.

'Wonderful hands,' he said suddenly, coming back to the artist. 'Do you notice anything characteristic about them now?'

'No,' I said. 'What?'

He did not answer, but applied for a refreshing moment or two to his grenadine.

'Ah!' he said, leaning back again, with a relishing motion of his lips. 'A comfortable seat and a cool glass, and we have here the best café-chantant in the world.'

'Well, it suits me,' I agreed—'to pass the time.'

'Ah!' he said, 'your friend is unpunctual?'

I yawned inexcusably.

'He always is. What would you think of an appointment, sir, three days overdue?'

'I should think of it with philosophy, having the Ritz cuisine and cellar to fall back upon.'

I turned to him interestedly, my hands behind my head.

'You have?'

'No, but you,' said he.

I was a bit puzzled and amused; but curious, too.

'You are not staying at the Ritz?' I asked. He shook his head good-humouredly. 'Then how do you know I am?'

'There is not much mystery in that,' said he. 'You happened to be standing on the steps when I happened to be passing. The rest you have admitted.'

'And among all these'—I waved my hand comprehensively—'you could remember me from that one glimpse?'

He laughed, but again ignored my question.

'How did you know,' I persisted, 'that my friend was a man?'

'You yourself,' said he, 'supplied the gender.'

'But not in the first instance.'

'No, not in the first instance,' he agreed, and said no more.

'You don't like the Ritz?' I asked after an interval, just to talk and be talked to. I was horribly bored, that is the truth, by my own society; and here was at least a compatriot to share some of its burden with me.

'I never said so,' he answered. 'But I confess it is too sumptuous for me. I lodge at the Hôtel Montesquieu, if you would know.'

'Where is that, may I ask?'

'It is in the Rue Montesquieu, but a step from here.'

'I should like, if you don't mind, to hear something of it. I am at the Ritz, true, but in a furiously economical mood.'

'Certainly,' he answered, with perfect good-humour. 'It would not suit all people; it does not even figure in the guides; but for those of an unexacting disposition—well it might serve—to pass the time. You can have your good bedroom there and your adequate *petit déjeuner*—nothing more. For meals, there is a Duval's across the road, or, more particularly, the Restaurant au Boeuf à la mode in the Rue de Valois close by, where such delicacies may be tasted as *sole à la Russe*, or *noisettes d'agneau à la Réjane*. Try it.'

I was half thinking I would, and wondering how I could express my sense of obligation to my new acquaintance, when a sudden crash and scream in the road brought us both to our feet. The hat-sketcher, having finished with his task and gone, had stepped thoughtlessly off the kerb right under the shafts of a passing cab.

For a tranquil body, my companion showed the most curious excitement over the accident. Uttering broken exclamations of reproof and concern, he hurried down, as fast as his bulk would permit him, to the scene of the mishap, about which a crowd was already swarming. I could see little of what followed; but, the press after a time dispersing, I made shift to inquire of an onlooker as to the nature of the victim's hurt, and was told that the man had been taken off to the St Antoine Hospital in the very cab which had run him down, my friend of the Panama hat accompanying him. And so there for the moment our acquaintance ended.

But we met again at the Montesquieu—whither I had actually transferred my quarters in the interval—a day or two later.

He came down into the hall just as I had entered it from the street, and greeted me and pressed my arm paternally.

'But this will not do at all,' he said. 'This will not do at all,' and summoned the hôtelier from his little dark room off the passage.

'I am sorry, Monsieur,' he said, when the bowing goodman appeared, 'to find such scant respect paid to my recommendation. If this is the treatment accorded to my patronage, I must convey it elsewhere.'

The proprietor was quite amazed, shocked, confounded. What had he done to merit this severe castigation from M. Le Sage? If M. le Baron would but condescend to particularise his offence, the resources of his establishment were at M. le Baron's command to remedy it.

'That is easily specified,' was M. le Baron's answer. 'I sing the modest praises of your hotel to my friend, Mr Bickerdike; on the strength of these my friend decides to give you a trial. What is the result? You put him into number 19, where the aspect is gloomy, where the paper peels off the wall; where to my certain suspicion there are bugs.'

I laughed, not quite liking this appropriation, but the landlord was profuse in his apologies. Not for a moment had he guessed that I was a friend of M. le Baron Le Sage; I had not informed him of the fact; it was a mere question of expediency: Number 19 happened to be the only room vacant at the moment; but since—in short, I was transferred straightway to a very good *appartement* in the front, where were ample space and comfort, and a powder-closet to poke my head into if I wished, and invoke the ghosts of the dead lords of Montesquieu, whose Hôtel this had once been.

Now I should have been grateful for M. le Baron's friendly offices, and I hope I was, but with a dash of reservation. I did not know what to make of him, in fact, and the uncertainty kept me on my guard. Nor was I the more reassured upon his commiserating me presently on the fact of my friend, Mr Kennett, not having yet turned up. So he had found out my friend's name? That might be possible through an inquiry at the Ritz, where Kennett was expected. But why was he interested in inquiring at all? Then, as to my own name; he might have ascertained that, of course, of my present landlord—a pardonable curiosity, only somehow coloured by his unauthorised examination of my room. What had he wanted in there in. the first instance? On the other hand, he was evidently held, for whatever reason, in high respect by the proprietor; and if the reason itself was to seek for me, I had certainly no grounds for suspecting its adequate claims. He *appeared* to be a man of education and some distinction, not to speak of his title, which, however, might be territorial and of small account. And, assuredly, he did not seem French, unless by deliberate adoption. His speech, appearance, habit of mind, were all as English as the shoes he wore on his feet.

I asked him, on that day of his service to me, how it had gone with the poor hat-sketcher whom, I had understood, he had accompanied to the hospital. He seemed to regard my question as if for a moment it puzzled him, and then he answered:

'O, the artist! O, yes, to be sure. I accompanied him, did I? Yes, yes. An old house this, Mr Bickerdike—a fragment of old Paris. If there is nothing more I can do for you, I think I will be going.'

So it always was on the few further occasions which brought us together. He could not, or would not, answer a direct question directly; he seemed to love secrecy and evasion for their own sake, and for the opportunity they gave him for springing some valueless surprises on the unsuspecting. Well, he should not have his little vanity for me. There is nothing so tiresome as that habit of meaningless reserve, of hoarding information which there can be no possible objection to disseminating; but some people seem to have it. I responded by asking no more questions of M. le Baron, and I only hope my incuriosity disappointed him. The next day, or the day after, Kennett turned up, and I left the Montesquieu for my original quarters.

CHAPTER II

MY SECOND MEETING WITH THE BARON

(*From Mr Bickerdike's Manuscript*)

It might have been somewhere near the anniversary of my first meeting with the Baron when I came upon him again—in London this time. I had been lunching at Simpson's in the Strand, and, my meal finished, had gone up into the smoking-room for a coffee and liqueur. This is a famous corner of a famous caravansary, being dedicate, like no other smoking-room I know, to the service of the most ancient and most royal game of chess, many of whose leading professors forgather therein, as it were, in an informal club, for the mixed purposes of sociability and play. There one may watch astounding mental conflicts which leave one's brain in a whirl; or, if one prefers it, may oneself join issue in a duel, whether for glory or profit; or, better still, like Gargantua, having a friend for adversary, for the mere serious diversion of the game, and for its capacity for giving a rare meditative flavour to one's tobacco. The room, too, for such a haunt of gravity, is a cheerful room, with its large window overlooking the Strand, and one may spend a postprandial hour there very agreeably, and eke very gainfully if one takes an idler's interest in other people's problems. That I may confess I do, wherefore Simpson's is, or was, a fairly frequent resort of mine.

Now, on this occasion I had hardly entered the room when my eyes fell on the figure of M. le Baron sitting profoundly absorbed over a game with one in whom I recognised a leading master in the craft. I knew my friend at once, as how could I fail to, for he sat before me in every detail the stranger of the Café l'Univers—bland, roomy, self-possessed, and unchanged as to his garb. I would not venture to break into his preoccupation, but passed him by and took a convenient seat in the window.

'Stothard has found his match,' remarked a casual acquaintance who lounged near me, nodding his head towards the pair.

'Who is it?' I asked. 'Do you know?

'I know his name,' was the answer, 'Le Sage, an out-of-pocket French Baron; but that's all.'

'O! out of pocket, is he?'

'I've no right to say it, perhaps, but I only surmise—he'll play you for a half-crown at any time, if you're rash enough to venture. He plays a wonderful game.'

'Is he new to the place?'

'O, no! I've seen him here frequently, though at long intervals.'

'Well, I think I'll go and watch them.'

Their table was against the wall, opposite the window. One or two devotees were already established behind the players, mutely following the moves. I took up a position near Le Sage, but out of his range of vision. He had never, to my knowledge, so much as raised his face since I entered the room; intent on his game, he appeared oblivious to all about him. Yet the moment I came to a stand, his voice, and only his voice, accosted me—

'Mr Bickerdike? How do you do, sir?'

I confess I was startled. After all, there was something disconcerting about this surprise trick of his. It was just a practised pose, of course; still, one could not help feeling, and resenting in it, that impression of the preternatural it was no doubt his desire to convey. I responded, with some commonplace acknowledgment, to the back of his head, and no more was spoken for the moment. Almost immediately the game came to an end. M. le Baron sat back in his chair with a 'My mate, I think?'—a claim in which his opponent acquiesced. Half the pieces were still on the board, but that made no difference. Your supreme chess expert will foresee, at a certain point in the contest, all the possible moves to come or to be countered, and will accept without dispute the inevitable issue. The great man Stothard was beaten, and acknowledged it.

M. le Baron rose from his seat, and turned on me with a beaming face.

'Happy to renew your acquaintance, Mr Bickerdike,' he said. 'You are a student of the game?'

'Not much better, I think,' I answered. 'I am still in my novitiate.'

'You would not care—?'

'O, no, I thank you! I'm not gull enough to invite my own plucking.'

It was a verbal stumble rather than a designed impertinence on my part, and I winced over my own rudeness the moment it was uttered, the more so for the composure with which it was received.

'No, that would be foolish, indeed,' said M. le Baron.

I floundered in a silly attempt to right myself.

'I mean—I only meant I'm just a rotten muff at the game, while you—' I stuck, at a loss.

'While I,' he said with a smile, 'have just, like David, brought down the giant Stothard with a lucky shot.'

He touched my arm in token of the larger tolerance; and, in some confusion, I made a movement as of invitation, towards the table in the window.

'I am obliged,' he said, 'but I have this moment recalled an appointment.' 'So,' I thought, 'in inventing a pretext for declining, he administers a gentle rebuke to my cubbishness.' 'You found your friend, I hope,' he asked, 'when you left the Montesquieu on 'that occasion?'

'Kennett? Yes,' I answered; and added, moved to some expiatory frankness; 'it is odd, by the by, M. le Baron, that our second meeting should associate itself with the same friend. I am going down tomorrow, as it happens, on a visit to his people.'

'No,' he said: 'really? That is odd, indeed.'

He shook hands with me, and left the room. Standing at the window a moment after, I saw him going City-wards along the Strand, looking, with his short thick legs and tailed morning coat, for all the world like a fat jaunty turtle on its way to Birch's.

Now I fancied I *had* seen the last of the man; but I was curiously mistaken. When I arrived at Waterloo Station the next day, there, rather to my stupefaction, he stood as if awaiting me, and at the barrier—*my* barrier—leading to the platform for *my* train, the two o'clock Bournemouth express. We passed through almost together.

'Hullo!' I said. 'Going south?'

He nodded genially. 'I thought, with your permission, we might be travelling companions.'

'With pleasure, of course. But I go no further than the first stop—Winton.'

'Nor I.'

'O, indeed? A delectable old city. You are putting up there?'

'No, O no! My destination, like yours, is Wildshott.'

'Wildshott! You know the Kennetts then?'

'I know Sir Calvin. His son, your friend, I have never met. It is odd, as you said, that our visits should coincide.'

'But you must have known yesterday—if you did not know in Paris. Why in the name of goodness did you not—' I began; and came to a rather petulant stop. This secrecy was simply intolerable. One was pulled up by it at every turn.

'Did I not?' he said blandly. 'No, now I come to think of it— O, Louis, is that an empty compartment? Put the rugs in, then, and the papers.'

He addressed a little vivid-eyed French valet, who stood awaiting his coming at an opened door of a carriage. Le Sage climbed in with a breathing effort, and I followed sulkily. Who on earth, or what on earth, was the man? Nothing more nor less than what he appeared to be, he might have protested. After all, not himself, but common gossip, had charged him with necessitousness. He might be as rich as Croesus, for all I knew or he was likely to say. Neediness was not wont to valet it, though insolvency very well might. But he was a friend of Sir Calvin, a most exclusive old Bashaw; and, again, he was said to play chess for half-crowns. O! it was no good worrying: I should find out all about him at Wildshott. With a grunt of resignation I sank into the cushions, and resolutely put the problem from me.

But the fellow was an engaging comrade for a journey—I will admit so much. He was observant, amusing, he had a fund of good tales at his command, and his voice, without unpleasant stress; was softly penetrative. Adapted to anecdote, moreover, his habit of secrecy, of non-committal, made for a sort of ghostly humour which was as titillating as it was elusive; and the faint aroma of snuff, which was never absent from him, seemed somehow the appropriate atmosphere for such airy quibbles. It surrounded him like an aura—not disagreeably; was associated with him at all times—as one associates certain perfumes with certain women—a particular snuff, Macuba I think it is called, a very delicate brand. So he is always recalled to me, himself and his rappee inseparable.

CHAPTER III

WILDSHOTT

WILDSHOTT, the Hampshire seat of the Kennetts, stands off the Winton-Sarum road, at a distance of some six miles from the former, and some three and a half from the sporting town of Longbridge, on the way to the latter. The house is lonely situated in wild but beautiful country, lying as it does in the trough of the great downs whose summits hereabouts command some of the most spacious views in the County. A mile north-east, footing a gentle incline, shelters the village of Leighway; less than a mile away, in a hollow of the main road, stands a wayside tavern called the Bit and Halter; and, with these two exceptions, no nearer neighbour has Wildshott than the tiny Red Deer inn, which perches on a high lift of the downs a mile and a half distant, rising north.

The stately, wrought-iron gates of Wildshott open from the main road. Thence a drive of considerable extent reaches to the house, which is a rectangular red-brick Jacobean structure, with stone string-courses and a fine porch, having a great shell over it. There are good stables contiguous, and the grounds about are ample and well timbered—almost too well timbered, it might be thought by some people, since the closeness of the foliage gives an effect of gloom and solemnity to a building which, amid freer surroundings, should have nothing but grace and frankness to recommend it. But settled as it is in the wash of the hills, with their moisture draining down upon it, growth and greenness have become a tradition of its life, and as such not to be irreverently handled by succeeding generations of Kennetts.

All down the west boundary of the upper estate—which, to its northernmost limit, breaks upon that bare hill on whose summit, at closer range now, the little Red Deer inn sits solitary—runs a wide fringe of beech-wood, which is continued to the high road, and thence, on the further side, dispersed among the miscellaneous plantations which are there situated. The highway itself roughly bisects the property—the best of whose grass and arable lands are contained in the southern division—and can be reached from the house, if one likes, through the long beech-thicket by way of a narrow path, which, entering near the stables, runs as far as the containing hedge, in which, at some fifty yards from the main entrance, is a private wicket, leading down by a couple of steps to the road. This path is known, through some superstitious association, as the Bishop's Walk, and is little used at any time, the fact that it offers a short cut from the house to the lower estate being regarded, perhaps, as inadequate compensation for its solitariness, its dankness, and the glooms of the packed foliage through which it penetrates. Opposite the wicket, across the road, an ordinary bar-gate gives upon a corresponding track, driven through the thick of a dense coppice, which, at a depth of some two hundred feet, ends in the open fields. It is useful to bear in mind these local features, in view of the event which came presently to give them a tragic notoriety.

At Winton a wagonette met the two gentlemen, and they were landed at Wildshott soon after four o'clock. Bickerdike was interested to discover that they were the only guests. He was not surprised for himself, since he and Hugo Kennett were on terms of unceremonial intimacy. He *did* wonder a little what qualities he and the Baron could be thought to possess in common that they should have been chosen together for so exclusive an invitation. But no doubt it was pure accident; and in any case there was his friend to explain. He was a bit down in the mouth, was Hugo—for any reason, or no reason, or the devil of a reason; never mind what—and old Viv was always a tower of strength to him in his moods—hence old Viv's citation to come and 'buck' his friend, and incidentally to enjoy a few days' shooting, which accounted for one half of the coincidence. Old Viv accepted his part philosophically; it was not the first time he had been called upon to play it with this up and down young officer, whose temporal senior he was by some six years, and whose elder, in all questions of sapience and self-sufficiency, he might have been by fifty. He did not ask what was the matter, but he said 'all right', as if all right were all reassurance, and gave a little nod to settle the matter. He had a well-looking, rather judicial face, clean shaven, a prim mouth, a somewhat naked head for a man of thirty, and he wore eyeglasses on a neatly turned nose, with a considerable prominence of the organ of eventuality above it. The complacent bachelor was writ plain in his every line. And then he inquired regarding the Baron.

'O! I know very little about him,' was young Kennett's answer. 'I believe the governor picked him up in Paris originally, but how or where I can't say. He's a marvel at chess; and you remember that's the old man's obsession. They're at it eternally while he's down here.'

'This isn't his first visit then?'

'No, I believe not; but it's the first time I've seen him. I'm quoting Audrey for the chess. Why, what's the matter? Is anything wrong with him?'

'There you go, you rabbit! Who said anything was wrong with him? I've met him before, that's all.'

'Have you? Where?'

'Why, in Paris. You remember the Montesquieu, and my French Baron?'

'I remember there *was* a Baron. I don't think you ever told me his name.'

'Well, it was Le Sage, and this is the man.'

'Is it? That's rather queer.'

'What is?'

'The coincidence of your meeting again like this.'

'O, as to that, coincidence, you know, is only queer till you have traced back its clues and found it inevitable.'

'Well, that's true. You can trace it in his case to the governor's being down with the gout again, and confined to the house, and wanting something and somebody to distract him.'

'There you are, you see. He thought of chess, and thought of this Le Sage, and wrote up to him on the chance. Your father probably knows more about his movements than we do. So we're both accounted for. No, what *is* queer to me is the man's confounded habit of secrecy. Why didn't he say, when I met him in Paris, that the friend I was waiting for was known to him? Why didn't he admit yesterday, admit until we actually met on the platform today, that we were bound for the same place? I hate a stupidly reticent man.'

Kennett laughed, and then frowned, and turned away to chalk his cue. The two men were in the billiard-room, playing a hundred up before dinner.

'Well,' he said, stooping to a losing hazard, 'I hope a fellow may be a good fellow, and yet not tell all that's in him.'

'Of course he may,' answered Bickerdike. 'Le Sage, I'm sure, is a very good fellow, a very decent old boy, and rare company when he chooses—I can answer for that. But there's a difference between telling all that's in one and not telling anything.'

'Well, perhaps he thinks,' said the other impatiently, 'that if he once opened the sluice he'd drain the dammed river. Do let him alone and attend to the game.'

Bickerdike responded, unruffled. He had found his friend in a curiously touchy state—irritable, and nervous, and moody. He had known him to be so before, though never, perhaps, so conspicuously. Hugo was temperamentally high-strung, and always subject to alternations of excitement and despondence; but he had not yet exhibited so unbalanced a temper as he seemed inclined to display on this occasion. He was wild, reckless, dejected, but seldom normal, appearing possessed by a spirit which in turns exalted or depressed him. What was wrong with the boy? His friend, covertly pondering the handsome young figure, found sufficient solution in the commonplace. He was in one of his nervous phases, that was all. They would afflict men subject to them at any odd time, and without apparent provocation. It was one of the mysteries of our organic being—a question of misfit somewhere between spirit and matter. No one looking at the young soldier would have thought him anything but a typical example of his kind—constitutionally flawless, mentally insensitive. He belonged to a crack regiment, and was popular in it; was tall, shapely-built, attractive, with a rather girlish complexion and umber-gold hair—a ladies' man, a pattern military man, everything nice. And yet that demon of nerve worked in him to his perfection's undoing. Perhaps it was the prick of conscience, like a shifting grit in one's shoe, now here, now there, now gone—for the boy had quite fine impulses for a spoilt boy, a spoilt child of Fortune—and spoilt, like Byron by his mother, in the ruinous way. His father, the General, alternately indulgent and tyrannical, was the worst of parents for him; he had lost his mother long ago; his one sister, flippant, independent—undervalued, it may be, and conscious of it—offered no adequate substitute for that departed influence. And so the good in Hugo was to his own credit, and stood perhaps for more than it might have in another man.

His father, Sir Calvin—he had got his K.C.B., by the way, after Tel-el-Kebir in '82, in reward for some signal feat of arms, and at the expense of his trigger-finger—was as proud as sin of his comely lad, and blind to all faults in him which did not turn upon opposition to himself. He designed great connexions for the young man, and humoured his own selfishness in the prospect. He was a martinet of fifty-five, with a fine surface polish and a heart of teak beneath it, a patrician of the Claudian breed, irascible, much subject to gout for his past misdeeds, and an ardent devotee of the game of chess, at which he could hold his own with some of the professed masters. It was that devotion which had brought him fortuitously acquainted with the French Baron—a sort of technical friendship, it might be called—and which had procured the latter an occasional invitation of late to Wildshott. Le Sage came for chess, but he proved very welcome for himself. There was a sort of soothing tolerance about him, the well-informed urbanity of a polished man of the world, which was as good as a lenitive to the splenetic invalid. But nobody, unless it were Sir Calvin himself, appeared to know anything concerning him; whether he were rich or indigent; what, if dependent on his wits, he did for a living; what was the meaning or value of his title in an Englishman, if English he were; whether, in short, he were a shady Baron of the *chevalier d' industrie* order, or a reputable Baron, with only some eccentricities to mark him out from the common. One of these, not necessarily questionable, was his sly incommunicativeness; another was his fondness for half-crowns. He invariably, whether with Sir Calvin or others, made that stake, no more and no less, a condition of his playing at all, and for the most part he carried it off. Vivian Bickerdike soon learned all that there was to be told about him, and he was puzzled and interested—'intrigued', as they would say in the horrible modern phrase. But being a young man of caution, in addition to great native curiosity, he kept his wits active, and his suspicions, if he had any, close.

The game proceeded—badly enough on the part of Hugo, who was generally a skilful player. He fouled or missed so many shots that his form presently became a scandal. 'Phew!' whistled his opponent, after a peculiarly villainous attempt; 'what's gone wrong with you?'

The young man laughed vexedly; then, in a sudden transition to violence, threw his cue from him so that it clattered on the floor.

'I can't play for nuts,' he said. 'You must get somebody else.'

'Hugh,' said his friend, after a moment or two of silence, 'there's something weighing on your mind.'

'Is there?' cried the other jeeringly. 'I wonder.'

'What is it? You needn't tell me.'

'O! thank you for that. I tell you what, Viv: I dreamed last night I was sitting on a barrel of gunpowder and smoking a cigarette, and the sparks dropped all about. Didn't I? That's what I feel, anyhow. Nerves, all nerves, my boy. O! shut up that long mug, and talk of something else. I told you I was off colour when I wrote.'

'I know you did, and I came down.'

'Good man. You'll be in at the kill. There's going to be a most infernal explosion—pyrotechnics galore. Or isn't there? Never mind.'

He appeared to Bickerdike to be in an extraordinary state, verging on the hysterical. But no more was said, and in a few moments they parted to dress for dinner.

M. le Baron, coming up to his room about the same time and for the same purpose, was witness of a little stage comedy, which, being for all his bulk a light treader, he surprised. The actors were his valet Louis and an under-housemaid, the latter of whom was at the moment depositing a can of hot water in the washing basin. He saw the lithe, susceptible little Gascon steal from his task of laying ready his master's dress clothes, saw him stalk his quarry like a cat, pounce, enfold the jimp waist, heard the startled squeal that followed, a smack like a hundred kisses, a spitting *sacré chein!* from the discomfited assailant, as he staggered back with a face of fury and a hand held to his ear, and, seeing, stood to await the upshot, a questioning smile upon his lips. Both parties realised his presence at the same instant, and checked the issue of hot words which was beginning to join between them. The girl, giving a defiant toss to her chin, hurried past Le Sage and out of the room; M. Louis Cabanis returned to his business with the expression of a robbed wild-cat.

Le Sage said nothing until he was being presently helped on with his coat, and then suddenly challenging the valet, eye to eye, he nodded, and congratulated him:

'That is better, my friend. It is not logical, you know, for the injurer to nurse the grievance.'

The Gascon looked at his master gravely.

'Will you tell me who is the injurer, Monsieur?'

'Surely,' answered Le Sage, 'it cannot be she, in these first few hours of your acquaintance?'

'But if she had appeared to encourage me, Monsieur?'

The Baron laughed.

'The only appearance to be trusted in a pretty woman, Louis, is her prettiness.'

'Monsieur, is her ravishing loveliness.'

'Well, well, Louis, as you will. Only bear it no grudge.'

He turned away from a parting keen scrutiny of the dark, handsome face, and left the room, softly carolling. The little episode had amused rather than surprised him. Certainly it had seemed to point, in respect of time, to a quite record enslavement on the Gascon's part; but then the provocation to that passionate impressionable nature! For the girl had been really amazingly pretty, with that cast of feature, that Hebe-like beauty of hair and eye and complexion about whose fascination no two properly constituted minds could disagree. She was a domestic servant—and she was a young morning goddess, fresh from the unsullied dawn of Nature, a Psyche, a butterfly, a Cressid like enough. 'If I were younger,' thought Le Sage, 'even I!' and he carolled as he went down to dinner.

CHAPTER IV

I AM INTERESTED IN THE BARON

(From the Bickerdike MS.)

I SEEMED conscious somehow, at dinner on the night of our arrival, of a feeling of electricity in the domestic atmosphere. Having no clue, such as the later course of events came to supply, to its origin, I diagnosed it, simply and vulgarly, as the vibrations from a family jar, of the sort to which even the most dignified and well-regulated households cannot always rise superior. Sir Calvin himself, exacting and domineering, could never at the best of times be considered a tactful autocrat: a prey to his hereditary foe, he appeared often to go out of his way to be thought detestable. When such was the case, his habit of harping on grievances could become an exquisite torture, his propensity for persisting in the unwelcome the more he saw it resented a pure malignancy. On this occasion, observing an obvious inclination in his son, my friend, to silence and self-obliteration, he took pleasure in drawing him out, with something of the savagery, I could not but think, of a fisherman who wrenches an obstinate hermit crab from its borrowed shell for bait. I saw how poor Hugh was rasped and goaded, but could do no more than take upon myself, where I could, the burden of response. Believing at the time that this aggravated fencing between the two was a part, or consequence, of some trouble, the serious nature of which might or might not have been implied in my friend's recent outburst, I made and could make but an inefficient second; yet, even had I known, as I came to know, that my surmise was wrong, and that the father's persistence was due to nothing but a perverse devil of teasing, it is not clear to me how else I could have helped the situation. I could not have hauled my host by the ears, as I should have liked to do, over his own dining-room table.

But the sense of atmospheric friction was not confined to these two. In some extraordinary way it communicated itself to the servants, the very butler, our young hostess. I had not seen Audrey at tea, and now greeted her for the first time. She came in late, to find us, by the Bashaw's directions, already seated, and to suffer a sharp reprimand for her unpunctuality which brought a flush to her young rebellious cheek. Nor did I better things, so far as she was concerned, by an ostentatious display of attentions; she seemed to resent my sympathy even more than the harshness which had provoked it. It is the way of cats and women to tear the hand that would release them from the trap.

The dinner, in short, began very uncomfortably, with an irascible host, a moody son, and an offended daughter, the butler taking his cue from his master, and the servants from the butler. They waited nervously, and got in one another's way, only the more flurriedly for their whispered harrying by the exacerbated Cleghorn. I was surprised, I confess, by the change in that usually immaculate dignitary. The very type and pattern of his kind, correct, imperturbable, pontifical, I had never before known Cleghorn to manifest the least sign of human emotion, unless it were when Mr Yockney, the curate from Leighway, had mixed water with his *Château Margaux* 1907. Now, preposterous as it appeared, I could have believed the great man had been crying. His globous eyes, his mottled cheeks, bore suspicious evidences of the fact; his very side-whiskers looked limp. Surely the domestic storm, if such, which had rocked the house of Kennett must have been demoralising to a hitherto unknown degree.

It was the Baron who redeemed the situation, winning harmony out of discord. He had, to do him justice, the reconciliatory faculty, chiefly, I think, because he could always find, as one should, a bright interest in differences of opinion instead of a subject for contention. I never knew him, then or thereafter, to be ruffled by opposition or contradiction. He accepted them placidly, as constituting possible rectifications of his own argumentative frontiers.

His opportunity came with a growl of Sir Calvin's over the lateness of the evening papers. The General had been particularly curious to hear the result of a local trial, known as the Antonferry Bank robbery case, which was just reaching its conclusion, and it chafed him to be kept waiting. Le Sage asked for information, and the supplying it smoothed the troubled waters. There is a relish for most people in being the first to announce news, whether good, bad, or indifferent.

The case, as stated, was remarkable for nothing but the skill with which it had been unravelled. A Bank in Antonferry—a considerable market town lying some eight or nine miles north of Wildshott—had been robbed, and the question was by whom. That question had been answered in the upshot by an astute Scotland Yard detective, who, in spite of the obloquy thrown upon his kind by Mr Sherlock Holmes, had shown considerable sagacity in tracing the crime to its source in the Bank's own manager—a startling *dénouement*. The accused, on the strength of this expert's evidence, had been committed to stand his trial at Winton Quarter Sessions, and it was the issue of that event which was interesting Sir Calvin. He had had some dealings with the Bank in question, and had even been brought into some personal contact with the delinquent official.

'It seems,' he ended, 'that there can be no doubt about the verdict. That Ridgway is a clever dog.'

'The detective?' queried Le Sage; and the General nodded. 'The sort I should be sorry, if a thief, to have laid on my trail.'

'But supposing you left none?' questioned the Baron, with a smile.

'Ah!' said Sir Calvin, having nothing better to reply.

'I have often thought,' said Le Sage, 'that if crime realised its own opportunities, there would be no use for detectives at all.'

'Eh? Why not?' asked his host.

'Because there would be nothing to find out,' answered the Baron.

'How d'ye mean? Nothing to find out?'

'Nothing whatever. My idea, now, of a successful crime is not a crime which baffles its investigators, but a crime which does not appear as a crime at all.'

'Instance, M. le Baron,' I ventured to put in.

'Why,' said Le Sage good-humouredly, 'a dozen may well present themselves to a man of average inventive intelligence. Direct murder, for example—how crude! when a hundred means offer themselves for procuring plausible ends to life. Tetanus germs and an iron tack; ptomaine, that toxicologic mystery, so easy to introduce; the edge of a cliff and a windy day; a frayed picture cord; a loosened nut or two; a scrap of soap left on the boards by an opened window—given adroitness, timeliness, a little nerve, would not any of these do?'

Audrey drew back in her chair, with a flushed little laugh.

'What a diabolical list!' she said, and made a face as if she had taken medicine.

'Yes,' said I. 'But after all, Baron, this is no more than generalising.'

'You want a concrete instance?' he answered, beaming on me. 'What do you say then to a swimmer being awarded the Humane Society's certificate for attempting to save the life of a man whom he had really drowned? It needs only a little imagination to fill in the details.'

'That is good,' I admitted. 'We put one to your credit.'

'Again,' said the Baron, 'I offer the case of a senseless young spendthrift. He gambles, he drinks, his life is a bad life from the insurance company's point of view. When hard pressed, he is lavish with his IOUs; when flush of money he redeems them; he pays up, he throws the slips into the fire with hardly a glance at them. One who holds a good deal of his paper observes this, and acts accordingly. He preserves the original securities, and on redemption, offers forgeries in their place, which he is careful to see destroyed. On the death of the young man he puts in his claim on his estate on the strength of the indisputable original documents. Thus he is paid twice over, without a possibility of any suspicion arising.'

'But one of the forged IOUs,' said Audrey, 'had been carried up the chimney without catching alight, and had been blown through the open window of the young man's family lawyer, who had kept it as a surprise.'

There was a shout of laughter, in which the Baron joined.

'Bravo, Audrey!' cried her brother. 'What about your average inventive intelligence, Baron?'

'I said, specifically, a man's,' pleaded Le Sage. 'Women, fortunately for us, are not eligible for the detective force.'

Audrey laughed at the compliment, but I think she liked the Baron for his pleasant good-nature. About that, for my part, I kept an open mind. Had he really invented these cases on the spur of the moment, or could it be possible that they touched on some experience of his own? One could not say, of course; but one could bear the point in mind.

The dinner went cheerfully enough after this *jeu d'esprit* of Audrey's. That had even roused Hugh from his glooms, and to quite exaggerated effect. He became suddenly talkative where he had been taciturn, and almost boisterously communicative where he had been reserved. But I noticed that he drank a good deal, and detected curiously, as I thought, a hint of desperation under his feverish gaiety.

In all this, it may be said, I was appropriating to myself, without authority, a sort of watching brief on behalf of a purely chimerical client. I had no real justification for suspecting the

Baron, either on his own account, or in association with my friend's apparent state; it was presumptive that Sir Calvin knew at least as much about the man as I did; still, I thought, so long as I preserved my attitude of what I may call sympathetic vigilance *à la sourdine*, nothing could be lost, and something even might be gained. The common atmosphere, perhaps, affected me with the others, and inclined me to an unusually observant mood; a mood, it may be, prone to attach an over-importance to trifles. Thus, I could find food for it in an incident so ordinary as the following. There was a certain picture on the wall, a genre painting, to which Le Sage, sitting opposite it, referred in some connexion. Sir Calvin, replying, remarked that so-and-so had declared one of the figures to be out of proportion—too short or too tall, I forget which—and, in order to measure the discrepancy, interposed, after the manner of the connoisseur, a finger between his eye and the subject. There was nothing out of the common in the action, save only that the finger he raised was the second finger of his right hand, the first having been shot away in some long-past engagement; but it appeared, quite obviously to me, to arrest in a curious way the attention of the visitor. He forgot what he was saying at the moment, his speech tailed off, he sat gazing, as if suddenly fascinated, not at the picture but at the finger. The next instant he had caught up and continued what he was observing; but the minute incident left me wondering. It had signified, I was sure, no sudden realization of the disfigurement, since that must have been long known to him, but of some association with it accidentally suggested. That, in that single moment, was my very definite impression—I could hardly have explained why at the time; but there it was. And I may say now, in my own justification, that my instinct, or my intuition, was not at fault.

Once or twice later I seemed to catch Le Sage manoeuvring to procure a repetition of the action, but without full success; and soon afterwards the two men fell upon the ever-absorbing subject of chess, and lapsed into vigorous discussion over the relative merits of certain openings, such as the Scotch, the Giuoco Piano, the Ruy Lopez attack, Philidor's defence, and the various gambits; to wit, the Queen's, the Allgaier, the Evans, the Muzio, the Sicilian, and God knows what else. They did not favour the drawing-room for long after dinner, but went off to the library to put their theories into practice, leaving Hugh and me alone with the lady. I cannot admit that I found the subsequent evening exhilarating. Hugh appeared already to be suffering a relapse from his artificial high spirits, and again disturbed me by the capricious oddity of his behaviour. He and his sister bickered, after their wont, a good deal, and once or twice the girl was brought by him near the verge of angry tears, I thought. I never could quite make out Audrey. She seemed to me a young woman of good impulses, but one who was for ever on the defensive against imagined criticism, and inclined therefore, in a spirit of pure perversity, to turn her worst side outermost. Yet she was a really pretty girl, a tall stalk of maiden-hood, nineteen, and athletically modern in the taking sense, and had no reason but to value herself and her attractions at the plain truth they represented. The trouble was that she was underestimated, and I think proudly conscious of the fact. With a father like Sir Calvin, it was, and must be, Hugo first and the rest nowhere. He bullied everyone, but there was no under-suggestion of jealous proprietorship in his bullying of Audrey as there was in his adoring bullying of his son. He did not care whether *she* felt it or not; with the other it was like a lover's temper, wooing by chastisement. Nor was Hugo, perhaps, a very sympathetic brother. He could enjoy teasing, like his father, and feel a mischievous pleasure in seeing 'the galled jade wince'. Audrey, I believe, would have worshipped him had he let her—I had observed how gratified she looked at dinner over his commendation of her jest—but he held her aloof between condescension and contempt, and the two had never been real companions. The long-motherless girl was lonely, I think, and it was rather pathetic; still, she did not always go the right way about it to avoid unfavourable criticism.

We were out for a day in the stubble on the morrow, and I made it an excuse for going to bed betimes. The trial of the Bank-Manager, I may mention by the way, had ended in a verdict of guilty, and a sentence of three years penal servitude. I found, and took the paper in to Sir Calvin before going upstairs. The servants never dared to disturb him at his game.

CHAPTER V

THE BARON CONTINUES TO INTEREST ME

(From the Bickerdike MS.)

We were three guns—Hugo, myself, and a young local landowner, Sir Francis Orsden of Audley, whom I had met before and liked. He was a good fellow, though considered effeminate by a sporting squirearchy; but that I could never see. Our shooting lay over the lower estate, from which the harvest had lately been carried, and we went out by the main gates, meeting the head gamekeeper, Hanson, with the dogs and a couple of boy beaters, in the road. Our plan was to work the stubble as far as possible in a south-westerly direction, making for Asholt Copse and Hanson's cottage, where Audrey and the Baron were to meet us, driving over in a pony trap with the lunch.

I perceived early enough that my chance of a day's sport wholly untrammelled by scruples of anxiety was destined to be a remote one. Hugh, it had been plain to me from the first, had not mastered with the new day his mood of the night before. His nervous irritability seemed to me even to have increased, and the truth was he was a trying companion. I had already made him some tentative bid for his confidence, but without result; I would not be the one again to proffer my sympathy uninvited. After all, he had asked for it, and was the one to broach the subject, if he wanted it broached. Probably—I knew him—the matter was no great matter—some disappointment or monetary difficulty which his fancy exaggerated. He hated trouble of any sort, and was quite capable of summoning a friend from a sick-bed to salve some petty grievance for him. So I left it to him to explain, if and when he should think proper.

It was a grey quiet day, chill, but without wind; the sort of day on which the echo of a shot might sound pretty deceptively from a distance—a point to be remembered. I was stationed on the left, Orsden on the extreme right, and Hugh divided us. His shooting was wild to a degree; he appeared to fire into the thick of the coveys without aim or judgment, and hardly a bird fell to his gun. Hanson, who kept close behind his young master, turned to me once or twice, when the lie of the ground brought us adjacent, and shook his head in a surprised, mournful way. Once Hugh and I came together at a gap in a hedge. I had negotiated it without difficulty, and my friend was following, when something caught my eye. I snatched at his gun barrel, directing it between us, and on the instant the charge exploded.

'Good God, man!' I exclaimed. '*You?*'

Like the veriest Cockney greenhorn, he had been pulling his piece after him by the muzzle, and the almost certain consequence had followed. I stood staring at him palely, and for the moment his face was distorted.

'Hugh!' I said stiffly, 'you didn't mean it?'

He broke into a mirthless laugh.

'Mean it, you mug! Of course I didn't mean it. Why should I?'

'I don't know. Mug for saving your life, anyhow!'

'I'll remember it, Vivian. I wish I owed you something better worth the paying.'

'That's infernal nonsense, of course. Now, look here; what's it all about?'

'All what?'

'You know.'

'I'll tell you by-and-by, Viv—on my honour, I will.'

'Will you? Hadn't you better go back in the meantime and leave your gun with Hanson?'

'No; don't be a fool, or make me seem one. I'll go more careful after this; I promise you on my sacred word I will. There, get on.'

I was not satisfied; but Hanson coming up at the moment to see what the shot had meant, I could have no more to say, and prepared silently to resume my place.

'It's all right, George,' said his master, 'only a snap at a rabbit.'

Had he meant to kill himself? If he had, what trouble so much more tragic than any I had conceived must lie at the root of the matter! But I would not dare to believe it; it had been merely another manifestation of the reckless mood to which his spoilt temper could only too easily succumb. Nevertheless, I felt agitated and disturbed, and still, in spite of his promise, apprehensive of some ugly business.

He shot better after this episode, however, and thereby brought some reassurance to my mind. Hanson, that astute gamekeeper, led us well and profitably, and the morning reached its grateful end in that worthy's little parlour in the cottage in the copse, with its cases of stuffed birds and vermin, and its table delectably laid with such appetising provender as ham, tongue, and a noble pigeon pie, with bottled beer, syphons, and old whisky to supply the welcome moisture. Audrey presided, and the Baron, who had somehow won her liking, and whom she had brought with her in the governess cart, made a cheerful addition to the company. He was brightly interested in our morning's sport, as he seemed to be generally in anything and everything; but even here one could never make out from his manner whether his questions arose from knowledge or ignorance in essential matters. They were not, I suppose—in conformity with his principle of *inwardness*—intended to betray; but the whole thing was to my mind ridiculous, like rattling the coppers in one's pocket to affect affluence. One might have gathered, for all proof to the contrary, that his acquaintance with modern sporting weapons was expert; yet he never directly admitted that he had used them, or was to be drawn into any relation of his personal experiences in their connexion. The subject of poachers was one on which, I remember, he exhibited a particular curiosity, asking many questions as to their methods, habits, and the measures taken to counter their dangerous activities. It was Orsden who mostly answered him, in that high eager voice of his, with just the suspicion of a stammer in it, which I could never hear without somehow being tickled. Hugh took no trouble to appear interested in the matter. He was again, I noticed with uneasiness, preoccupied with his own moody reflections, and was drinking far too much whisky and soda.

The Baron asked as if for information; yet it struck me that his inquiries often suggested the knowledge they purported to seek, as thus:

'Might it not be possible, now, that among the quiet, respectable men of the village, who attend to their business, drink in moderation, go punctually to church, and are well thought of by the local policeman, the real expert poacher is mostly to be found—the man who makes a study and a business of his craft, and whose depredations, conducted on scientific and meteorological lines, should cause far more steady havoc among the preserves than that wrought by the organised gangs, or by the unprofessional loafer—"moocher", I think you call him?'

Or thus: 'This country now, with its mixture of downlands and low woods, and the variety of opportunities they afford, should be, one might imagine, peculiarly suited to the operations of these gentry?'

Or thus: 'I wonder if your shrewd poacher makes much use of a gun, unless perhaps on a foggy morning, when the sound of the report would be muffled? He should be a trapper, I think, *par excellence*'—and other proffered hypotheses, seeming to show an even more intimate acquaintance with the minutiae of the subject, such as the springes, nets, ferrets, and tricks of snaring common to the trade—a list which set Orsden cackling after a time.

'On my word, Baron,' said he, 'if it wasn't for your innocent way of p-putting things, I could almost suspect you of being a poacher yourself.'

Le Sage laughed.

'Of other men's games, in books, perhaps,' he said.

'Well,' said Orsden, 'you're right so far, that one of the closest and cunningest poachers I ever heard of was a Leighway hedge-carpenter called Cleaver, and he was as quiet, sober, civil-spoken a chap as one could meet; pious, too, and reasonable, though a bit of a village politician, with views of his own on labour. Yet it came out that for years he'd been making quite a handsome income out of Audley and its neighbours—a sort of D-Deacon Brodie, you know. Not one of their preserves, though; you're at fault there, Baron. Your local man knows better than to put his head into the noose. His dealings are with the casual outsiders, so far as pheasants are concerned. When he takes a gun, it's mostly to the birds; and of course he shoots them sitting.'

'Brute!' said Audrey.

'Well, I don't know,' said the young Baronet. 'He's a tradesman, isn't he, not a sportsman, and tradesmen don't give law.'

'How did he escape so long?' asked the girl.

'Why, you see,' answered Orsden, 'you can't arrest a man on suspicion of game-stealing with nothing about him to prove it. He must be caught in the act; and if one-third of his business lies in poaching, quite two-thirds lie in the art of avoiding suspicion. Fellows like Cleaver are cleverer hypocrites than they are trappers—J-Joseph Surfaces in corduroys.'

'Do you find,' said Le Sage, 'men of his kind much prone to violence?'

'Not usually,' replied Orsden, 'but they may be on occasion, if suddenly discovered at work with a gun in their hands. It's exposure or murder then, you see; ruin or safety, with no known reason for anyone suspecting them. I expect many poor innocent d-devils were hanged in the old days for the sins of such vermin.'

'Yes,' said Le Sage, 'a shot-gun can be a great riddler.'

One or two of us cackled dutifully over the *jeu de mot*. Could we have guessed what tragic application it would receive before the day was out, we might have appreciated it better, perhaps.

I shall not soon forget that afternoon. It began with Audrey and the Baron driving off together for a jaunt in the little cart. They were very merry, and our young Baronet would have liked, I think, to join them. I had noticed Le Sage looking excessively sly during lunch over what he thought, no doubt, was an exclusive discovery of his regarding these two. But he was wrong. They were good friends, and that was all; and, as to the young lady's heart, I had just as much reason as Orsden—which was none whatever—for claiming a particular share in its interest. Any thought of preference would have been rank presumption in either of us, and the wish, I am sure, was founded upon no such supposition. It was merely that with Hugh in his present mood, the prospect of spending further hours in his company was not an exhilarating one.

He was flushed, and lethargic, and very difficult to move to further efforts when the meal was over; but we got him out at last and went to work. It did not last long with him. It must have been somewhere short of three o'clock that he shouldered his gun and came plodding to me across the stubble.

'Look here, Viv,' he said, 'I'm going home. Make my apologies to Orsden, and keep it up with him; but I'm no good, and I've had enough of it.'

He turned instantly with the word, giving a short laugh over the meaning expressed obviously enough, I dare say, in my eyes, and began to stride away.

'No,' he called, 'I'm not going to shoot myself, and I'm not going to let you make an ass of me. So long!'

I had to let him go. Any further obstruction from me, and I knew that his temper would have gone to pieces. I gave his message to Orsden, and we two continued the shoot without him. But it was a joyless business, and we were not very long in making an end of it. We parted in the road—Orsden for the Bit and Halter and the turning to Leighway, and I for the gates of Wildshott. It was near five o'clock, and a grey still evening. As I passed the stables, a white-faced groom came hurrying to stop me with a piece of staggering news. One of the maids, he said, had been found murdered, shot dead, that afternoon in the Bishop's Walk.

CHAPTER VI

'THAT THUNDERS IN THE INDEX'

LE SAGE, in the course of a pleasant little drive with Audrey, asked innumerable questions and answered none. This idiosyncrasy of his greatly amused the young lady, who was by disposition frankly outspoken, and whose habit it never was to consider in conversation whether she committed herself or anyone else. Truth with her was at least a state of nature—though it might sometimes have worn with greater credit to itself a little more trimming—and states of nature are relatively pardonable in the young. A child who sees no indecorum in nakedness can hardly be expected to clothe Truth.

'This Sir Francis,' asked the Baron, 'he is an old friend of yours?'

'O, yes!' said Audrey; 'quite an old friend.'

'And favourite?'

'Well, he seems one of us, you see. Don't you like him yourself?'

'I suppose he and your brother are on intimate terms?'

'We are all on intimate terms; Hugh and Frank no more than Frank and I.'

'And no less, perhaps; or perhaps not quite so much?'

'O, yes they are! What makes you think so? '

'Not quite so intimate, I will put it, as your brother and Mr Bickerdike?'

'I'm sure I don't know. Hugh is great friends with them both.'

'Tell me, now—which would you rather he were most intimate with?'

'How can it matter to me?'

'You have a preference, I expect.'

'I certainly have; but that doesn't affect the question. It was Hugh you were speaking of, not me.'

'Shall I give your preference? It is for Mr Bickerdike.'

'Well guessed, Baron. Am I to take it as a compliment to my good taste?'

'He is a superior man.'

'Isn't he? And always wishes one to know it, too.'

'Aha! Then the Baronet is the man?'

'How absurd you are! Do you value your friends by preference? Nobody is the *man*, as you call it. Because I don't much like Mr Bickerdike, it doesn't follow that I particularly like anybody else.'

'Why don't you like him?'

'I don't know. Perhaps because he likes himself too much.'

'Conceited, is he?'

'Not quite that: a first-rate prig I should call him—always wanting to appear cleverer than he really is.'

'Isn't he clever?'

'O, yes! Clever after a sort; but frightfully obtuse, too. I wouldn't trust him with a secret. He's so cocksure of himself that he'd always be liable to give it away with his blessing. But I oughtn't to speak like that of him. He's a great friend of Hugh's, and he does really like to help people, I think, only it must be in his own way and not theirs. Do *you* like him?'

'I am rather surprised that he and your brother should be on such close terms of friendship.'

'Are you? Why?'

'Is not Mr Hugo, now, without offence, a rather passionate, self-willed young gentleman?'

'Very, I should say.'

'Balance and instability—there you are.'

'You mean they are not at all alike. I should have thought that was the best reason in the world for their chumming. One of oneself is quite enough for most people. Fancy the horror of being a Siamese twin!'

'Is that why you and Sir Francis are on such good terms—because there is nothing in common between you?'

'Isn't there? What, for instance?'

'He presents himself to me, from what little I have seen and heard of him, as a rather gentle, spiritual young man, with a taste for books and the fine arts, and a preference in sport, if any, for angling. *In aere piscari.*'

'What does that mean?'

'I should fancy him a fisherman, by choice, of ideas rather than of streams.'

'And me, I suppose, a cross-tempered, empty-headed country hoyden, who thinks of nothing but dogs and stables?' But she laughed as she bent to Le Sage, looking mockingly into his smiling eyes. 'M. le Baron, what a character!'

'It is not of my giving,' he said. 'A spirited Diana should have been *my* antithesis.'

'But why should you contrast us at all? Frank and I are not going to live together.'

'You are bearing in mind, I hope,' he said, 'that I promised your father to be back at Wildshott by half-past two?'

'For chess again? What can you find in it?' She pulled up the pony, and, halting in the road, determinedly faced her companion. 'Do you know you never answer anything that's asked of you? Why don't you?'

'I didn't know I didn't.'

'Don't fib, sir.'

He chuckled aloud. 'You are a frank young lady.' He took her slim left hand between his cushiony palms, and patted it paternally. 'When a suspected man is arrested, my dear, the first warning he receives from the police is that anything he says may be used in evidence against him. Supposing we apply that rule to common converse? Then at least we shall avoid self-committal.'

'But are we all, every one of us, suspected people?'

'One never knows what may lie in a question. For instance, you ask me what can I find in chess. Very seeming innocent; but, O, the suspicion it may embody!'

'What suspicion?'

'Why, that chess represents my poor wits, and that I live upon them.'

Audrey tinkled with laughter. 'I never guessed I was such a serpent. But I am afraid I was only thinking of the dullness of it. To sit for ten minutes looking at a board, and then to move a pawn a single inch on it! Ugh! By that time I should be screaming for "Grab".'

'Let us play "Grab" one night,' said the Baron gaily.

They drove on by the pleasant lanes, and presently came out into the High Road near Wildshott. As they passed the wicket in the hedge, a gleam of something, quickly seen and quickly withdrawn among the green beyond, caught Le Sage's attention. He laid a hand on the reins, suggesting a halt.

'Was that a private way to the house?' he asked. 'There, where the little gate stood?'

Audrey told him yes. That it was called the Bishop's Walk, and that he, might lift the latch and go by it if he pleased. She twinkled as she spoke, and the Baron looked roguish.

'Inquisitive?' said he; 'I admit it, if it is the word for an inquiring mind. But not conceited, I hope. I am going to explore.'

He was out in the road, to the dancing relief of the governess-cart springs, and waved *au revoir* to his companion. She nodded, and drove on, while he turned to go back to the wicket. He hummed as he went, a little philandering French air, droning the words in a soft, throaty way, and was still recalling them as he mounted the two steps from the road, opened the gate, and passed through. His eyes, moving in an immobile face, were busy all the time. '*Dites moi, belle enchanteresse*,' he sang, '*Qui donc vous a donné vos yeux?*' just above his breath and suddenly, at a few yards in, eighteen or twenty, swerved from the close narrow track and stepped behind a beech-trunk. And there was a girl hiding from view, her eyes wide, her forefinger crooked to her lip.

'*Vos doux yeux, si pleins de tendresse*,' hummed M. le Baron, and nodded humorously. 'I thought I recognised you from the road.'

She did not flush up or exclaim '*Me!*' or exhibit any of the offensive-defensive pertness of the ordinary housemaid surprised out of bounds. She just stood looking at the intruder, a wonder on her rosy lips, and Le Sage for his part returned her scrutiny at his leisure. His impression of the night before he found more than confirmed by daylight: she was a very Arcadian nymph, with a sweet-briar complexion and eyes and hair of thyme and honey; shapely as a doe, ineffably pretty. He wondered less than ever over Louis's infatuation.

And what was she doing here? Her head was bare; a light waterproof veiled her official livery: it might be concluded without much circumspection that a tryst was in the air.

'I am sorry,' said M. le Baron. 'I did not come to be a spoil-sport. I ought, perhaps, to have pretended to see nothing and pass by. But that rudeness of my man last night sticks in my mind, and it occurred to me to apologise for him.'

She laughed, with a tiny toss of her head. 'Thank you, sir, but I can look after myself.'

'So I perceive,' he said. 'You tone very well with the trees. No eyes, except perhaps the favoured ones, could possibly guess you were here.'

'Except yours, sir,' she said, with just a tiny sauce of irony.

'Except mine, of course,' he agreed; and left her to wonder why, if she would.

'Well,' he said, after a smiling moment, 'that was an unpardonable act of Louis's, only don't visit it further on his head. I have wanted to warn you, and here is my opportunity. He comes of a hot-blooded race, and there's no knowing— But you can look after yourself; I will take your word for it.'

He believed she could, though she made no further answer to assure him; and, with a nod, he went on his way, taking up again the little murmured burden of his song: '*Yeux, yeux,—Astres divins tombés des cieux.*' 'O, eyes!' he said. 'Sweetest eyes were ever seen! From what heaven did you fall to flower in a housemaid's face?' There was something suggestive about the girl, more than her surprising beauty—a 'towniness', a hint, both in speech and manner, of some shrewd quality which was not of the soil. 'When Lamia takes to country service,' thought the Baron, 'let more than rustic hearts look to their locks!' With whom, he wondered, could be her assignation? What if, after all, it were with Louis himself? Would that surprise him? Perhaps not. Cabanis was a handsome and compelling fellow, and women, like the Lord, could chasten whom they loved. But he devoutly hoped it was not so; he desired no amorous complications in his train; and, disturbed by the thought, he inquired for his valet the moment he reached the house—only to learn that the man had gone out some time before and had not yet returned. Somewhat disquieted, Le Sage entered the hall, where he was met by his host.

'Ah, Baron!' hailed Sir Calvin. 'Punctuality itself! Go into my study, will you, and I'll join you in a moment.'

The study was a comfortable room on the ground floor, with a large bay window overlooking the gardens. Here the table for chess was set ready, with a brace of high easy chairs and, handily contiguous, a smoker's cabinet. There were trophies of the chase and some good sporting pictures on the walls, against them a couple of mahogany bookcases containing well-bound editions of Alken, Surtees, and others, and, let into an alcove of that one of them which included the fireplace, a substantial safe. Le Sage knew it was there, though it was hidden from sight behind a shallow curtain; and now, as he moved humming about the room, his hands behind his back, his eyes scrutinising a picture or two while he awaited his host's coming, he gravitated gradually towards its place of concealment. Arrived there, he lifted very delicately, and still humming, the hem of the curtain, just exposed the keyhole, and bent to examine it with singular intentness. But a moment later, when the General entered, he was contemplating a coaching print by Flavell over the mantelpiece.

'Indifferent art, I suppose you will admit,' he said. 'But there is something picturesquely direct about these old Sporting pieces.'

'Well, they suit me,' answered Sir Calvin, 'because I understand them. Red's red and blue's blue to me, and if any artist tells me they are not, I've nothing to answer the fellow but that he's a damned liar.'

Le Sage laughed—'What is the colour of a black eye, then?'—and they settled down to their game. The General was a good player; all the best of his mental qualifications—which were otherwise of the standard common among retired officers of an over-bearing, obstinate, and undiscerning disposition—were displayed in his astute engineering of his small forces. He was a tactical Napoleon in miniature when it came to chess; he seemed to acquire then a reason and a dignity inconspicuous in his dealings with living people. The chessmen could not misrepresent him; their movements were his movements, and their successes or failures his. If he lost, he had no one but himself he could possibly blame, and his understanding of that condition seemed to bring out the best in him. He was never choleric over the fortunes of the game. For the rest, he was not a wise man, or an amenable man, or anything but a typical despot of his class, having an inordinate pride of family, which owed less than it should have to any moral credit he had brought it in the past. In person he was a leanish, clean-built soldier of fifty-five, with bullying eyebrows and a thick blunt moustache of a grizzled blonde.

He and the Baron were very fond of devising problems, which they would send up for solution to the *Morning Post*.

They set to elaborating a tough one now, a very difficult changed-mate two-mover, which kept them absorbed and occupied over the board for a considerable time. Indeed, a full hour and a half had passed before they had settled it to their satisfaction; and then the Baron, taking a refreshing pinch of Macuba, rose to his feet.

'That is it, my friend,' said he; 'an economical B.P. at K. Knight 4, and the thing is done.'

The clock on the mantelpiece chimed a quarter past four as he spoke, and on the tinkling reverberation of its one stroke someone opened the door. It was Hugo Kennett: the young man's face was ghastly; his hands shook; he came into the room hurriedly, as if overweighted with some dreadful piece of intelligence.

'Good God, Hughie!' exclaimed his father, and rose, staring at the boy, his eternal cigarette caught between his teeth.

The young soldier made an effort to speak; his breath fluttered audibly in him like the leaf of a ventilator; his nerve seemed for the moment gone utterly beyond his control.

'Steady, sir!' commanded the General; and his masterful tone had its visible effect. 'Now,' he said, after a rallying pause. 'What is it?'

Hugh swallowed once or twice, and answered. Le Sage, observant of him, could see what immense force he had to put upon himself to do so.

'The Bishop's Walk! Can you come at once, sir? There's been what looks like a dreadful murder there.'

Sir Calvin never so much as blenched or exclaimed. One might at least admire in him the self-possessed soldier, not to be rattled by any sudden call upon his nerve.

'Murder!' he said. 'Whose murder?'

The young man's lips quivered; he looked physically sick.

'It's one of the maids, sir. I saw her; I came upon her myself. I had forgotten my gun, and went back to fetch it, and there she was lying on her face, and—' He put his hands before his own face and shuddered horribly.

'Look here,' said the father, 'you must pull yourself together. This won't do at all. Baron, get me my hunting flask, if you'll be so good. It's in the right-hand top drawer of my desk.'

He poured into the cup, with an unshaking hand, a full half gill of liqueur brandy, and made his son drink it down. It wrought a measure of effect; a tinge of colour came to Hugh's cheek; his hurried respirations steadied.

'Now,' said Sir Calvin, 'try to be coherent. What do you mean by forgetting your gun?'

'I mean, sir,'—he looked down; his features still twitched spasmodically, 'I mean—it was like this. I was no good at the shoot, and I left it and came back by myself—came back by the Bishop's Walk. Just a little way inside, I stopped to light a cigarette, and rested my gun against a tree and forgot it; but an hour later I remembered that I had left it there, and went back to fetch it, and saw—O, it was ghastly!'

'Steady, man! Was the girl there when you first entered the path?'

Le Sage listened for an answer in the affirmative, and could hardly hear it when it came.

'And you stopped to light a cigarette?' The father looked keenly into the son's face. 'You haven't yet told us what girl, Hughie.'

The good liquor was working. The young fellow lifted his head, a new passionate expression in his eyes:

'It was Annie, sir—that good-looking housemaid. You wouldn't wonder over my horror if you saw. He must have fired at short range, the damned villain, and when she was turned from him. There is a hole in her back that one could put—ah, I can't tell you!'

M. le Baron exclaimed, 'That would have been,' said he, speaking for the first time, 'between three and four, when you discovered the body?'

'Just now,' answered Hugh, addressing his father. 'I have come straight from it. They are waiting for you, sir, to know what to do.'

'It was done with your gun? Is that the assumption?' suggested the Baron.

'I don't know,' replied the young man feverishly, again not to the questioner. 'I suppose so; I dare say. Both barrels are discharged, and one I am pretty sure I left loaded. Are you coming, sir?'

Sir Calvin, frowning a stiff moment, moved to acquiesce. They all went out together. At the entrance to the track a group of frightened maid-servants stood white-lipped and whispering, afraid to penetrate farther. One or two grooms and a couple of gardeners had already gone in, and were awaiting about the body the arrival of their master. It lay, face downwards, close beside the beech-trunk behind which the living girl had sought to hide herself from Le Sage. That stood at a point in the winding path some twenty-five yards from the wicket, and was nowhere remotely visible from the road. She might have been making her way back to the house when she was fired on and shattered. It was a pitiful, ugly sight; but death must have been instantaneous—that was one comfort. Le Sage made the most of it to himself, though he was really distressed and moved. 'Poor eyes!' he thought, '*si pleins de tendresse*: but an hour ago so beautiful, and now quenched in death. So this was the tryst you kept! Why, it can hardly be cold yet about your heart.'

Sir Calvin, stern and wrath, gave brief directions. A shutter was to be brought, a doctor fetched from Longbridge by one servant, the county police informed by another. He asked a short question or two—one of his son. Was this the tree against which he had left his gun leaning? Hugh answered no, while Le Sage listened. He had left it, he said, propped against a smaller trunk, four or five yards nearer the gate. He had had to pass the body to recover it, and had then taken it home, and thrust it into the gun-room as he had hurried by to raise an alarm. He spoke with extreme agitation, averting his eyes from the dead girl; and, indeed, it was a sight to move a tougher heart than his. Sir Calvin's next question was to the group at large. It was to ask if anyone knew of any enemy the unfortunate victim had raised against herself, or of any possible reason for the attack. But no one knew or guessed, or, if he felt a suspicion, would have dared to formulate it. It would have been too risky a venture at this stage of the affair. Their master looked from face to face, and grunted and spoke a warning word. If that were so, he said, let them avoid all loose discussion of the matter until the police had taken it in hand. It might, after all, prove no murder, but only an accident, the perpetrator of which, terrified by the deed which he had unwittingly committed, might be keeping silence only until assured that he could tell the truth without danger to himself. Le Sage ventured to applaud that suggestion, turning to Hugh to ask him if he did not think it a quite reasonable one. But the young man refused to consider it; he was very excited; it was murder, he said, gross, palpable, open, and it was mere criminal sophistry to pretend to account for it on any other theory. His father steadied him once more with a word, and the three turned to go back to the house together as they had come, leaving the men to follow with the body. On issuing from the copse they found the little group of frightened sobbing women reinforced by Cleghorn. The butler wore a cloth cap and a light overcoat. His face was the colour of veal, and his lower jaw hung in a foolish incapable way.

'Ha, Cleghorn!' said his master. 'This is a bad business.'

'It's knocked me all of a heap, sir,' answered the man. His voice shook and wheezed. 'I've only this moment heard of it, sir.'

Hugo hung behind as they entered the hall. His father, steady as a rock, marched on to his study, and was followed by M. le Baron. The latter shut the door upon them.

'An ugly business,' he said.

'A cursed interruption to our game,' damned the General. He was greatly incensed. That such a vulgar scandal should have come to pollute the sacred preserves of Wildshott seemed to him the incredible outrage.

'What am I to do?' he said. 'What is the infernal procedure? There will have to be an inquest, I suppose, and then—'

'And then to indict the murderer,' said Le Sage, answering the pause.

'You think it *is* a murder?'

'What do you think?'

'I don't know; I suppose so. It may prove a devil of a business to find out. Ought we to have a detective?'

'These provincial police are excellent men, but their normal training— Still, it may prove a quite simple affair.'

'I have a feeling somehow that it won't. I'd better write up to Scotland Yard.'

'If you're decided on it, why not apply? There is, or was, in the neighbourhood the very man.'

'You mean that fellow Ridgway? By Jove, yes—a clever dog! I'll motor into Winton first thing tomorrow, and find out. In the meantime—where's Hugo?'

'I think I saw him go upstairs. I'll have him sent to you, if you'll allow me. I was wanting to write some letters.'

He retreated, with a smile which left his face the moment he was outside. Finding a servant, he gave her Sir Calvin's message, and then put a question of his own:

'Do you know where my man is, my dear?'

'I think Mr Cabanis is out, sir,' answered the girl. Her cheeks were still mottled with the fright of things. 'He went out some time ago.'

'O, to be sure! About three o'clock, wasn't it?'

'Earlier than that, sir—directly after dinner in the servants' hall.'

Her manner appeared a little odd, disordered; but that might have been due to the shock they had all received.

'And he has not yet returned?' said the Baron cheerily. 'Well, send him to me the moment he comes in, if you will be so good. And he moved to mount the stairs, humming as he went. But again, though his song was light, he turned a dark face to the wall.

CHAPTER VII

THE BARON VISITS THE SCENE OF THE CRIME

(*From the Bickerdike MS.*)

I CONFESS that the man's communication, coming on the top of my concern for my friend, fairly, in the first moment of it, took me aghast. The state in which I had found Hugh, that disquieting business of the gun, his insistence on sticking to his weapon—it was inevitable that any mind should instinctively leap to some association between these and a catastrophe so seemingly their corollary in its nature and instrumentality. It was odd, but ever since my meeting with the Baron in Simpson's smoking-room a sense as of some vague fatality had seemed to overcloud me. It was formless, impalpable, but it was there, like that unnerving atmosphere which precedes, according to people who know, an earthquake. But that first sick alarm was not long in dissipating itself in me in a fine scorn. The thing, to my recovered judgment, was simply incredible. Apart from the brutal clumsiness, the unthinking recklessness of such a deed, what was there in my knowledge of my friend to justify such a horrible assumption?

Spoilt he was, selfish he was, no doubt, but always the last man in the world to incline to personal violence. A sensitiveness to pain, almost morbid, on account of himself or others, was rather his characteristic; an excess of affection, his charm and his weakness. He could not have done it, of course, for whatever mad reason.

But, as I came to learn the particulars of the tragedy, so far as they were known or guessed, another suspicion, less base though still discomposing, *would* occur to me. The poor girl, according to all accounts, had been a great beauty; and it appeared probable—from evidence freely volunteered by M. le Baron, who had passed through the copse some short time before the murder must have been committed, and who had seen and spoken with her there—that she was keeping an assignation. With whom? Who could as yet say? But I had too good reason to dread my friend's susceptibility where the adorable feminine was concerned, and I could not forget how the time of the assignation, if such it were, had coincided with that of his leaving the shoot. 'This,' I thought, 'may be as unjustified an assumption as the other; still, for the sake of argument, admit it, and one thing at least is accounted for. With such a wire-strung nature as Hugh's, the consciousness of a guilty intrigue would be quite enough to induce in him that state of recklessness and excitability which had so bothered and perplexed me.'

It was still, in fact, perplexing me at dinner on the night of the murder, when, after the withdrawal of Audrey and the servants, much discussion of the tragic subject took place, and later, when he and I were for a brief time alone together in the billiard-room. It was not so much that he was not shocked and horrified with the rest of us, as that his emotions were expressed in such an extraordinary form. They made him lament one moment, and go into half hysterical laughter the next; now utter raging imprecations against the dastard capable of so damnable a crime, now assert that jealousy was probably responsible for it, and that no man who had not felt jealousy had a right to sit in judgment on a passion which was after all not so much a passion as a demoniac possession. Then he would declare that, the thing being done, it was no good making oneself miserable about it, and rally me on my long face, which, he said, made him feel worse than a hundred murders. The horror of the thing had no doubt unhinged him, coupled with the knowledge that it was through his own carelessness in leaving a loaded gun within reach of temptation that the deed had been made possible. With such a nature as his, that consciousness must have counted for much, though still, and at the same time, I could never quite rid myself of the feeling that, beneath all his expressed remorse and pity, a strange little note of—I will not call it relief, but ease from some long haunting oppression, made itself faintly audible. However, remembering his late promise of confidence to me, I determined to abide in patience its coming, only wondering in the interval what had instigated his remarks on jealousy, and if it were possible that they had been inspired by any suspicion of the criminal, and if so, on what personal grounds. He came down quite quiet to breakfast the next morning, and from that time onwards was his own rational hospitable self.

Early in the afternoon of that day Sir Calvin came back with the detective, Sergeant Ridgway, in tow. The latter had been retrieved, by good luck, from Antonferry, whither, after the trial, he had returned from Winton to settle for the lodgings he had occupied during the Bank investigations. The General had been fortunate in encountering him at the very moment of his departure, and had at once secured from him, contingent on the receipt of official authority, a promise to undertake the case. A prepaid telegram to Scotland Yard had brought the necessary sanction, and within a couple of hours of its despatch the Sergeant was safe at Wildshott, and already engaged over the preliminaries of the business. Personally, I admit, I felt greatly relieved by his appearance on the scene. A notable writer has somewhat humoured a belief in the fatuity of the professional detective; but that was with a view, I think, to exalt his own incomparable amateur rather than to discredit a singularly capable body of men, having a pretty persistent record of success to justify their being. Intellectuality was at least not absent by inference from this face. When I saw it, I felt that the case was in safe hands, and that henceforth we might, one and all of us, cast whatever burden of personal responsibility had unwittingly overhung our spirits. The Sergeant was installed in the house, and lost no time in getting to work in a reassuring, business-like way. He went in the first instance to view the body, which had been laid on a table in the gun-room, with a policeman—one of two brought over the night before by the Chief Constable, a friend of Sir Calvin's, in person—to watch the door. Thereafter, established in the General's study, he briefly reviewed the evidence of such witnesses as could supply any topical information that bore on the crime—Le Sage, to wit, Hugo himself, Mrs Bingley the housekeeper, and one or two of the servants, including the men who, on their young master's alarmed summons, had first entered the copse to remove the body.

I was present during the whole, I think, of this examination, and for the following reason. It happened that I and the Baron, on his way to the study, met in the hall, when he attacked me, I thought rather impertinently, on a question of punctilio.

'Do you not think, my friend,' he said, 'that under the circumstances it would be decent of us to offer to terminate our visit? Supposing we both, here and now, address Sir Calvin on the subject?'

I was very much annoyed. 'Baron,' I said, 'I am not accustomed to seek advice in matters of conduct, and I certainly shall not do as you propose. Apart from the question of deserting my friend in a crisis, I think that any suggestion of our leaving now would look like a desire to avoid inquiry—which I, for my part, am far from wishing to do—and would bear a very bad complexion. You can act as you like; but it is my intention to see this thing through.'

'O, very well!' he said. 'Then I will speak for myself alone.'

Why should he wish to escape? All my instinctive suspicion of him reawakened on the moment; and I wondered. True, he could not himself have perpetrated the crime; Hugo's evidence would not permit of such a supposition; but could he not be somehow implicated in it as instigator or abettor? I determined then and there to keep a very close observation on M. le Baron.

We entered the room together, since I would not suffer his going in alone to misrepresent me. Sir Calvin was there, with his son and the detective. I saw the last for the first time. He was quite the typical Hawkshaw, and handsome at that—a lithe man of middle height, with a keen, dark, aquiline face, and clean-shaven jaws and chin. I could have thought him a young man for his work and reputation; he did not look more than thirty-five, and might have been less; but about his mental ability, if one could judge by indications, there was no question. A certain rather truculent dandyism in his dress contrasted oddly with this intellectuality of feature; it showed itself a little over-emphatic in the matter of trouser-crease and collar and scarf-pin, and it tilted his black plush Homburg hat, when out of doors, at a slightly theatrical angle. But taste, after all, is a question not of mind but of breeding, and the man who has, like Disraeli, to stand on his head for a living, may be excused a little ostentation in the process. He looked at us both searchingly as we entered.

'This, Sergeant,' said Sir Calvin, 'is the Baron Le Sage, whom I mentioned to you as having encountered the unfortunate young woman in the copse a little before—'

The detective nodded. 'I should like to ask a question of you, sir.'

Le Sage told what he knew. It was very little, and only of value in so far as it touched upon the evidence of time.

'It must have been a little before half-past two when we met,' he said.

'And shortly after three,' said the detective, turning to Hugo, 'when you came by the same path, sir, and had your little talk with her, like this gentleman?'

'My talk,' said the Baron, smiling, 'was of the briefest. We exchanged but a pleasant word or two, and I passed on.'

'And yours,' said the detective to Hugh, 'was perhaps of a more prolonged sort?'

'It may have been, Sergeant,' was my friend's answer. He was looking pale but composed; and his manner was absolutely frank and unequivocal. 'You see,' said he, 'poor Annie was, after all, one of the household, and there was nothing out of the way in my stopping to speak with her. We may have chatted for ten minutes—I should think no longer—while I put down my gun and lighted a cigarette. I was back at the house by a quarter past three or thereabouts.'

'And you remembered, and returned for your gun?'

'That must have been just about four o'clock.'

'So that the murder, if murder it was, must have been committed sometime between 3.15 and 4 p.m.'

'That is so, I suppose.'

The detective stood as if mutely weighing the few facts at his disposition for a moment or two, then turned to the General.

'We shall want evidence of identity, Sir Calvin,' he said. 'Your housekeeper, I suppose, engaged the young woman? Can I see her?'

Mrs Bingley was rung for, and in the interval, while awaiting her appearance, Le Sage approached our host.

'Pardon me, Sir Calvin,' said he; 'but before you proceed any further, would you not prefer that I should withdraw? I cannot but feel that my visit itself is proving untimely, and that it were better that I should relieve you of the embarrassment of—'

But the General broke in forcibly.

'Not a bit of it! There's nothing to conceal. Damn it, man! Beyond helping this Sergeant what we can to find out the truth, I don't see why the even tenor of our ways need disturb itself by so much as a thought. No, no; you came for chess, and you'll stay for chess!' A sentiment which, while justifying my own attitude, pretty effectually disposed of the Baron's affected, and perhaps interested scruples.

He smiled, with a tiny shrug. 'Well, if I am not in the way!' and addressed the detective; 'the ruling passion, you see, Sergeant Ridgway. Do you play chess?'

'A little,' answered the man, cautious even in his admission. 'It's a great game.'

'It's *the* game,' said the Baron. 'We'll play, you and I, one of these days, when you're needing some distraction from your labours.'

'Very well, sir,' responded the detective civilly, and at that moment Mrs Bingley entered the room.

Wildshott was, by common assent, fortunate in its housekeeper. She was a good soul and a good manager, strict but tolerant, ruling by tact alone. Spare and wiry, her virgin angularity (despite her courtesy title) was of the sort one associates with blessed women in old painted manuscripts. Firmness and patience showed in her capable face, to which agitation had now lent a rather red-eyed pallor. She bowed to Sir Calvin, and faced the detective quietly:

'You wanted to speak with me, sir?'

'Just a few words,' he answered. 'This young woman's name, Mrs Bingley—?'

'Was Annie Evans, sir.'

'And her age?'

'She was just, by her own statement, turned twenty-three.'

'You have communicated with her relations?'

'No, indeed. She never referred to any, and I have no means of finding them out. Annie was a very reserved girl.'

'But surely, when you engaged her—'

'I did so by advertisement, sir, through the *Ladies' Times* newspaper. We were in immediate need of an under-housemaid, and there was a difficulty about local girls. I put an advertisement in the paper, as I had often done before, preferring that method to the agencies, and she answered it. That was about two months ago.'

'And her former employer?'

'That was a Mrs Wilson, sir. She had gone to New Zealand, and left a written character with Annie. It was quite against my custom to take a servant with only a written character; but in this instance I was persuaded to break my rule, the character given was so excellent, and the girl herself so modest and attractive.'

'H'm! Then you saw her before engaging her?'

'I went up to see her at the office of the paper itself by her own appointment, and was so struck by her manner and appearance that I settled with her then and there. She was to come down two days later. To the best of my memory, I never inquired about her people.'

'But she must have spoken of them—received letters?'

'She never spoke of them to my knowledge, or that of her fellow servants, to whom I have put the question. As to letters, Annie certainly did receive one now and again—one or two quite recently; but I have been looking, and can find no trace of any. It would have been just like her funny sensitive ways to destroy every one of them.'

The detective was silent for a moment, his dark scrutinizing eyes fixed on the speaker's face, as if he were pondering some significance, to him, in the answer.

'What became of the written character?' he asked presently.

'I returned it to her, sir. It is customary to do so.'

'In case she should want to use it again? That being so, I should have thought she would have kept it?'

'Yes, sir.'

'But you have not come across it?'

'It may be in her boxes. I have not looked.'

'You and I must overhaul those boxes, Mrs Bingley. Did you think, now, of making any inquiries about this Mrs Wilson?'

'No, it would have been useless; she had already sailed for New Zealand.'

'Do you remember her address?'

'She wrote, so far as I can recollect, from the Savoy Hotel.'

Sergeant Ridgway took an envelope from his pocket, and making a note on the back of it, returned it into keeping.

'Well, you can leave that to me,' he said, and, resting his right elbow in the palm of the other hand, softly caressed his chin, bending an intent look on his witness.

'Now, ma'am,' he said. 'I want to ask you a particular question. Has Annie Evans's conduct, while in this service, always continued to justify you in your first good opinion of her?'

'Always,' answered the housekeeper with emphasis. 'She was a thoroughly good straightforward girl, and during the short time she was here I have never had any trouble with her that was of her own procuring.'

'Will you tell me quite what you mean by that?'

'Well, sir, she could not help being pretty and admired, and if it led to some quarrels among the men on her account, the blame was theirs, and never in the smallest degree to be charged to her conduct with them. She always did her best to keep them at a distance.'

'O, quarrels, were there? Can you tell me of any particular quarrel, now?'

'I could—' began the housekeeper, and stopped.

'Come, Mrs Bingley,' said her master. 'You must speak out without fear or favour.'

'I know it, sir,' said the housekeeper, distressed. 'I will try to do my duty.'

'Hey!' cried the General. 'Of course you must. You wouldn't want to risk hanging the wrong man? *What* particular quarrel—hey?'

'It was between Mr Cleghorn and the Baron's gentleman, sir.'

'Cleghorn, eh? Great Scott! Was he sweet on the girl?'

'I think for some time he had greatly admired her, sir. And then Mr Cabanis came; and being a young man, with ways different from ours—' again she hesitated.

'Out with it!' cried Sir Calvin. 'Don't keep anything back.'

'On the night before—before the deed,' said the housekeeper, with an effort, 'Annie had come down into the kitchen, I was told, red with fury over Mr Cabanis having tried to kiss her. She had boxed his ears for him, she said, and he had looked murder at her for it. He came down himself later on, I understand, and there was a fine scene between the two men. It was renewed the next day at dinner, when Annie wasn't there, and in the end, after having come to blows and been separated, they both went out, Cabanis first, and Mr Cleghorn a little later. That is the truth, sir, and now may I go?'

I think we were all sorry for the Baron; it appeared so obvious whither the trend of the detective's inquiries must henceforth carry him. But he sat quite quiet, with only a smile on his face.

'Louis is not vindictive,' was the sole thing he contented himself with saying.

Sir Calvin turned to the detective. 'Do you need Mrs Bingley any more?'

'Not for the present,' answered the Sergeant, and the housekeeper left the room. I had expected from him, on her disappearance, some significant look or gesture, betokening his acceptance of the inevitable conclusion; but he made no such sign, and merely resumed his business conduct of the case. He knew better than we, no doubt, that in crime the most obvious is often the most unreliable.

'We must find the girl's relations, if possible, Sir Calvin,' he said. 'You can leave that to me, however. What I would advise, if her boxes yield no clue, would be an advertisement in the papers.'

An examination of some of the servants ensued upon this; but beyond the fact of their supplying corroborative testimony as to the quarrel, their evidence was of little interest, and I omit it here. The Baron disappeared during the course of the inquiry, so secretively that I think I was the only one who noticed his going. At the end the detective expressed a desire to examine the scene of the crime. If one of us, he said, would conduct him there, he would be satisfied and would ask no more. He did not want a crowd. I ventured to volunteer, and was accepted. Sir Calvin had looked towards his son; but Hugh, with reason sufficient, had declined to go. He had sat throughout the inquiry, after giving his own evidence, perfectly still, and with a sort of white small smile on his lips. Thinking my own thoughts, I was sorry for him.

The Sergeant and I made for the coppice. Passing the constable at the gun-room door, he nodded to him. 'That's a poor thing inside,' he said, as we went on. 'What a lot of trouble she'd save if she could speak! Well, I suppose that him that did it thinks she's got her deserts.'

'I hope he'll get his,' I answered.'

'Ah!' he agreed,' I hope he will.' We turned a bend as we came near the fatal beech-tree and there was the Baron before us!

The detective stopped with a smart exclamation, then went on slowly.

'Doing a little amateur detective work on your own, sir?' he asked sarcastically.

'I was considering, my friend,' answered the Baron. 'It becomes interesting to me, you see, since my man is involved.'

'Who said he was involved, sir?'

'Ah! Who, now? You can see very distinctly, Sergeant, where the body lay—just the one ugly token. No signs of a struggle, I think; and the ground too hard to have left a trace of footprints. But I won't disturb you at your work.'

'I wouldn't, sir,' said the detective pretty bluntly. 'You can undertake, I fancy, to leave it all to me.'

'I'm sure I can,' answered the Baron pleasantly, and he went, off towards the house, humming softly to himself a little French air.

'Who is he?' asked the detective, when the odd creature was out of hearing.

'I know little more about him than you do,' I answered; 'and Sir Calvin's acquaintance with him is, I think, almost as casual as my own. We both met him abroad at different times. He may be a person of distinction, or he may be just an adventurer for all I know to the contrary.'

'Well,' said the officer, 'whoever he is, I don't want him meddling in my business, and I shall have to tell Sir Calvin so.'

'Do,' I said. 'Chess is the Baron's business, and it's that that he's here for.'

But I kept my private suspicions, while duly noting as much as might or might not be implied in Le Sage's curious interest in the scene of the crime. No doubt the last thing he had expected was our sudden descent upon him there.

CHAPTER VIII

AN ENTR'ACTE

JAKE was a boy of imagination, though one would never have thought it to look at his jolly rubicund face and small sturdy form. The very gaiters on his stout calves, spruce and workmanlike, would have precluded any such idea. His master, Sir Francis Orsden—the son of one of whose gamekeepers he was—would never, though a young man of imagination himself, have guessed in Jake a kindred spirit. Yet, when Sir Francis played on the organ in the little church at Leighway, and Jake blew for him, it was odds which of the two brought the more inspiration to his task. Sir Francis would practise there occasionally, and bring the boy with him, because Jake was dogged and strong of muscle, and not easily tired. He never knew what secret goad to endurance the small rascal possessed in his imagination. The business in hand-blowing was to watch a plummet's rise and fall: you pumped for the fall and slackened for the rise. That was the hard prose of it; but Jake knew a better way. He would imagine himself blowing up a fire with a bellows. When a full organ was needed, he had to blow like the devil to keep the plummet down, and then the fire roared under his efforts; otherwise, a gentle purring glow was easily stimulated. At another time he would be filling a bucket at a well for a succession of thirsty horses, and would so nicely time the allowance for each that the bucket was descending again on the very point of its being sucked dry. Or he would be the landlord of the Bit and Halter, dozing over his parlour fire, nodding, nodding down in little jerks, and then recovering himself with an indrawn rising sigh. Sometimes, when the music was very liquid, he would work a beer engine—one or two good pulls, and then the upward flow through the syphon; sometimes he would fish, and, getting a bite, pull in. These make-believes greatly ameliorated the tedium of his office by importing a sense of personal responsibility into it. It was not so much the music he had to keep going as his fancy of the moment.

One morning he was blowing for his master—and pretending, rather gruesomely, to be an exhausted swimmer struggling for a few strokes, and then relaxing and drifting until agonised convulsively to fresh efforts—when he became aware of a young lady standing by him and amusedly watching his labours. Jake ducked, even in the process of pumping, and Miss Kennett put a finger to her lips. She was quite a popular young lady among the villagers, whom she treated on terms of sociability which her father would strongly have disapproved had he known. There was nothing of Touchstone's rosy Audrey about Miss Kennett, but there was a good deal of the graceful and graceless rebel. Grievance, mutely felt, had thrown her into another camp than that of her order.

Sir Francis played on, unconscious of his listener; until presently, with a whispered 'Give it me, Jacob,' the young lady appropriated the pump-handle and began herself to inflate the lungs of the music. The change did not make for success; her strokes, femininely short and quick, raced against the rising plummet, and presently gave out altogether at a critical moment of full pressure. The wind went from the pipes in a dismal whine; Miss Kennett sat back on the pump-handle in a fit of helpless laughter, and Sir Francis came dodging round the organ in a fume.

'Great Scott!' he exclaimed; and the asperity in his face melted into an amiable grin.

'My mistake,' said Audrey. 'Do go on!'

'How did you know I was here?'

'I didn't; but I heard someone grinding the organ, and came in to see.'

'Jake,' said his master, 'Miss Kennett is going to blow for me, so you can cut along.'

The boy touched his forehead, secured his cap, and departed.

'A good youngster,' said Sir Francis.

'I love him,' said Audrey.

'Ah!' sighed the young Baronet, 'lucky Jake!'

'Frank, don't be tiresome. Do you really want me to blow for you? No, not for ever. I know you are going to say it, and it would simply be silly. If I am going to stop here, you must talk sense.'

'I have hardly said anything yet.'

'Well, don't say it. Sit down and play.'

'I don't want to play: I want to be serious. Why am I so obnoxious to you, Audrey?'

'Now I shall go.'

'No. Do be patient. Really, you know, you have never yet said, in so many words, why you won't marry me.'

'Yes I have. It is because I couldn't possibly call myself Audrey Orsden of Audley.'

'Well, if you will be flippant.'

She stood looking at him a moment. 'I didn't mean to be flippant, Frank—nothing but kind. Shall we go a walk together? It's such a lovely morning. Only you must promise.'

'I think I know what you mean by kind, Audrey—kind in forbearing. Very well, I will promise.'

He stowed his music away, and they went out together—out through the green and shadowed churchyard, with its old headboards and epitaphs. There was one to a merry maid dead at sixteen, whose thoughtless laughter had served some mortuary rhymster for a theme on the perishableness of sweet things, with an earnest recommendation to the Christian to be wise while he might—as if wisdom lay in melancholy. There was a fine opportunity for drawing a moral; but Sir Francis did not draw it. Perhaps he thought he would rather have marriage as a jest than no wife at all.

Soon they were outside the village and making for the free Downs. Audrey was always at her best and frankest on the Downs.

'I had wanted to speak to you,' said her companion. 'Is it really true that our friend the Baron's man has been arrested in connexion with this horrible affair?'

'Yes, it is quite true. Poor Baron! I am not allowed to know much about it all; but it seems that everything points to this Louis being the culprit. He went out on the afternoon of the murder with the express purpose of seeking Annie, and did not come home till long afterwards. The police have taken him into custody on suspicion.'

'It must be awkward for you all, having the Baron for a guest.'

'It is, in a way; but we can't very well ask him to go elsewhere while his man is in peril. He offered; but papa wouldn't hear of it. He said the best thing for them both was to go on playing chess.'

'How's Hugo?'

'He's all right. Why shouldn't he be?'

'I don't know. Only he struck me as being upset about something on that day we shot together.'

'Well, he doesn't give me his confidence, you know.'

'No, I know. Poor Audrey!'

'Why do you call me poor Audrey?' asked the girl angrily. 'I don't want your pity, or anybody's.'

'You don't want anything of mine, I'm sure; and yet it's all there for your acceptance—every bit.'

'Is this keeping your promise? No, I don't. I want what I want, and it's nothing that you can give me.'

'Not my whole love and submission, Audrey?'

She flounced her shoulder, and seemed as if about to leave him, but suddenly thought better of it, and faced him resolutely.

'It's that, Frank, though you don't seem to understand it. I don't want any man's submission! I want his mastership, if I want him at all.' Her eyes softened, and she looked at him pityingly.' I hate to pain you, dear; but I can't marry you. You have a thousand good qualities; you are gentle and true and just and honourable, and you have a mind to put my poor little organ to shame. Why you should possibly want me, I can't tell; but I'm very sure of one thing—that I am wise in disappointing you. We should be the brass and the earthenware pots, Frank, and you would be the one to be broke. I know it. You are a poet, and I am the very worst of prose. You have a right to despise me, and I have a right—not to despise you, but to see what you are not—from my point of view.'

'That is to say, a sportsman,' he replied.

'You know I could never pretend to any sympathy with your real tastes—books and music and musty old prints, and all that sort of thing.'

He laughed. 'Well, I shall try again.'

His persistence goaded her to cruelty.

'If you want to know the truth, I like a man to be a man, as my brother is.'

His face twitched and sobered. 'And I am not one.'

'Why do you make me say these things?' she cried resentfully. 'You drive me to it, and then take credit, I suppose, for your larger nature.'

'I take credit for nothing,' said he. 'My account with you is all on the debit side. Audrey, dear, please forgive me for having broken my word. It shall be the last time.'

'I believe it has been the first,' she said, with a rather quivering lip. 'I will say that for you, Frank. Your word is your bond. Now do let us talk about something else. I came out to get rid of all that horrible atmosphere, of police, and detectives, and suspicions about everybody and everything, and this is my reward. The inquest is taking place this very day, and how glad I shall be when the whole sick business is over, and the poor thing decently buried, words can't say. Now, one, two, three, and let us race for that clump.'

CHAPTER IX

THE INQUEST

THE Bit and Halter was seething with excitement. Its landlord, Joe Harris, selected foreman of the jury about to sit on the poor remains of that which, five days earlier, had been the living entity known as Annie Evans, had all the bustling air of a Master of the Ceremonies at some important entertainment. The tap overflowed as on an auction day—occasion most popular for bringing together from near and far those birds of prey to whom a broken home or a bankrupt farm stock offers an irresistible attraction. Here it was another sort of calamity, but the moral was the same. It turned upon that form of Epicurism which consists in watching comfortably from an auditorium the agonies of one's martyred fellow-creatures in the arena. There are sybarites of that complexion who, if they cannot be in at the death, will go far to be in at the burying.

The case, both from its local notoriety and the agreeable mystery which surrounded it, had aroused pretty widespread interest. Speculation as to its outcome was rife and voluble. Quite a pack of vehicles stood congregated in the road, and quite a crowd of their owners in and about the inn enclosure. Each known official visage, as it appeared, was greeted with a curious scrutiny, silent until the newcomer had passed, and then rising garrulous in the wake of his going. There was no actual ribaldry heard, but plenty of rather excited jocularity, with odds given and taken on the event. If the poor shattered voiceless thing, which lay so quietly in its shell in an outhouse awaiting the coming verdict, could only once have pleaded in visible evidence for itself, surely the solemnity of that mute entreaty for peace and forgetfulness would have found its way even to those insensate hearts. But charity is as much a matter of imagination as of feeling, and many an unobtrusive need in the world fails of its relief through the lack of that penetrative vision in the well-meaning. Our souls, it may be, are not to be measured within the limits of our qualities.

At near eleven o'clock the deputy District Coroner, Mr Brabner, drove up in a fly. He was a small important-looking bewhiskered man, in large round spectacles of such strength as to impart to his whole face a solemn owlish look, very sapient and impressive. A hush fell upon the throng as he alighted with his clerk and, ushered by the landlord, entered the inn. But he had hardly disappeared when a more thrilling advent came, like Aaron's serpent, to devour the lesser. This was of the arrested man, in the charge of a couple of officers from the County police-station. The unhappy little Gascon looked frightened and bewildered. His restless, vivacious, brown eyes glanced hither and thither among the people, seeming to deprecate, to implore, to appeal for pity from a monstrous terror which had trapped and was about to devour him. But his emotions had hardly found scope for their display when he was gone—hurried in by his escort.

Thereafter—the party from the house, with all necessary witnesses, being already assembled in the inn—no time was lost in opening the proceedings, which were arranged to take place in the coffee-room, the one fair-sized chamber in the building, though still so small that only a fraction of the waiting public could be allowed admittance to it, the rest hanging disconsolately about the passages and windows, and getting what information they could by deputy. The Coroner took his seat at one end of the long table provided; the jury—*probi et legales homines* to the number of twelve, good farm-hands and true, the most of them, and ready to believe anything they were told—were despatched to view the body; and the business began. Mr Redstall, a Winton solicitor, watched the case on behalf of Sir Calvin, the deceased's family being unrepresented, and Mr Fyler, barrister-at-law, appeared for the police. A report of the subsequent proceedings is summarised in the following notes:

Evidence of identification being in the first instance required, Sergeant Ridgway, of the Scotland Yard detective force, stated that it had been found impossible so far, in spite of every effort made, to trace out the deceased's relations. He had himself made a journey to London, whence the girl had been originally engaged, for the express purpose of inquiring, but had failed wholly to procure any information on the subject. All agencies had been communicated with, and the name did not figure anywhere on their books. An advertisement, appealing to the next of kin, had been inserted in a number of newspapers, but without as yet eliciting any response. He called on Mrs Bingley to repeat the statement she had already made to him regarding the deceased's engagement by her, and the housekeeper having complied, he asked the Coroner, in default of any more intimate proof, to accept the only evidence of identification procurable at the moment. Further attempts would be made, of course, to elucidate the mystery, as by way of the deceased's former employer, Mrs Wilson; but that lady, being gone to New Zealand, might prove as difficult to trace as Evans's own connexions; and in any event a long time must elapse before an answer could be obtained from her. A search of the girl's boxes and personal belongings, though minutely conducted by himself and the housekeeper, had failed to yield any clue whatsoever, and, in short, so far as things went, that was the whole matter.

The Sergeant spoke, now as hereafter, always with visible effect, not only on the jury but on the Coroner himself. His cool, keen aspect, his pruned and essential phrases, the awful halo with which his position as a great London detective surrounded him, not to speak of the local reputation he had lately acquired, weighted his every word to these admiring provincial minds with a gravity and authority which were final. If he said that such a thing was, it was. The Coroner's clerk entered on his minutes the name of Annie Evans, domestic servant, age twenty-three, family and condition unknown; and the case proceeded.

Mr Hugo Kennett was the first witness called. He gave his evidence quietly and clearly, though with some signs of emotion when he referred to his discovery of the dead body. His relation of the event has already been given, and need not here be repeated. The essential facts were that he had entered the Bishop's Walk on the fatal afternoon, shortly after three o'clock; had encountered and stood talking with the girl for a period estimated at ten minutes; had then continued his way to the house, which he may have reached about 3.15, and later, just as it struck four, had suddenly remembered leaving his gun in the copse, and had returned to retrieve it, with the result known. The body was lying on its face, and from its attitude and the nature of the injury it would appear that the shot had been fired from the direction of the road. He went at once to raise an alarm.

At the conclusion of this evidence, Counsel rose to put a few questions to the witness.

Q. You say, Mr Kennett, you left at once, on discovering the body, to give the alarm?

A. Yes.

Q. Leaving your gun where it was?

A. No, I forgot. I spoke generally, not realising that the point might be important

Q. You see that it may be?

A. Quite.

Q. You secured your gun first, then?

A. Yes, I did. I had to pass the body to do it, not liking the job, but driven to it in a sort of insane instinct to get the thing into my safe keeping when it was too late. You see, I blamed myself for having in a sort of way contributed to the deed by my carelessness. I was very much agitated.

Q. You mean that, in your opinion, the crime might never have been committed had not the gun offered itself to some sudden temptation?

A. Yes, that is what I mean.

Q. You are convinced, then, that the shot was fired from this particular weapon?

A. It seems reasonable to conclude so.

Q. Why?

A. I had left it with one of the barrels loaded, and when I saw it again they had both been discharged.

Q. You will swear to the one barrel having been loaded when you left it leaning against the tree?

A. To the best of my belief it was.

Q. You will swear to that?

A. No, I cannot actually swear to it, but I am practically convinced of the fact.

Q. Did you notice, when you took up the gun again, if the barrels, or barrel, were warm?

A. No, I never thought of it.

Q. Don't you think it would have been well if it *had* occurred to you? Don't you think you would have done better to leave the gun alone altogether, until the police arrived?

A. *(The witness for the first time exhibiting a little irritability under this catechism)* I dare say it would have been better. I was agitated, I tell you, and the situation was new to me. One doesn't think of the proper thing to do on such an occasion unless one is a lawyer. I just took the gun with me, and chucked it into the gun-room as I passed, hating the infernal thing.

Q. Very natural under the circumstances, I am sure. Now, another question. The shot was fired, you consider, from the direction of the road. At what distance from the deceased would your knowledge as a sportsman put it?

A. Judging roughly, I should say about fifteen feet.

Q. About the distance, that is to say, between the tree against which you had leaned your gun and the spot where the body was found?

A. Yes.

Q. Then the inference is that the gun had suddenly been seized by someone from its position, fired, and replaced where it was?

A. I suppose so.

Q. You reached the house, you say, about 3.15, and left it again, on your way to the copse, just as it struck four. Would you mind telling us how you disposed of the interval?

A. *(With some temper)* I was in my own den all the time. What on earth has that to do with the matter?

Q. Everything, sir; touching on the critical movements of witnesses in a case of this sort matters. I wish to ask you, for instance, if, during that interval from 3.15 to 4 o'clock, you heard any sound, any report, like that of a gun being discharged?

A. If I had, I should probably have paid no attention to it. The sound of a gun is nothing very uncommon with us.

Q. I ask you if you were aware of any such sound?

A. Not that I can remember.

Mr Fyler was an advocate of that Old Bailey complexion, colourless, black-eyebrowed, moist, thick rinded, whose constant policy it is to provoke hostility in a witness with the object of bullying him for it into submission and self-committal. With every reason, in the present case, to *res*pect, and none to *sus*pect, the deponent, his professional habit would nevertheless not permit him to cast his examination in a wholly conciliatory form.

Q. Now, Mr Kennett, I must ask you to be very particular in your replies to the questions I am about to put to you. You came upon Annie Evans, I understand, shortly after entering the copse, and put down your gun with the purpose of speaking to her?

A. With the purpose of lighting a cigarette.

Q. But you did speak with her?

A. Yes, I have said so.

Q. You placed your gun against the tree where you afterwards found it?

A. Yes.

Q. Was the deceased then standing near you, or further in by the tree where her body was found?

A. She was standing— *(Some amazing purport in the question seemed suddenly here to burst upon the witness, and he uttered a violent ejaculation)* —Great God! Are you meaning to suggest that I fired the shot myself? *(Sensation.)*

Q. I am suggesting nothing of the sort, of course. Will you answer, if you please, whether, after you had put aside your gun, she came towards you or you walked towards her?

A. *(Recovering himself with obvious difficulty)* She came towards me.

Q. So as to bring herself within view, we will say, of anyone who might be watching from the road, or thereabouts?

A. Just possibly she might, if the person had come inside the gate.

Q. Would you mind telling us what was the subject of your brief conversation with the deceased?

A. I asked her what she was doing there.

Q. Just so. And she answered, Mr Kennett?

A. O! what one might expect.

Q. Evasively, that is to say?

A. Yes.

Q. Did you twit her, possibly, with being there for an assignation?

A. Something of the sort I might.

Q. And she admitted it?

A. Of course not. *(Laughter.)*

Q. What else, would you mind saying?

A. I understood from her that she had come out to escape the company in the kitchen. It seemed there had been a row regarding her between Cleghorn our butler and the prisoner, and she wanted to get away from them both. She said that the foreigner had paid her unwelcome attentions, and had tried to kiss her, for which she had boxed his ears, and that ever since she had gone in fear of her life from him. *(Sensation.)* I took it more for a joke than a formal complaint, and did not suppose her to be serious. It did not occur to me that she was really frightened of the man, or I should have taken steps for her protection.

Q. And that was all?

A. All that was essential.

Q. Thank you, Mr Kennett. I will not trouble you any further.

Witness turned and retired. His evidence had yielded something of the unexpected, in its incredulous little outburst and in its conclusion. As to the first, it was patent that Counsel's object in putting the question which had provoked it was to suggest maddened jealousy as a motive for the crime on the part of someone to whom the girl's actions had become suddenly visible through her movement towards the witness, between whom and herself had possibly occurred some philandering passages. Such, at least, from the witness's own implied admission of a certain freedom in his conversation with the deceased, would appear a justifiable assumption. His final statement—though legally inadmissible—inasmuch as it supplied the motive with a name, caused a profound stir in Court.

Mrs Anna Bingley, housekeeper to Sir Calvin Kennett, was the next witness called. Her evidence repeated, in effect, what has already been recorded, and may be passed over. Where it was important, it was, like the other, evidence of hearsay, and inadmissible.

Jane Ketchlove, cook to Sir Calvin, gave evidence. She had never seen the prisoner till the night of his arrival, though she had seen his master once or twice on the occasion of former visits. He, the Baron, had not at those times come accompanied by any gentleman. Mr Cabanis made himself quite at home like: he was a very lively, talkative person, and easily excited, she thought. He showed himself very forward with the ladies, and they remarked on it, though putting it down to his foreign breeding. On the night of his arrival the valet went up to lay out his master's things about seven o'clock. Shortly afterwards Annie followed him with the hot water. She, witness, rather wondered over the girl's assurance in going alone, after the way the man had been acting towards her. He had seemed like one struck of a heap with her beauty; for the poor creature was beautiful, there was no denying it. It was as if he claimed her for his own from the first moment of his seeing her, and dared anyone to say him nay. A few minutes later Annie came down, red with fury over his having tried to kiss her. She had boxed his ears well for him, she said. Mr Cleghorn was in the kitchen, and he flew into a fury when he heard. He said she must have encouraged the man, or he never would have dared. He was a great admirer of Annie himself, and it was always said among us that they would come to make a match of it. Annie answered up, asking him what business it was of his, and there was a fine row between the two. In the middle this Cabanis came down. His cheek was red as fire, and he looked like a devil. He said no one had ever struck him—man, woman, or child—without living to repent it. He and Mr Cleghorn got at it then, and the rest of us had a hard ado to part them; but we got things quiet after a time, though it was only for a time, Mr Cleghorn having to go upstairs, upset as he was. They simmered like, and came on the boil again the next day at dinner in the servants' hall. Annie was not there, and that seemed to give them the chance to settle things in her absence. Mr Cleghorn began it, insisting on his prior claim to the girl, and Cabanis answered that, if he couldn't have her, nobody else should; he would see her dead first. That led to a struggle, ending in blows between them; and at the last Cabanis broke away, declaring he was going out then and there to find the girl and put the question to her.

Q. What question?

A. Whether it was to be himself or Mr Cleghorn, sir.

Q. Did he utter any threat against the girl, in case her choice was against him?

A. Not in so many words, sir; but we were all terrified by his look and manner.

Q. They struck you as meaning business, eh?

A. That was it, sir.

Q. About what time was that?

A. As near as possible to two o'clock.

Q. And Mr Cleghorn followed?

A. After waiting a bit, sir, to recover himself. Then he got up sudden, saying he was going to see this thing through, and, putting on his cap and coat, out he went.

Q. At what time was that?

A. It may have been ten minutes after the other.

Q. Did you form any conclusion as to what he meant by seeing the thing through?

A. We all thought he meant, sir, that he was going to follow Cabanis and get the girl herself to choose between them.

Q. When did you see him again?

A. It was at half after four, when, as some of us stood waiting and shivering at the head of the path, he came amongst us.

Q. In his cap and overcoat?

A. Yes, sir. Just as he had gone out. We told him what had happened.

Q And how did he take it?

A. Very bad, sir. He turned that white, I thought he would have fallen.

Q. And when did the prisoner return?

A. It may have been five o'clock when I saw him come in.

Q. Did his manner then show any signs of agitation or disturbance?

A. No, sir, I can't say it did. On the contrary, he seemed cheerful and relieved, as if he had got something off his mind.

Q. Did you tell him what had happened?

A. Yes, to be sure.

Q. And how did *he* take it?

A. Very quiet—sort of stunned like.

Q. Did he make any remark?

A. He said something in his own language, sir, very deep and hoarse. It sounded like—but I really can't manage it.

M. le Baron. (interposing) It was '*Non, non, par pitié!*'

Counsel. (tartly) I shall be obliged, sir, if you will keep your evidence till it is asked for. *(M. le Baron admitted his error with a bow.)*

Q. Was that all?

A. One of the maids told him, sir, that his master was asking for him, and he went off at once, without another word.

Q. And he has never referred to the subject since?

A. He would not talk of it. It was too horrible, he said.

Jessie Ellis, parlour-maid, and a couple of house-maids (they kept no male indoor servants, except the butler, at Wildshott), Kate Vokes and Mabel Wheelband, gave corroborative evidence, substantiating in all essential particulars the last witness's statement.

Reuben Henstridge, landlord of the Red Deer inn, was the next witness summoned. He was a big cloddish fellow, unprepossessing in appearance, and reluctant and unwilling in his answers, as though surlily suspecting some design to ensnare him into compromising himself. He deposed that on the afternoon of the crime he was out on the hill somewhere, below his inn 'taking the air', when he saw a man break through the lower beech-thicket skirting Wildshott, and go down quickly towards the high road. That man was the prisoner. He parted the branches savage-like, and jumped the bank and trench, moving his arms and talking to himself all the time. Witness went on with his business of 'taking the air', and, when he had had enough, returned to his own premises. Later, Mr Cleghorn, whom he knew very well as a casual customer, came in for a glass. He did not look himself, and stayed only a short time, and that was the whole *he* knew of the matter.

Q. What time of day was it when you saw the prisoner come from the wood?

A. Ten after two, it might be.

Q. And he went down towards the road?

A. Aye.

Q. Did you notice what became of him?

A. No, I didn't. I had my own concerns to look after.

Q. Taking the air, eh?

A. That's it.

Q. You weren't taking it with a wire, I suppose? *(Laughter.)*

A. No, I weren't. You keep a civil tongue in your head.

The witness, called sharply to order by the Coroner, stood glowering and muttering.

Q. Where is your inn situated?

A. Top o' Stockford Down.

Q. How far is it from the high road?

A. Call it a mile and a half.

Q. Where were you on the hill when you saw the prisoner?

A. Nigher the road than the inn. Three-quarters way down, say.

Q. Were you anywhere near the prisoner when he emerged?

A. Nigh as close as I am to you.

Q. Did he see you?

A. No, he didn't. I were hid in the ditch. *(Laughter.)*

Q. You didn't recognise him?

A. Not likely. I'd never seen him before.

Q. Did anything strike you in his manner or expression?

A. He looked uncommon wild.

Q. Did he? Now, what time was it when you started to return to your inn?

A. It may have been an hour later.

Q. A little after three, say?

A. Aye.

Q. Did you pass anybody by the way?

A. No.

Q. The Red Deer is very lonely situated, is it not?

A. Lonely enough.

Q. High up, at the meeting of four cross roads, I understand?

A. That's it.

Q. You don't have many customers in the course of a day?

A. Maybe, maybe not.

Q. Not so many that you would forget this one or that having called yesterday or the day before?

A. What are you trying to get at?

Q. I must trouble you to answer questions, not put them. What time was it on that day when Mr Cleghorn looked in?

A. Put it at four o'clock.

Q. And you thought he looked unwell?

A. He said himself he was feeling out of sorts. The liquor seemed to pull him round a bit.

Q. Did he say anything else?

A. Not much. He went as soon a'most as he'd drunk it down. I thought he'd tired himself walking up the hill.

Q. What made you think that?

A. I see'd him a'coming when he was far off. I was crossing the yard to the pump at the time. That might have been at a quarter before four. He looked as if he'd pulled his cap over his eyes and turned his coat collar up; but I couldn't make him out distinct.

Q. How did you know, then, that it was Mr Cleghorn?

A. Because he come in himself a quarter of an hour or twenty minutes later. Who else could it be?

Q. What sort of coat and hat or cap was this figure wearing?

A. What I see when Mr Cleghorn come in, of course—same as he's got now.

Q. Colour, style—the same in every particular?

A. That's it.

Q. You made out the figure in the distance to be wearing a coat and cloth cap like Mr Cleghorn's?

A. Nat'rally, as it were Mr Cleghorn himself.

Q. Now attend to me. Will you swear you could distinguish the colour of the coat and cap the figure was wearing?

A. I won't go so far as to say that. It were a dull day, and my eyesight none of the best, and he were too far off, and down in the shadder of the hollers. He looked all one colour to me—a sort o' misty purple. But I knew him for Mr Cleghorn, sure enough, when he walked into the tap.

Q. Wonderfully sagacious of you. *(Laughter.)* How far away was this figure when you saw it?

A. Couple o' hundred yards, maybe.

Q. Was it climbing the hill fast?

A. What you might call fast—hurrying.

Q. Didn't it strike you as odd, then, that it should take it a quarter of an hour or twenty minutes to cover that short distance between the spot where you saw it and your inn?

A. No, it didn't. I didn't think about it. Mr Cleghorn, he might have stopped to rest himself, or to tie a bootlace, or anything.

Q. After seeing the figure did you return to the bar?

A. No. I went into the parlour to make tea.

Q. And remained there till Mr Cleghorn entered?

A. That's it.

Counsel nodded across at the detective, as if to say, 'Here's possible matter for you, Sergeant,' and with that he closed the examination, and told the witness he might stand down.

Samuel Cleghorn, butler to Sir Calvin, was then called to give evidence. Witness appeared as a substantial, well-nourished man of forty, with a full, rather unexpressive face, a fixed eye (literally), and a large bald tonsure—not at all the sort of figure one would associate with a romantic story of passion and mystery. He admitted his quarrel with the prisoner, pleading excessive provocation, and that he had followed him out on the fatal afternoon with the intention actually suggested by the witness Ketchlove. He had failed, however, to discover him, or the direction in which he had gone, and had ultimately, after some desultory prying about the grounds, withdrawn himself to the upper kitchen gardens, where he had taken refuge in a tool-shed, and there remained, nursing his sorrow, until 3.30 or thereabouts, when, feeling still very overcome, he had decided to go up to the Red Deer for a little refreshment, which he had done, afterwards returning straight to the house.

Q. How did you leave the kitchen garden?

A. By a door in the wall, sir, giving on the downs; and by that way I returned.

Q. During all this time, while you were looking for the prisoner, or mourning in the tool-shed *(Laughter)* did you encounter anyone?

A. Not a soul that I can remember, sir.

Q. You were greatly attached to the deceased?

A. *(With emotion)* I was.

Q. And wished to make her your wife?

A. Yes.

Q. Though your acquaintance with her extended over only a couple of months?

A. That is so.

Q. Almost a case of love at first sight, eh?

A. As you choose, sir.

Q. Did she return your attachment?

A. Not as I could have wished.

Q. She refused you?

A. I never offered myself to her in so many words.

Q. Had you reason to suspect a rival?

A. None in particular—till the Frenchman came.

Q. Rivals generally, then?

A. Naturally there were many to admire her.

Q. But no one in especial to excite your jealousy?

A. No.

Q. Did the deceased give you her confidence?

A. Not what you might call her confidence. We were very friendly.

Q. She never spoke to you of her past life, or of her former situations, or of her relations?

A. No, never. She was not what you might call a communicative young woman.

Q. You had no reason to suspect that she was carrying on with anybody unknown to you?

A. No *reason*, sir. I can't answer for my thoughts.

Q. What do you mean by that?

A. Why, I might have wondered now and again *why* she was so obstinate in resisting me.

Q. But you suspected no rival in particular? I ask you again.

A. A man may think things.

Q. Will you answer my question?

A. Well, then, I didn't.

Q. Are you speaking the truth?

A. Yes.

Witness was subjected to some severe cross-questioning on this point, but persisted in his refusal to associate his suspicions with any particular person. He argued only negatively, he said, from the deceased's indifference to himself, which (he declared amid some laughter) was utterly incomprehensible to him on any other supposition than that of a previous attachment. Counsel then continued:

Q. When, after leaving the garden, you were making for the Red Deer, did you observe any other figure on the hill, going in the same direction as yourself, but in advance of you?

A. There may have been. I won't answer for sure.

Q. Will you explain what you mean by that?

A. I was what you might call preoccupied—not thinking much of anything but my own trouble. But—yes, I have an idea there was someone.

Q. How was he dressed?

A. I can't say, sir. I never looked; it's only a hazy sort of impression.

Q. Was he far ahead?

A. He may have been—very far; or perhaps it was only the shadows. I shouldn't like to swear there was anyone at all.

Q. You have heard the witness Henstridge's evidence. Are you sure you are not borrowing from it the idea of this second figure, a sort of simulacrum of yourself?

A. Well, I may be, unconscious as it were. I can't state anything for certain.

Q. Were you walking fast as you got near the inn?

A. I dare say I was fast—for me. *(Laughter.)* What with one thing and another, my throat was as dry as tinder.

Q. Did you stop, or linger, for any purpose when approaching the inn?

A. Not that I can remember. I may have. What happened afterwards has put all that out of my head.

Q. You mean the news awaiting you on your return?

A. Yes.

Q. So that you can't tell me, I suppose, whether or not, as you climbed the hill, your coat-collar was turned up and the peak of your cap pulled down?

A. It's like enough they were. I had put the things on anyhow in my hurry. But it's all a vague memory.

Counsel. Very well. You can stand down.

Daniel Groome, gardener, was next called. He stated that he was sweeping up leaves in the drive to the east side of the house—that is to say, the side furthest from the copse—on the afternoon of the murder. Had heard the stable clock strike three, and shortly afterwards had seen the young master come out of the head of the Bishop's Walk and go towards the house, which he entered by the front door. He was looking, he thought, in a bit of a temper: but the young master was like that—all in a stew one moment over a little thing, and the next laughing and joking over something that mattered. Had wondered at seeing him back so soon from the shooting, but supposed he had shot wild, as he sometimes would, and was in a pet about it. Did not see him again until he, witness, was summoned to the copse to help remove the body.

Q. During the time you were sweeping in the drive, did you hear the sound of a shot?

A. A'many, sir. The gentlemen was out with their guns.

Q. Did any one shot sound to you nearer than the others?

A. One sounded pretty loud.

Q. As if comparatively close by?

A. Yes, it might be.

Q. From the direction of the Bishop's Walk?

A. I couldn't rightly say, sir. It wasn't a carrying day. Sounds on such a day travel very deceptive. It might have come from across the road, or further.

Q. At what time did you hear this particular shot?

A. It might have been three o'clock, or a little later; I couldn't be sure.

Q. Think again.

A. No, I couldn't be sure, sir. I shouldn't like to swear.

Q. Might it have been nearer half-past three?

A. Very like. I dare say it might.

This point was urged, but the witness persisted in refusing to commit himself to any more definite statement.

John Tugwood, coachman, Edward Noakes, groom, and Martha Jolly, lodge-keeper, were called and examined on the same subject. They had all distinguished, or thought they had distinguished, the louder shot in question; but their evidence as to its precise time was so hopelessly contradictory that no reliance whatever could be placed on it.

Sergeant-Detective Ridgway deposed that, having been put in charge of the case by Sir Calvin Kennett, he had proceeded to make an examination of the spot where the body had been found. This was some twenty-four hours after the commission of the alleged crime, and it might be thought possible that certain local changes had occurred during the interval. He understood, however, that the police had, when first called in, conducted an exhaustive investigation of the place, and that their conclusions differed in no material degree from his own, so that he was permitted to speak for them in the few details he had to place before the jury. Briefly, his notes comprised the following observations: The measured distance from the wicket in the boundary hedge to the tree against which the witness, Mr Hugo Kennett, had stated that he rested his gun was nineteen and a quarter yards: thence to the beech-tree by which the body had been found was another fifteen feet. Between the wicket and the first tree there was a curve in the track, sufficient to conceal from anyone standing by the second, or inner, tree the movements of one approaching from the direction of the gate. All about this part of the copse, down to the hedge, was very dense thicket, which in one place, in close proximity to the first tree supporting the gun, bore some tokens as of a person having been concealed there. If such were the case, the movements of the person in question had been presumably stealthy, the growth showing only slight signs of disturbance, not easily detected. His theory was that this person had entered possibly by the gate from the road, had crept along the path, or track, until he had caught a glimpse through the trees of the deceased in conversation with Mr Kennett, had then slipped into the undergrowth and silently worked his way to the point of concealment first mentioned, where he would be both eye and ear witness of what was passing between the two, and had subsequently, whether torn by the passion of revenge or of jealousy, issued noiselessly forth, some few minutes after Mr Kennett's departure, seized up the gun, and either at once, or following a brief altercation, shot the deceased dead as she was moving to escape from him. Conformably with this theory, there was no sign of any struggle having occurred; but there *were* signs that the murderer had moved and conducted himself with great caution and circumspection. Unfortunately no evidence as to footprints could be adduced, the ground being in too hard and dry a state to record their impression. Finally, he was bound to say that there was nothing in his theory incompatible with the assumption that the prisoner was the one responsible for the deed. On the other hand, it was true that the man's movements between the time when the witness Henstridge had seen him descending towards the road, and the time of the commission of the crime—which could not have been earlier than three o'clock—had still to be accounted for. But it was possible, of course, that he had occupied this interval of three-quarters of an hour in stalking, and in finally running to earth his victim. If he could produce witnesses to prove the contrary, the theory of course collapsed.

The Sergeant delivered his statement with a hard, clear-cut precision which was in curious and rather deadly contrast with the nervous hesitation displayed by other witnesses. There was a suggestion about him of the expert surgeon, demonstrating, knife in hand, above the operating table; and in a voice as keen and cold as his blade.

Raymond, Baron Le Sage, was the next witness called. It was noticed once or twice, during the course of the Baron's evidence, that the prisoner looked reproachfully and imploringly towards his master.

Q. The prisoner is your servant?
A. He is my servant.
Q. Since when, will you tell me?
A. He has been in my service now over a year.
Q. You took him with a good character?
A. An excellent character.
Q. He is a Gascon, I believe?
A. Yes, a Gascon.
Q. A hot-blooded and vindictive race, is it not?
A. A warm-blooded people, certainly.

Q. Practising the vendetta?

A. You surprise me.

Q. I am asking you for information.

A. I have none to give you.

Q. Very well; we will leave it at that. On the afternoon of the murder, about half-past two, you entered the Bishop's Walk?

A. I had been out driving with Miss Kennett, and, passing the gate, asked her whither it led. She told me, and I decided to go by the path, leaving her to drive on to the house alone.

Q. Why did you so decide?

A. I had caught a glimpse among the trees, of, as I thought, the maid, Annie Evans, and I wished to speak with her.

Q. Indeed? *(Counsel was evidently a little taken aback over the frankness of his admission.)* Would you inform me on what subject?

A. I had been accidental witness the night before of the scrimmage between her and Louis already referred to, and I wished at once to apologise to her for Louis's behaviour, and to warn her against any repetition of the punishment she had inflicted.

Q. On what grounds?

A. On the grounds that, the man being quick-tempered and impulsive, I would not answer for the consequences of another such assault. *(Sensation.)*

Q. And what was the deceased's answer?

A. She thanked me, and said she could look after herself.

Q. Anything further?

A. Nothing. I went on and joined my friend, Sir Calvin, in the house.

Q. The deceased, while you were with her, offered no sort of explanation of her presence in the copse?

A. None whatever.

Q. And you did not seek one?

A. O, dear, no! I should not have been so foolish. *(Laughter.)*

Q. Did you speak to the prisoner on the subject of the assault?

A. At the time, yes.

Q. And what did you gather from his answer?

A. I gathered that, in his quick ardent way, he was very much enamoured of the girl's beauty.

Q. And was correspondingly incensed, perhaps, over her rejection of his advances?

A. Not incensed. Saddened.

Q. He uttered no threat?

A. No.

Q. On the afternoon of the murder, on your return to the house, as just described, you inquired for the prisoner?

A. I inquired for him, then, and again later on our return from the copse after we had been to view the body.

Q. You were troubled about him, perhaps?

A. I was uneasy, until I had seen and questioned him.

Q. When was that?

A. He came in about five o'clock, and was immediately sent up to me.

Q. You asked him, perhaps, to account for his absence?

A. I did.

Q. And what was his explanation?

A. He made a frank confession of his quarrel with Mr Cleghorn, described how his first intention on rushing from the house had really been to find the girl and throw himself upon her mercy; but how, once in the open air, his frenzy had begun to cool, and to yield itself presently to indecision. He had then, he said, gone for a long walk over the downs, fighting all the way the demon of rage and jealousy which possessed him, and had finally, getting the better of his black unreasoning mood, grown thoroughly repentant and ashamed of his behaviour, and had returned to make amends.

Q. And you credited that wonderful story?

A. I believed it implicitly.

Q. Well, indeed, sir! Did he appear overcome by the *news* which had greeted him on his return?

A. He appeared stupefied—that is the word.

Q. Did he comment on it at all?

A. If you mean in the self-incriminating sense, he did not.

Q. In what sense, then?

A. He cursed the assassin capable of destroying so sweet a paragon of womanhood. *(Laughter.)*

Q. Very disinterested of him, I'm sure. Thank you, sir; that will suffice.

Counsel sitting down, Mr Redstall, for Sir Calvin, rose to put a question or two to the witness:

Q. You have never had reason, M. le Baron, to regard the prisoner as a vindictive man?

A. Never. Impulsive, yes.

Q. And truthful?

A. Transparently so—to a childish degree.

Q. He would have a difficulty in dissembling?

A. An insuperable difficulty, I should think.

Dr Harding, of Longbridge, was the last witness called. He deposed to his having been summoned to the house on the afternoon of the murder, and to having examined the body within an hour and a half of its first discovery in the copse. The cause of death was a gunshot wound in the back, from a weapon fired at short range. Practically the whole of the charge had entered the body in one piece. Death must have been instantaneous, and must have occurred, from the indications, some two hours before his arrival; or, approximately, at about 3.30 o'clock. The wound could not possibly have been self-inflicted, and the position of the gun precluded any thought of accident. He had since, assisted by Dr Liversidge of Winton, made a *post-mortem* examination of the body. Asked if there was anything significant in the deceased's condition, his answer was yes.

This completed the evidence, at the conclusion of which, and of some remarks by the Coroner, the jury, after a brief consultation among themselves, brought in a verdict that the deceased died from a gunshot wound deliberately inflicted by the prisoner Louis Victor Cabanis, in a fit of revengeful passion; which verdict amounting to one of wilful murder, the prisoner was forthwith, on the Coroner's warrant, committed to the County gaol, there to await his examination before the magistrates on the capital charge. The jury further—being local men—added a rider to their verdict respectfully commiserating Sir Calvin on the very unpleasant business which had chosen to select his grounds for its enactment; and with that the proceedings terminated.

CHAPTER X

AFTERWARDS

THE Inquest was over, the provisional verdict delivered, and all that remained for the time being was to put the poor subject of it straightway to rest under the leafless trees in Leighway churchyard. It was done quietly and decently the morning after the inquiry, with some of her fellow-servants attending, and Miss Kennett to represent the family; and so was another blossom untimely fallen, and another moral—a somewhat ghastly one now—furnished for the reproof of the too hilarious Christian.

Audrey, coming back from the sad little ceremony, met Le Sage walking by himself in the grounds. The Baron looked serious and, she thought, dejected, and her young heart warmed to his grief. She went up to him, and, putting her hands on his sleeve, 'I am so sorry,' she said, 'so very, very sorry.'

He smiled at her kindly, then took her hand and drew it under his arm.

'Let us walk a little way, and talk,' he said; and they strolled on together. 'Poor Louis!' he sighed.

'It is not true, is it, Baron?'

'I don't think it is, my dear. But the difficulty is to prove that it isn't.'

'How can it be done?'

'At the expense only, I am afraid, of finding the real criminal.'

'Have you any idea who that is?'

He laughed; actually laughed aloud.

'Have I not had enough of cross-examination?'

'I could not help wondering why, as I have been told, you confessed to the warning you gave the poor girl.'

'About the danger of tempting hot blood, and so forth?'

'Yes, that.'

'It was the truth.'

'Yes, but—'

He put a finger to his lips, glancing at her with some solemnity.

'You were not going to say that it is my way to repress the truth?'

'No,' answered the girl, with a little flush; 'but only not to blurt it out unnecessarily.'

'My dear,' he said, 'take my word for it that I always speak the truth.'

'O! I only meant to say—' she began; but he stopped her.

'What would you do if a question were put to you which, for some reason of expediency, or good-feeling, you did not wish to answer?'

'I am afraid I should fib.'

'Try my plan, and answer it with another question. It saves a world of responsibility. That is a secret I confide to you. An answer may often be interpreted into an innuendo which is as false to the speaker's meaning as it is unjust to its subject. I love truth so much that I would not expose it to that misunderstanding. In this instance, to have left the truth for someone else to discover might have cast suspicion on us both, thereby darkening the case against Louis. But, in general, not to answer is surely not to lie?'

'No, I suppose not, Baron'—she thought a little— 'I wonder if you would answer me just *one* question?'

'What is that?'

'Do you put any faith in that talk about there having been another man on the hill besides Cleghorn?'

He did not reply for awhile, but went softly patting the hand on his arm. Presently he looked up.

'If I were to say yes, I should not speak the truth, and if I were to say no, I should not speak the truth. So I follow my bent, and you will not be offended with me. Are you going to take me for a drive today, I ask?'

'Certainly, if you wish it.'

'What a question! I can answer that without a scruple. I wish it with such fervour, seeing my companion, as my years may permit themselves. Where shall we go?'

'You shall choose.'

'Very well. Then we will go north by the Downs, that we may take the great free air into our lungs, and realise the more sympathetically the condition of my poor Louis.'

'O, don't! It would kill me to be in prison. Baron, you are going to stop with us, are you not, until the trial is over?'

'Both you and your father are very good. I may have, however, to absent myself for a short time presently. We will see. In the meanwhile I am your grateful Baron.' He took vast snuff, making his eyes glisten, and somehow she liked him for it.

'I shall be glad,' she said, 'when that detective goes. One will feel more at peace from the squalor of it all.'

He shook his head.

'I do not think he means to go just yet.'

'Not? Why not?'

'Ah! that is his secret.'

'But what can he have to do now?'

'You must ask him, not me. All I can tell you is that he considers his work here not yet finished; in fact, from words I heard him let fall to your father this morning, little more than just begun.'

'How very strange! What can it mean?'

'Let us hazard a conjecture that he is not wholly satisfied with the evidence against my Louis. It would be a happy thought for me.'

'O, yes, wouldn't it! But—I wonder.'

'What do you wonder?'

'If the question of that other figure on the hill is puzzling him too.'

Le Sage laughed. 'Well, we are permitted to wonder,' he said, and, humming a little tune, changed the subject to one of topography, and the situation of various places of interest in the neighbourhood.

Audrey was perplexed about him. That he felt, and felt deeply, not only the unhappy position of the prisoner, but the disturbance which he himself had been the innocent means of introducing into the house, she could not doubt; yet the patent genuineness of this sentiment was unable, it seemed, wholly to deprive him of that constitutional serenity, even gaiety, habitual to his nature. It was as if he either could not, or would not, realise the black gravity of the affair; as if, almost, holding the strings of it in his own hands, he could afford to give this or that puppet a little tether before reining it in to submit to his direction. And then she thought how this impression was probably all due to that unanswering trick of his which they had just been discussing, and which might very well seem to inform his manner with a significance it did not really possess or intend. She left him shortly, being called to some duty in the house, and he continued his saunter alone, an aimless one apparently, but gradually, after a time, assuming a definite direction. It took him leisurely down the drive, out by the lodge gates into the road as far as the fatal wicket, and so once more into the Bishop's Walk. Going unhurried along the track, he suddenly saw the detective before him.

The Sergeant, bent over, it seemed, in an intent observation of the ground, was fairly taken off his guard. He showed it, as he came erect, in a momentary change of colour. But the little shock of surprise was mastered as soon as felt: self-possession is not long or easily yielded by one trained in self-resourcefulness.

'Were you wanting me, sir?' he said; 'because, if not—'

'Because, if not,' took up the Baron, wagging his head cheerfully, 'what am I doing here, interrupting you at your business?'

'Well, sir, it's you have said it, not I.'

'So your business is not yet over, Sergeant? Am I to borrow any hope for my man from that?'

'Was it the question, sir, you were looking for me to answer?'

'Excellent! My own way of meeting an awkward inquiry.'

'What do you mean by awkward?'

'Why, you won't answer me, of course. What sensible detective would, and give away his case? Still, I am justified in assuming that there is something in the business which, so far, does not satisfy you; and I build on that.'

'O! you do, do you?' He rubbed his chin grittily, pulling down his well-formed lower jaw, and stood for a moment or two speculatively regarding the face before him. 'I wonder now,' he said suddenly, 'if you would answer a question I might put to you?'

'I'll see, my friend. Chance it.'

'What made you so interested in this business before even your man was charged on suspicion?'

'You allude—?'

'I allude to my finding you already on the spot here when I came down to make my own examination of it.'

'Surely I have no reason to hide what I have already admitted in public? I was uneasy about Louis.'

'And wanted to look and see, perhaps, if he'd left any evidences of his guilt behind him?'

'I admit I was anxious to assure myself that there were no such evidences.'

'And you did assure yourself?'

Quite.'

'You found nothing suspicious?'

'Nothing whatever to connect with his presence here.'

'Found nothing at all?'

'Yes, I did: I found this.'

The Baron took from a pocket a common horn coat-button, and handed it to the other, who received it and turned it over in silence.

'I picked it up,' said Le Sage, 'near the tree where the gun had stood.'

'Why,' said the detective, looking up rather blackly, 'didn't you produce this at the Inquest?'

'I never supposed for the moment it could be of any importance.'

'H'mph!' grunted the Sergeant, and after a darkling moment, put the button into his own pocket. 'I don't know; it may or may not be; but you should have told me about it, sir. For the present, by your leave, I'll take charge of the thing. And now, if you've nothing more to show me—'

'Nothing.'

'Then I should like to get on with my work, if it's all the same to you.'

'And I with my walk,' said the Baron, and he tripped jauntily away.

CHAPTER XI

THE BARON DRIVES

(*From the Bickerdike MS.*)

On the day following the Inquest, the plot thickened. It became really entertaining. One did not know whether to appear the more scandalised or amused. On the one hand there was a certain satisfaction in knowing that the last word was apparently not said in what had seemed to be a perfectly straightforward affair; on the other one's sense of fitness had received a severe blow. In short, the impeccable Cleghorn had been arrested, and was detained on suspicion. I saw him go off in a fly in the charge of a couple of policemen, and never did hooked cod-fish on the Dogger Bank look more gogglingly stupefied than he over the amazing behaviour of the bait he had swallowed. Sir Calvin stormed, and blasphemed, and demanded to know if the whole household of Wildshott was in a conspiracy to shame him and tarnish his escutcheon; but his objurgations were received very civilly and sensibly by the detective, who explained that he must act according to his professional conscience, that detention did not necessarily mean conviction, or even indictment, and that where a sifting of the truth from the chaff imposed precautionary measures, he must be free to take them, or abandon his conduct of the case. Whereon the wrathful General simmered down, and contented himself only with requesting sarcastically a few hours' grace to settle his affairs, when it came to be his turn to wear the official bracelets.

And so, for the while, we were without a butler; nor could one, on reviewing the evidence, be altogether surprised, perhaps, over that deprivation. Certainly Cleghorn's account of his own movements could not be considered wholly satisfying or convincing, and he had admitted his lack of any witness to substantiate it. It seemed incredible, with a man of his substance and dignity; but is not the history of crime full of such apparent contradictions? After all, he had had the same provocation as the other man, and had departed, apparently, the same way to answer it; and, as to his moral condition *after* the event, all testimony went to prove that it was worse than that of the Gascon. Anyhow, this new development, however it was destined to turn out, added fifty per cent to the excitement of the business. Cleghorn! It seemed inexpressibly comic.

As day followed day succeeding this terrific event, however progressively other things might be assumed to be moving, no ground was made in the matter of tracing out the dead girl's origin or connexions—and that in spite of the publicity given to the affair. It was very strange, and I was immensely curious to know what could be the reason. Her portrait was published in the *Police Gazette*, and exhibited outside the various stations, but without result. I saw a copy of it, and did not wonder. It had been reproduced, enlarged, it seemed, from a tiny snapshot group, taken by one of the grooms, in which she had figured quite inconspicuously, and was like nothing human. I spoke to Ridgway about it, and he said it was the best that could be done, that no other photograph of her could be traced, though all the photographers in London had been applied to, and he owned frankly that there seemed some mystery about the girl. I quite agreed with him, and hinted that it was not the only one that remained to be cleared up. He did not ask me what I meant, but I saw, by his next remark, that he had understood what was in my mind.

'Why don't you persuade him, sir,' he said, 'to throw this business off his chest, and get back to his old interests? He takes it too much to heart.'

It was to Hugo he referred, of course, and I did not pretend to misapprehend him. To tell the truth, I was a little smarting from my friend's treatment of me, and not in the mood to be indulgent of his idiosyncrasies. I might have my suspicions as to his involvement in a discreditable affair, but I had certainly not made him a party to them, or even touched upon the subject of the scandal to him save with the utmost delicacy and consideration. If he had chosen to give me his confidence then and there, I would have honoured it; as it was, since he showed no disposition to keep his promise to me made on the day of the shoot, I considered myself as much at liberty to canvass the subject as anyone else who had heard, and formed his own conclusions, from the doctor's evidence. It was true that, to me at least, Hugh was doing his best to give his case away by his behaviour. He seemed to make little attempt to rally from the gloom with which the tragedy had overcast him, but mooned about, silent and aimless, as if for the moment he had lost all interest in life. It was only that morning that, moved by his condition, I had come at last to the resolution to remind him of his promise, and get him to share with me, if he would, the burden that was crushing his soul. His answer showed me at once, however, the vanity of my good intentions. 'Thanks, old fellow,' he had said; 'but a good deal has happened since then, and I've nothing to confide.'

Now, that might be true, in the sense that the danger was past, and I could have forgiven his reticence on the score of the loyalty it might imply to a reputation passed beyond its own defence; but he went on with some offensive remark about his regret in not being able to satisfy my curiosity, and ended with a suggestion which, however well-meaning it might have been, I considered positively insulting.

'You are wasting yourself here, old boy,' he said. 'I'm not, truth to tell, in the mood for much, and we oughtn't to keep you. I feel that I got you here under false pretences; but I couldn't know what was going to happen, could I? and so I won't apologise. I think, I really think, that, for the sake of all our feelings, it would be better if you terminated your visit. You don't mind my saying so, do you?'

'On the contrary, I mind very much,' I answered. 'Have you forgotten how, at considerable inconvenience to myself, I responded at once to your invitation, and came down at a moment's notice? The reason, as you ought to know, Hugh, was pure regard for yourself and a desire to help, and that desire is not lessened because I find you involved in a much more serious business than I had anticipated.'

'O, if you put it in that way—' he began.

'I do put it in that way,' I said, 'and I don't take it very friendly of you that you should talk of denying me a privilege which you were ready enough to grant to that precious new Baron of yours—even pressing him to stay.'

'It was not I who asked him,' he murmured.

'No,' I insisted, 'I came to be helpful, and I am going to remain to be helpful. I don't leave you till I have seen this thing through.'

'Well,' he said very equivocally, 'I hope that will be soon'—and he left me to myself to brood over his ingratitude. I was sore with him, I confess, and my grievance made me more unguarded perhaps in my references to him than otherwise I should have been.

'I dare say he does,' I answered the detective; 'but after all, I suppose, it is his heart that is affected.'

He looked at me keenly.

'You mean, sir?'

'O! what *you* mean,' I answered, 'and that I can see that you mean. What's the good of our beating about the bush? My friend wouldn't be the first young fellow of his class to have got into trouble with a good-looking servant girl.'

'No,' he said, 'no,' in a hard sort of way. 'They are not the kind to bother about the consequences to others where their own gratification is concerned. I've knocked up against some pretty bad cases in my time. So, that's what you gather from the medical report?'

'Partly from that; not wholly.'

'Ah! I dare say now, being on such friendly terms with Mr Kennett, you've been taken into his confidence?'

'Not directly; but in a way that invited me to form my own conclusions. What then? It doesn't affect this case, does it, except in suggesting a possible motive for the crime on the part of some jealous rival?'

'That's it. It's of no consequence, of course—except to the girl herself—from any other point of view.'

His assurance satisfied me, and, taken by his sympathetic candour, I could not refrain from opening my rankling mind to him a bit.

'The truth is,' I said, 'that the moment I came down, I saw there was something wrong with my friend. Indeed, he had written to me to imply as much.'

'He was upset like, was he?' commented the detective.

'He was in a very odd mood,' said I— 'an aggravated form of hysteria, I should call it. I had never known him quite like it before, though, as I dare say you have gathered, his temperament is an excitable one, up and down like a see-saw. He talked of his dreaming of sitting on a gunpowder barrel smoking a cigarette, and of the hell of an explosion that was coming. And then there was his behaviour at the shoot the next day.'

'I've heard something about it,' said Ridgway. 'Queer, wasn't it?'

'More than queer,' I answered. 'I don't mind telling you in confidence that I had reason at one time to suspect him of playing the fool with his gun, with the half intention—you know—an accident, and all the bother ended. He swore not, when I tackled him about it; but I wasn't satisfied. I tried to get him to go home, leaving his gun with the keeper, but he absolutely refused; and he refused again to part with it when, in the afternoon, he finally did leave us, saying he was good for nothing, and had had enough of it. If only then he had done what I wanted him to do, and left his gun behind, this wretched business might never have happened.'

'Ah!' said the detective, 'he feels that, I dare say, and it doesn't help to cheer him up. Well, sir, I'd get him out, if I was you—distract his thoughts, and make him forget himself. He won't mend what's done by moping.'

'All very well,' I answered, 'to talk about making him forget himself; but when I'm forced to affect an ignorance of the very thing he wants to forget—if we're right—what am I to do? You might think that after having had me down for the express purpose of advising him—as I have no doubt was the case—in this scrape, he would take me more into his confidence, and not at least resent, as seemingly he does, any allusion to it.'

'Well, you see,' said the detective, 'from his point of view the scrape's ended for him, and so there isn't the same need for advice. But I'd keep at it, if I was you, and after a time you may get him to unburden himself.'

I had not much hope, after what had passed between us; but I held the Sergeant's recommendation in mind, and resolved to watch for and encourage the least disposition to candour which might show itself on my friend's part. Perhaps I had gone a little further than I should have in taking the detective into my confidence about a scandal which, after all, was no more than surmise; but it was so patent to me that his judgment ran, and must run, with my own, that it would have been simply idle to pretend ignorance of a situation about which no two men of intelligence could possibly have come to differing conclusions. And, moreover, as Ridgway himself had admitted, true or not, the incident had no direct bearing on the case.

These days at Wildshott, otherwise a little eventless for me as an outsider, found a certain mitigation of their dullness in the suspicion still kept alive in me regarding the Baron's movements, and in the consequent watchfulness I felt it my duty to keep on them. I don't know how it was, but I mistrusted the man, his secretiveness, the company he kept, the mystery surrounding his being. Who was he? Why did he play chess for half-crowns? Why had he come attended—as, according to evidence, never before—by a ruffianly foreign man-servant, ready, on the most trifling provocation, to dip his hands in blood? That had been outside the programme, no doubt: men who use dangerous tools must risk their turning in their hands; but what had been his purpose in bringing the fellow? Throat-cutting? Robbery?—I was prepared for any revelation. Abduction, perhaps: the Baron was for ever driving about the country with Audrey in the little governess cart. In the meanwhile, following that miscarriage of his master's plans, whatever they might be, Mr Louis Victor Cabanis had been had up before a full bench of magistrates, and, the police asking for time in which to compact their evidence, had been remanded to prison for a fortnight. The delay gave some breathing space for all concerned, and was, I think, welcomed by everyone but Hugo. I don't know by what passion of hatred of the slayer my friend's soul might have been agitated. Perhaps it was that, perhaps mere nervous tension; but he appeared to be in a feverish impatience to get the business over. He did not say much about it; but one could judge by his look and manner the strained torment of his spirit. We were not a great deal together; and mostly I had to make out my time alone as best I could. Sometimes, in a rather pathetic way, he would go and play chess with his father, a thing he had never dreamed of doing in his normal state. I used to wonder if the General had guessed the truth, and how he was regarding it if he had. According to all accounts, he had been no Puritan himself in his younger days.

I have said that Audrey and the Baron were about a good deal together. They were, and the knowledge troubled me so much that I made up my mind to warn her.

'You appear to find his company very entertaining,' I said to her one day.

Audrey had a rather disconcerting way of responding to any unwelcome question with a wide-eyed stare, which it was difficult to undergo quite stoically.

'Do I?' she said presently. 'Why?'

'You would hardly favour it so much otherwise, would you?'

'Perhaps not. You see I take the best there is. I can't help it if the choice is so limited.'

'That's one for me. But never mind. I'm content he should do the entertaining, if I can do the helpful.'

'To me, Mr Bickerdike?'

'I hope so—a little. As Hugo's friend I feel that I ought to have some claim on your forbearance, not to say your good will. I think at least that, on the strength of that friendship, you need not resent my giving you a word of advice on a subject where, in my opinion, it's wanted.'

'I have a father and brother to look after me, Mr Bickerdike.'

'I'm aware of it, Audrey; and also of the fact that—for reasons sufficient of their own, no doubt—they leave you pretty much as you like to go your own way. It may be an unexceptionable way for the most part; but the wisest of us may occasionally go wrong from ignorance, and then it is the duty—I dare say the thankless duty—of friendship to interpose. You are very young, you know, and, one can't help seeing, rather forlornly situated—'

'Will you please to leave my situation alone, and explain what this is all about?'

'Frankly, then—I offer this in confidence—I don't think the Baron very good company for you.'

'Why not?'

'It's a little difficult to say. If you had more knowledge of the world you would understand, perhaps. There's an air about him of the shady Continental adventurer, whose purpose in society, wherever he may seek it, is never a disinterested purpose. He's always, one may be sure, after something profitable to himself—in one word, spoil. What do we any of us know about the Baron, except that he plays chess for money and consorts with doubtful characters? Your father knows, I believe, little more than I do, and that little for me is summed up in the word "suspect". One can't say what can be his object in staying on here when common decency, one would have thought, seeing the trouble he has been instrumental in causing, should have dictated his departure; but, whatever his object, it is not likely, one feels convinced, to be a harmless one, and one cannot help fearing that he may be practising on your young credulity with a view to furthering it in some way. I wish you would tell me—will you?—what he talks to you about.'

She laughed in a way which somehow nettled me. 'Doesn't it strike you,' she said, 'as rather cheek on the part of one guest in a house to criticize the behaviour of another to his hostess?'

'O, if you take it in that way,' I answered, greatly affronted, 'I've nothing more to say. Your power of reading character is no doubt immensely superior to mine.'

'Well, I don't think yours is very good,' she answered; 'and I don't see why the question of common decency should apply to him more than to another.'

'Don't you?' I said, now fairly in a rage: 'then it's useless to prolong the discussion further. This is the usual reward of trying to interpose for good in other people's affairs.'

'Some people might call it prying into them,' she answered, and I flung from her without another word. I felt that I really hated the girl—intolerable, pert, audacious young minx; but my rebuff made me more determined than ever to sift the truth out of this questionable riddle, and face her insolent assurance with it at the proper time.

CHAPTER XII

THE BARON WALKS

(*From the Bickerdike MS.*)

I WAS still in this resolved mood, when something happened one night which confirmed my worst suspicions, showing me how faithfully I had weighed and measured the character of the man posing as a benevolent guest in the house, the hospitality of which he was designing all the time, in some mysteriously villainous way, to abuse. On that night I had gone to bed rather late, outstaying, in fact, the entire family and household, whose early country ways my degenerate London habits found sometimes rather irksome. It was past midnight when I turned out the lights in the billiard room, and, taking a candle, made my way upstairs. There was a double flight rising from a pretty spacious hall, and both the Baron's room and my own gave upon the corridor which opened west from the first-floor landing. As I passed his door I noticed that a thread of light showed under it, proving him to be either still awake, or fallen asleep with his candle unextinguished. Which? For some unaccountable reason a thrill of excitement overtook me. No sound came from behind the door; the whole house was dead quiet. I stooped to peer through the key-hole—a naked light burning beside one's bed is a dangerous thing—but the key being in the lock prevented my seeing anything. Soft-footed I went on—but not to sleep. I determined to sit up and listen in my own room for any possible developments. I don't know why it was, but my heart misgave me that there was some rascality afoot, and that I had only to wait patiently, and go warily, to unmask it. And I was not mistaken.

Time passed—enough to assure the watcher at last of my being long in bed and asleep—when I was aware of a stealthy sound in the corridor. All my blood leaped and tingled to the shock of it. I stole, and put my ear to my own keyhole; and at once the nature of the sound was made clear to me. He had noiselessly opened his door and come out into the passage, down which he was stealthily creeping in a direction away from me. I don't know how I recognized all this, but there is a language in profound stillness. When silence is at its deathliest, one can hear almost the way the earth is moving on its axis. I waited until I felt that he had turned the corner to the stairs, then, with infinite care, manipulated, a fraction at a time, the handle of my own door, and, slipping off my pumps, emerged and followed, hardly breathing, in pursuit.

At the opening to the stairs I paused discreetly, to give my quarry 'law', and, with sovereign caution, peered round the corner—and saw him. He was in his pyjamas, and carried an electric torch in his hand, reminding me somehow, thus attired, of the actor Pellissier, only a little squatter in his build. He descended soundlessly, throwing the little beam of light before him, and, reaching the foot of the flight, turned to his left at the moment that I withdrew my head. But I could see from my eyrie the way he was going by the course of the travelling light, and I believed that he was making for Sir Calvin's study. And the next moment there came to my ears the tiniest confirmatory sound—the minute bat-like screak of a rusty door-handle. I had noticed that very day how the one in question needed oiling, and the evidence left me no longer in doubt. It was for the study he was bound, and with what sinister purpose? That remained to see; but I remembered the hidden safe in the room. I had happened upon it once when left alone there.

A minute I paused, to allow him time to settle to his business; then descended the stairs cat-footed. At the newel post, crowned with a great carved wyvern, the Kennett device, I stood to reconnoitre, pressing my face to the wood and looking round it with one eye. And at once I perceived that I neither could nor need venture further. He stood, sure enough, at the desk in the study, fairly revealed in the diffused glow from his torch, whose little brilliant facula was turned upon a litter of papers that lay before him. But the door of the room—he had left it so in his fancied security—stood wide open, precluding any thought of a closer espionage on my part. I could only stay where I was, concentrating all my vision on the event.

Suddenly he seemed to find what he sought, and I saw a paper in his hand. Something appeared to tell me at the same moment that he was about to return, and I yielded and—judging discretion, for the occasion, to be the better part of valour—went up the stairs on my hands and feet as fast as I could paddle, in a soft hurry to regain my room and extinguish the light before so much as the ghost of a suspicion could occur to him. It would not have served my purpose to face him then and there, and I had learnt as much as for the time being I needed. To have detected our worthy friend in a secret midnight raid on his host's papers was proof damning enough of the correctness of my judgment.

Listening intently, I heard him re-enter his room, as he had left it, with supreme caution. I was feeling a good deal agitated, and the moisture stood on my forehead. How was I to proceed; what course to take? My decision was not reached until after much debating within myself. It might be guided by the General's chance assertion that some important document had been lost or mislaid in his room, in which case I must act at once; but if, on the other hand, he made no such statement, it might very well be days or weeks before his loss were brought home to him. In that event I would say nothing about my discovery, trusting to lead the criminal on, through his sense of immunity, to further depredations. By then I might have acquired what at present I lacked, some insight into the nature and meaning of his designs, holding the key to which I could face him with any discovery. No, I would not tell Sir Calvin as yet. In such a case premature exposure might very easily prove more futile than unsuspicion itself. The keystone being wanting, all one's structure might fall to pieces at the first test.

But what a stealthy villain it was! As I recovered, it was to plume myself a little, I confess, on my circumventing such a rogue. I would have given a good deal to know what was the character of the paper he had stolen. Hardly a draft, for such would not have been left about, not to speak of the crude futility of such a deed. No, there was some more subtle intention behind it—blackmail perhaps—but it was useless to speculate. He had not at least touched the safe, and that was so much to be thankful for.

Now I came to my resolution. I would speak to Sir Calvin on the subject when the moment was ripe, and not before: and then, having so far justified my remaining on as his guest, I would go. In the meanwhile I would make it my especial and individual province to expose this rascal, and thereby refute Audrey's detestable calumny of me as a sort of unpleasant eavesdropper and hanger-on. Perhaps she would learn to regret her insult when she saw in what fashion I had retaliated on it.

CHAPTER XIII

ACCUMULATING EVIDENCE

WEDNESDAY of the third week following the Inquest was appointed for the magisterial inquiry, and during the interval Sergeant Ridgway was busily occupied, presumably in accumulating and piecing together various evidence. Of what it consisted no one but himself knew, nor did it appear whether or not its trend on the whole was favourable or disastrous to the unhappy prisoner, at the expense possibly of Cleghorn, or possibly to the complete exculpation of that injured man. The detective kept his own counsel, after the manner of his kind; and if any had thought to extract from the cover of that sealed book a hint of its contents, no reassuring message at least could have been gathered from its unlettered sombreness. But nobody asked, fearful of being thought to profane the majestic muteness of the oracle; and the labouring atmosphere lowered unlightened as the days went on. Even M. le Baron, most individually concerned in the fate of his henchman, made no attempt to plumb the official profundity, in spite of his curiosity about most things. He seemed, indeed, oddly passive about the whole business, never referring to it but indirectly, and, so far as appeared, taking no steps to interview the prisoner or supply him with the means of defence. If any sneering allusion was made to this insensibility by Mr Bickerdike or another, Audrey, were she present, would be hot in her friend's vindication. It may have been that, in the course of their queer association, he had confided to her sufficient reasons for his behaviour; old Viv, on the other hand, saw in her attitude only proof of the process of corruption he had suspected. But, whatever the case, cheerfully detached the Baron remained, asking no questions of the detective, and taking chess and life with as placid a gaiety as if no Louis Victor Cabanis lay caged a few miles away, awaiting his examination on a charge of wilful murder.

Whether it were in some apology for a darkness which he could not afford to illuminate, or to avoid teasing inquiries, or for any other reason, the Sergeant came gradually to give the house less and less of his company. He seemed rather to avoid contact with its inmates, and his manner, when he rarely appeared, was sombre and preoccupied. No one, perhaps, felt this withdrawal more than the housekeeper, Mrs Bingley, with whom he had been accustomed to take his meals, and who had found him, when once her awe of his office was overcome, a most entertaining guest, full of intelligence, rich in anecdote, and deeply interested in everything appertaining to Wildshott, from its family portraits and accumulated collections to the beauty of its grounds and of the country in which it lay situated.

'It must have been,' she said one day to her master, to whom she was lamenting the Sergeant's prolonged absences, 'such a relief to a man of his occupations to be able to forget himself, even for an hour or two, in such noble surroundings. But perhaps he wants to show us that he's taking no advantage of the attentions paid him, lest we might think he was trying to worm himself into our confidence.'

'Or can it be that he has already found out from you all that he wants to know?' observed Le Sage, who was present on the occasion, with a humorous look.

'I'm sure, sir,' said Mrs Bingley with asperity, 'that he is incapable of the meanness. If you had heard him express the sentiments that I have you would never hint such a charge. No, there is some delicacy of feeling, take my word for it, at the bottom of this change in him; and I can't help fearing that it means he has found out something fresh, something even more distressful to the family, which makes him chary of accepting its hospitality. I only hope—' she paused, with a little sigh.

'You're thinking of Cleghorn!' broke in her master. 'Damme! I'll never believe in respectability again if that man's done it.'

'God forbid!' said the housekeeper. 'But I wish Sergeant Ridgway would appear more, and more in his old way, when he *does* honour me with his company.'

Her wish, however, was not to be fulfilled. The detective more and more absented himself as the days went on, and became more and more of an Asian mystery in the fleeting glimpses of his presence vouchsafed the household. Dark, taciturn, abysmal, he flitted, a casual shadow, through the labyrinthine mysteries of the crime, and could never be said to be here before an echo of his footfall was sounding in the hollows far away. A picturesque description of his processes, perhaps, but consorting in a way with the housekeeper's fanciful rendering. Perhaps delicacy rather than expediency *was* the motive of his tactics; perhaps, having virtually completed his case, he was keeping out of the way until the time came to expound it; perhaps a feature of its revision *was* that distressful something, menacing, appalling, foreseen by the housekeeper. He had plenty otherwise to do, no doubt, in the way of collecting evidence, consulting Counsel, and so forth, which alone gave plenty of reason for neglecting the social amenities. Whatever the explanation, however, the issue was not to be long delayed.

The Baron came upon him unexpectedly one morning in the upper grounds, where the fruit gardens were, and the espaliers, and all the signs of a prosperous vegetable order. There was a fair view of the estate to be gained from that elevation, and the Sergeant appeared to be absorbed for the moment in the gracious prospect. He waited unmoving for the other to join him, and nodded as he came up.

'It's pleasant to snatch a minute, sir,' he said, 'to give to a view like this. People of my profession don't get many such.'

'I suppose not,' answered Le Sage, 'nor of a good many other professions. Proprietary views, like incomes, are very unfairly distributed, don't you think?'

'Well, that's so, no doubt; and among the wrong sort of people often enough.'

Le Sage laughed.

'Are you one of the right sort of people, Sergeant?'

'I won't go so far as to say that, sir, but I will go so far as to say that, if *I* owned this property, I'd come to feast my eyes on it here more often than what Sir Calvin does.'

The Baron, without moving his head, took in the face of the speaker. He saw a glow, a subdued passion in it which interested him. What spirit of romance, to be sure, might lurk unsuspected under the hard official rind. Here was the last man in the world whom one would have credited with a sense of beauty, and he was wrought to emotion by a landscape!

'You talk,' said he, 'of your profession not affording you many such moments as this. Now, to my mind, it seems *the* profession for a man romantically inclined.'

'Does it, indeed, sir?'

'Why, don't you live in a perpetual atmosphere of romance? Think of the mysteries which are your daily food.'

'That's it—my daily food, and lodging too. The men who pull on the ropes for a living don't think much, or see much, of the fairy scene they're setting. That's all for the prosperous folks in front.'

'You'd rather be one of them?'

'Which would you rather, sir—be a police-officer, or the owner of an estate like this? If such things were properly distributed, as you say, there'd be no need perhaps for police-officers at all. You read the papers about a case like ours here, and you see only a romance: we, whose necessity puts us behind the scenes, see only, in nine cases out of ten, the dirty mishandling of Fate. Give a man his right position in the world, and he'll commit no crimes. That's my belief, and it's founded on some experience.'

'I dare say you're right. It's comforting to know, in that case, that my valet has always fitted into *his* place like a stopper into a bottle.'

The detective stood silent a moment; then turned on the speaker with a queer enigmatic look.

'Well, I wouldn't lose heart about him, if I was you,' he said drily.

'That's good!' said Le Sage. 'I can leave him with a tolerably safe conscience then.'

'What, sir—you're going away before the inquiry?'

'I must, I am afraid. I have business in London which I can no longer postpone.'

'But how about your evidence?'

'After what you have said, cannot you afford to do without it?'

The detective considered, frowning and rubbing his chin; then said simply, 'Very well,' and made a movement to go.

They went down the garden together, and parted at the door in the wall. This was on the Saturday. On the following Monday the officer appeared for the last time to arrange for his witnesses on the Wednesday ensuing. He carried his handbag with him, and intimated that it was not his purpose to return again before the event. They were all—Mrs Bingley perhaps excepted—glad to see the last of him, and the last of what his presence there implied, and welcomed the prospect of the one clean day which was to be theirs before their re-meeting in Court.

The Sergeant's manner at his parting was restrained, and his countenance rigidly pale. Sir Calvin, receiving his formal thanks for the courtesy shown him, remarked upon it, and asked him if he were feeling overdone.

'No, sir,' he replied: 'never better, thank you. I hope you yourself may never feel worse than I do at this moment.'

Something in his way of saying it, some significance of tone, or look, or emphasis, seemed to cast a sudden chill upon the air. The General turned away with a slightly wondering, puzzled expression, and shrugged his shoulders as if he were cold. There were one or two present who remembered that gesture afterwards, identifying it with some vague sensation in themselves.

That same night the Baron caused a considerable stir by announcing his intention of leaving them on the morrow. They all had something to say in the way of surprise and remonstrance except Mr Bickerdike, and he judiciously held his tongue. Even Hugo showed a certain concern, as a man might who felt, without quite realizing what it was he felt, the giving way of some moral support on which he had been unconsciously leaning. He looked up and asked, as the detective had asked, 'What about your evidence?'

'It is said to be immaterial,' answered Le Sage. 'I am speaking on the authority of the Sergeant himself.'

Hugh said no more; but he eyed the Baron in a wistful, questioning way. He was in a rather moving mood, patently looking forward to Wednesday's ordeal with considerable nervousness and apprehension, and not altogether without reason. The Inquest had been trying enough; yet that had been a mere local affair, conducted amid familiar surroundings. To stand up in public Court and repeat, perhaps be forced to amplify, the evidence he had already given was a far different and more agitating prospect. What was in his mind, who could know? There was something a little touching in the way he clung to his family, and in the slight embarrassment they showed over his unaccustomed attentions. Audrey, falling in for her share, laughed, and responded with only a bad grace; but the glow in her eyes testified to feelings not the less proud and exultant because their repression had been so long a necessity with her.

Coming upon the Baron in the hall by-and-by, as he was on his way upstairs to prepare for the morrow's journey, she stopped and spoke to him.

'Can you manage without a valet, Baron?'

'As I have managed a hundred times before, my dear.'

'Must you really go?'

'I must, indeed.'

'Leaving Louis to shift for himself?'

'I leave him in the hands of Providence.'

'Yes, but Providence is not a lawyer.'

'Heaven forbid! God, you know, like no lawyer, tempers the wind to the shorn lamb—*à brebis tondue Dieu mesure le vent*. That is a good French proverb, and I am going to France in the faith of it.'

'But you will come back again?'

'Yes, I will come back. It will be all right about Louis—you will see.'

She did not answer. She had been holding him by the lapels of his coat, running her thumbs down the seams, and suddenly, feeling a little convulsive pressure there, he looked up in her face and saw that thick tears were running down her cheeks. Very softly but resolutely then he captured the two wandering hands and held them between his own.

'My dear,' he said, 'my dear, I understand. But listen to this—have confidence in your friend the Baron.'

And on the morrow morning he left, accompanied by Mr Vivian Bickerdike's most private and most profound misgivings. That he was going to London on some business connected with the stolen document was that gentleman's certain conviction. But what was he to do? Expose at once, or wait and learn more? On the whole it were better to wait, perhaps: the fellow was coming back—he had said so, and to the same unconsciousness of there being one on his track who at the right moment could put a spoke in his nefarious wheel.

He was still considering the question, when something happened which, for the time being, put all considerations but one out of his head. By the first post on the very morning of the inquiry he received, much to his astonishment, a *subpoena* binding him to appear and give evidence in Court. About what? If any uneasy suspicion in his mind answered that question, to it was to be attributed, no doubt, his rather white conscience-troubled aspect as he presently joined the party waiting to be motored over to the Castle in the old city where the case was to be tried.

CHAPTER XIV

THE EXPLOSION

THE Magistrates assembled to hear the case were four in number, two of them being local magnates and personal friends of Sir Calvin, who was accorded a seat on the Bench. They took their places at eleven o'clock, the Court being then crowded to its utmost capacity. The case stood first on the list, and no delay was experienced in opening it. As before, Mr Fyler appeared for the police, and Mr Redstall for Sir Calvin. The prisoner was undefended.

At the outset of the proceedings a surprise awaited the public. The prisoner having been brought up from the cells beneath the Court, and placed in the dock, Sergeant Ridgway asked permission to speak. Addressing the Bench, he said that since the inquiry before the Coroner, which had ended, as their Worships were aware, in a verdict by the jury of wilful murder against the prisoner Louis Victor Cabanis, facts had come to his knowledge which entirely disposed of the theory of the prosecution, proving, as they did, an unquestionable *alibi* in the prisoner's favour. Under these circumstances he proposed to offer no evidence against the accused, who, with their Worships' permission, would be discharged.

Smart in aspect, concise in phrase, the detective stood up and made his avowal, and again, though in an auguster atmosphere, with a marked impression upon his hearers. Some of them had already encountered him, no doubt, and were prepared to concede to his every statement the force and value of an official fiat.

'Very well, Sergeant,' was the reply, while the public wondered if they were going to be defrauded of their feast of sensation, or if some spicier substitute were about to be placed before them. They were not kept long in suspense.

Following the Sergeant's declaration, brief evidence was given by Andrew Marie, shepherd, and Nicholas Penny, thatcher. The former deposed that on the afternoon in question he was setting hurdles on the uplands above Leighway, at a point about three miles north-east of Wildshott Park as the crow flies, when he saw prisoner. That was as near three o'clock as might be. Prisoner had stood watching him for a few minutes while exchanging a remark or two, and had then gone on in a northerly direction.

Penny gave evidence that, on the same afternoon, at three-thirty, he was working in the garden of his cottage at Milldown, two miles beyond the point mentioned by the last witness, when prisoner came by and asked him the time. He gave it him, and prisoner thanked him and continued his way, still bearing north by east until he was out of sight. He was going leisurely, both witnesses affirmed, and there appeared nothing peculiar about him except his foreign looks and speech. Neither had the slightest hesitation in identifying the prisoner with the man they had seen. There was no possibility of mistaking him.

This evidence, said the detective, addressing the justices again at the end of it, precluded any idea of the prisoner's being the guilty party, the case for the prosecution holding that the murder was committed at some time between three and four o'clock in the afternoon. At three o'clock the accused was proved to have been at a spot good three miles away from the scene of the crime, and again at 3.30 at a spot five miles away, representing a distance which, even on an extravagant estimate, he could hardly have covered within the period remaining to him if the theory of the prosecution was to be substantiated. There was no case, in fact, and the prosecution therefore withdrew the charge.

A Magistrate put the question somewhat extra-judicially, why had he not pleaded this *alibi* in the first instance. The accused, who appeared overwhelmed by the change in his situation, was understood to say, with much emotion and gesticulation, that he had not been advised, nor had he supposed that the deposition of a prisoner himself would count for anything, and, moreover, that he had been so bewildered by the labyrinth of suspicion in which he had got himself involved, that it had seemed hopeless to him to think of ever extricating himself from it. He seemed a simple soul, and the justices smiled, with some insular superiority, over his naïve declaration. He was then given to understand that he was discharged and might go, and with a joyous expression he stepped from the dock and vanished like a jocund goblin down the official trap.

Counsel for the prosecution then rose, and stated that, the charge against Cabanis being withdrawn, it was proposed to put in his place Samuel Cleghorn, against whom, although no definite charge had as yet been preferred by the police, a *prima facie* case existed. His examination, and the examination of the witnesses concerned, would probably prove a lengthy affair, and he asked therefore that the case might be taken next on the list. The justices concurring, Samuel Cleghorn was brought up from the cells, and stood to undergo his examination.

Confinement and anxiety, it was evident, had told upon the prisoner, whose aspect since the Inquest had undergone a noticeable change. He looked limp and deteriorated, like a worn banknote, and his lips were tremulous. Respectability in a sidesman caught pilfering from the plate could not have appeared more self-conscious of its fall. He bowed deferentially to the Bench, with a slight start on seeing his master seated there, and, making some ineffectual effort to appear at ease, clasped his plump white hands before him and fixed a glassy eye on the wall. The public, reassured, settled down, like a music-hall audience to a new exciting 'turn', the Bench assumed its most judicial expression, and Counsel, adjusting its wig for the fray, proceeded to open the case

It is not proposed to recapitulate *in extenso* the evidence already given. In bulk and essentials the two hardly differed, the only marked changes being in the order of the witnesses examined, and in the absence from their list of the Baron Le Sage, who, however, inasmuch as his sole use had been to testify to the character of his servant, was no longer needed. There was the same reference to the insuperable difficulty—experienced and still unsurmounted—in tracing out the deceased's connexions, the same statement by Sergeant Ridgway as to the fruitlessness of the measures taken, and the same request that, in default of further information, such evidence of identification as was at present available should be provisionally accepted. The Bench agreed, the detective sat down, and Counsel rose once more, this time with a formidable eye to business.

Mr Fyler began by reconstructing, so far as was possible, the history of the crime from the evidence already adduced, into the particulars of which it is unnecessary to follow him. In summarising the known facts, he made no especial point, it was observed, of bringing them to bear on the presumptive guilt of the prisoner, but used him rather as a convenient model or framework about which to shape his story. Indeed, when he sat down again, it might have been given as even odds whether the conviction or acquittal of the accused man was the thing foreshadowed. And what then? After two attempts, was the whole business to end in a fiasco? Incredible! Someone must have killed the girl. The very atmosphere of the Court, moreover, fateful, ominous—derided such a conclusion. 'Attend and wait!' it seemed to whisper.

Counsel was no sooner down than he was up again, and calling now upon his witnesses to appear. They came one by one, as summoned—Mrs Bingley, Jane Ketchlove, Jessie Ellis, Kate Vokes, Mabel Wheelband; and there the order was broken. The examination of these five was in all essentials a replica of that conducted at the Inquest, but, to the observant, with one significant note added. For the first time Counsel showed, as it were, a corner of the card up his sleeve by suggesting tentatively, insinuatively, *à propos* the question of a guilty intrigue, that one or other of them might possibly have her suspicions as to the identity of the second party implicated in it. The hint was disowned as soon as rejected; but it had left a curious impression here and there of more to come, of its having only been proffered to open and prepare the way to evidence, the stronger, perhaps, for some such moral corroboration. Not one of the women, however, would own to the subtle impeachment, and the question for the moment was dropped.

But it was dropped only tactically, in accordance with a pre-arranged plan, as became increasingly apparent with the choice of the next witness. This was Dr Harding, who had made the *post-mortem* examination, and whose evidence repeated exactly what he had formerly stated. It added, moreover, a detail which, touching upon a question of time, showed yet a little more plainly which way the wind was setting; and it included an admission, or correction, no less suggestive in its import. The question was asked witness: 'At the Inquest you stated, I believe, that death must have occurred at 3.30 o'clock, or thereabouts. Is that so?'

A. I said 'approximately', judging by the indications.

Q. Just so. I am aware that, in these cases, a certain latitude must be granted. It might then, in fact, have occurred somewhat earlier or somewhat later?

A. Yes. By preference, somewhat earlier.

Q. How much earlier?

Witness, refusing to submit to any brow-beating on the question, finally, at the end of a highly technical disputation, conceded a half hour as the extreme limit of his approximation; and with that the matter ended. As he stepped from the box the name of a new witness—a witness not formerly included in the inquiry—was called, and public interest, already deeply stimulated, grew intensified.

Margaret Hopkins, widow, deposed on oath. She was landlady of the Brewer's Dray inn at Longbridge. The inn was situated to the east of the town and a little outside it on the Winton Road. One afternoon, about five weeks ago, a lady and gentleman had called at her inn wanting tea, and a private room to drink it in. They were shown up to a chamber on the first floor, where the gentleman ordered a fire to be lighted. Tea was brought them by witness herself, and they had remained there shut in a long time together—a couple of hours perhaps. They were very affectionate with one another, and had gone away, when they did go, very lovingly arm in arm. The gentleman was Mr Hugo Kennett, whom she now saw in Court, and whom she had recognised for the male stranger at once. The name of the lady accompanying him she had had no means of ascertaining, but her companion had addressed her as Annie.

Mr Redstall, rising to cross-examine witness, put the following questions:

Q. Will you swear to Mr Kennett having been the gentleman in question?

A. Yes, on my oath, sir.

Q. You already knew Mr Kennett by sight, eh?

A. No, I did not, sir. I had never seen him before, and have never seen him since till today. I hadn't been settled in Longbridge not a two-month at the time he come.

Q. You say the two appeared to be on affectionate terms. On companionable terms would perhaps be the truer expression, eh?

A. As you choose, sir, if that means behaving like lovers together. *(Laughter.)*

Q. What do you mean by like lovers? They would hardly have made a display of their sentiments before you.

A. Not intentional perhaps, sir; but I come upon them unexpected when I brought in the tea; and there they was a'sitting on the sofy together, as close and as fond as two turtle-doves. *(Laughter.)*

Mrs Bingley, recalled, reluctantly admitted having given deceased an afternoon off about the date in question. The girl had returned to the house before six o'clock.

Reuben Henstridge called, repeated his evidence given on the day of the Inquest, omitting only, or abridging, such parts of it as bore on the movements of the Frenchman, and excluding altogether—by tacit consent, it seemed—those references to the butler's approach which had brought such a confusion of cross-questioning about his ears. The following bodeful catechism then ensued:

Q. You say it was ten minutes past two when you saw Cabanis break from the copse and go down towards the road?

A. Aye.

Q. And that, having hung about after seeing him, you eventually returned to the Red Deer inn, reaching it at about 3.30?

A. That's it.

Q. At what time did you start to return to the inn?

A. Three o'clock, or a bit after.

Q. What had you been doing in the interval?

A. *(Sulkily)* That's my business.

Q. I ask you again. You had better answer.

A. *(After a scowling pause)* Setting snares, then. *(Defiantly)* Weren't it the open downs?

Q. I'm not entering into that question. We'll assume, if you like, that the downs and your behaviour were equally open. You were setting snares, that's enough. Did anything suddenly occur to interrupt you at your task?'

A. Yes, it did.

Q. What was that?

A. The sound of a gun going off.

Q. From what direction?

A. From down among the trees near the road.

Q. Quite so. Now will you tell the Bench exactly what time it was when you heard that sound?

A. The time when I started to go home.

Q. About three o'clock or a little after?

A. That's it.

Q. You state that on your oath?

A. Yes, I do.

It was as if a conscious tremor, like the excitement of many hearts leaping in unison, passed through the Court, dimly foretelling some approaching crisis. The examination was resumed:

Q. What makes you so certain of the time?

A. The stable clock had just gone three.

Q. And, following on the sound of the gun, you left your snare-setting and made for home?

A. Aye.

Q. For what reason?

A. Because I thought they might be working round my way.

Q. Whom do you mean by 'they'?

A. The party as was out shooting. I made sure at first it come from them.

Q. What made you alter your opinion?

A. I see them, as I went up the hill, afar off nigh Asholt wood.

Q. Now, tell me: why didn't you mention all this at the Inquest?

A. Because I weren't asked.

Q. Or was it because you feared having to confess to what made you bolt, and from what occupation, when the shot startled you? *(No answer.)* Very well. Now attend to this. You have heard it propounded, or assumed, that the murder took place sometime between 3.15 and 4 o'clock. Do you still adhere to your statement that it was just after three when you heard the sound of the gun?

A. Aye.

Q. You are on your oath, remember.

A. All right, master.

Q. And you adhere to it?

A. Yes, I do.

Q. That is enough. You can stand down.

A sibilation, a momentary rustling and shuffling, as on the close of an engrossing sermon when tension is relaxed and the hymn being prepared for, followed the dismissal of the witness. A few glanced furtively, hardly realizing yet why they were moved to do so, at a rigid soldierly figure, seated upright and motionless beside the justices on the Bench. But the sense of curious perplexity was hardly theirs when the next witness was claiming their attention. This was Daniel Groome, the gardener, whose evidence, generally a repetition of what he had formerly stated, was marked by a single amendment, the significance of which he himself hardly seemed to realize. It appeared as follows:

Q. You stated before the Coroner that this louder shot heard by you occurred at a time which you roughly estimated to be anything between three and half-past three o'clock. Is that so?

A. No, sir.

Q. What do you mean by 'no'?

A. I've thought it over since, sir, and I've come to the conclusion that my first impression was nearer the correct one.

Q. Your impression, that is to say, that the shot was fired somewhere about three o'clock?

A. Yes, sir.

Q. What is your reason for this change of opinion?

A. Because I remembered afterwards, sir, having heard the clock in the master's study strike the quarter past. I had gone round by then to the back of the house.

Q. And you had heard the shot fired while at the front?

A. Yes, sir.

This witness was stiffly cross-examined by Mr Redstall, who sought to shake his evidence on the grounds that he was, consciously or unconsciously, seeking to adapt it to what was expected of him. But the poor fellow's honesty was so transparent, and his incomprehension of the gravity of his statement so ingenuous, that the only result of his harrying was to increase the impression of his disinterested probity. He said what he believed to be the truth, and he adhered to it.

He went, and the usher, tapping with his wand on the floor, called in a loud voice on Vivian Bickerdike to appear and give evidence.

A famous writer has asserted that there are two kinds of witness to whom lawyers take particular exception, the reluctant witness and the too-willing witness. To these may be added a third, the anxious witness, who, being oppressed with a sense of responsibility of his position, fears at once to say too much or too little, and ends by saying both. Bickerdike entered the box an acutely anxious witness. The trend of some recent evidence had left him in no doubt as to the lines on which his own examination was destined to run, and he foresaw at once the use to which a certain conversation of his with the detective was going to be put. Now it was all very well to hold the Sergeant guilty in this of a gross breach of confidence, but his conscience would not thereby allow him to maintain himself blameless in the matter. He should have known quite well, being no fool, that a detective did not ask questions or invite communications from a purely altruistic point of view, and that the apparent transparency of such a man's sentiments was the least indication of their depth. By permitting pique a little to obscure that fact to him he had done his friend—for whom he had a real, very warm regard—a disservice, to which he had now, in that friend's hearing, to confess. So far, then, it only remained to him to endeavour to repair, through his sworn evidence, the mischief to which he had made himself a party.

But could any reparation stultify now a certain issue, to which—he had seen it suddenly, aghast—that too-open candour of his had been seduced into contributing? What horrible thing was it which was being approached, threatened, in the shadow of his friend's secret? The thing was monstrous, damnable; yet he could not forget how it had appeared momentarily adumbrated to himself on his first hearing of the murder. But he had rejected the thought with incredulous scorn then, as he would reject it now. Of whatever sinful weakness Hugh might be capable, a crime so detestable, so cruel, was utterly impossible to him. He swore it in his heart; but his faith could not relieve him of the weight of responsibility which went with him into the witness box. It was like a physical oppression, and he seemed to bend under it. Counsel took the witness's measure with a rolling relish of the lips, as he prepared, giving a satisfied shift to his gown, to open his inquisitions:

Q. You are on very intimate terms, I believe, Mr Bickerdike, with Sir Calvin and his family?

A. With Sir Calvin's permission, I think I may say yes.

Q. You have seen the prisoner before?

A. Many times.

Q. Could you, as a guest, speak to his general character?

A. It has always appeared to me quite unexceptionable.

Q. Not a violent man?

A. O! dear, no.

Q. At dinner, on the night before the murder, did you notice anything peculiar about him?

A. He appeared to me to be upset about something.

Q. And you wondered, perhaps—having only arrived that afternoon, as I understand—what domestic tribulation could have discomposed so stately a character? *(Laughter.)*

A. I may have. I had always considered Cleghorn as immovable an institution as the Monument.

The laughter which greeted this sally appeared to reassure witness somewhat, as did the unexpected lines on which his rather irregular examination seemed to be developing. But his confidence was of short duration. The very next question brought him aware of the true purpose of this preliminary catechism, which was merely to constitute a pretext for getting him into the witness box at all.

Q. Was your arrival that afternoon, may I ask, in response to a long invitation or a sudden call?

A. (With a sudden stiffening of his shoulders, as if rallying his energies to meet an ordeal foreseen) A sudden call. I came down in response to a letter from my friend Mr Hugo Kennett, inviting me to a few days' shooting.

Q. Mr Hugo Kennett is a particular friend of yours, is he not?

A. We have known one another a long time.

Q. Intimate to that degree, I mean, that you have few secrets from one another?

A. That may be.

Q. And can depend upon one another in any emergency?

A. I hope so.

Q. There was a question of emergency, perhaps, in this case?

A. I am bound to say there often is with Mr Kennett.

Q. Will you explain what you mean by that?

A. I mean—I hope he will forgive my saying it—that his imagination is a little wont to create emergencies which nothing but his friends' immediate advice and assistance can overcome. He is apt to be in the depths one moment and on the heights the next. He is built that way, that's all.

Q. Was this a case of an emergency due to his imagination?

A. I won't go quite so far as to say that.

Q. Then there was really a reason this time for his having you down at short notice?

A. I may have thought so.

Q. We will come to that. Had he mentioned the reason in his letter to you?

A. No. The letter only said that he badly wanted 'bucking', and asked me to come down at once.

Q. He gave no explanation?

A. None whatever.

Q. In the letter, or afterwards when you met?

A. No.

Q. You found him in an uncommunicative mood?

A. Somewhat.

Q. Kindly say what you mean by 'somewhat'.

A. I mean that, while he told me nothing definite about his reason for having me down, he did seem to hint that there was trouble somewhere.

Q. What were his exact words?

A. I can't remember.

Q. Were they to the effect that he was in a devil of a fix with a girl, and could only see one way out of it? *(Sensation.)*

A. *(Aghast)* Nothing of the sort. Now I recall, he described himself as sitting on a barrel of gunpowder, smoking a cigarette and waiting for the explosion that was to come.

Q. Thank you. Another effort or two, Mr Bickerdike, and your memory may need no refreshing. Did you find your friend's manner, now, as strange as his talk?

A. It might often have seemed strange on such occasions to those who did not know him.

Q. Answer my question, please.

A. *(Reluctantly)* Well, it was strange.

Q. Stranger than you had ever known it to be before?

A. Perhaps so.

Q. I suggest that it was wild and reckless to a degree—the manner of a man who had got himself into a hopeless scrape, and saw no way out of it but social and material ruin?

A. It was very strange: I can say no more.

Q. Would you have considered his state compatible with that of a young man of good position and prospects, who had entangled himself with a girl greatly his social inferior, and was threatened by her with exposure unless he, in the common phrase, made an honest woman of her?

Mr Redstall rising to object, the Bench ruled that the question was inadmissible. It had created, however, a profound impression in Court, which from that moment never abated. Counsel, accepting their worships' decision, resumed:

Q. Had you any reason to suspect a woman in the case?

A. It was pure conjecture on my part.

Q. Then you *did* entertain such a suspicion?

A. Not at that time. Later perhaps.

Q. After the murder?

A. Yes, after the murder.

Q. When?

A. The moment I heard it had been committed. I was told by a groom.

Q. About the woman or the murder?

A. About the murder.

Q. When was that?

A. When I returned from shooting that day.

Q. You returned alone, I believe?

A. Yes.

Q. Mr Kennett having left you shortly before three o'clock?

A. I fancy about that time.

Q. And at the moment you heard there had been this murder committed, that conjecture, that association between your friend and the murdered girl came into your mind?

A. It was wholly preposterous, of course. I dismissed the idea the moment it occurred to me.

Q. You dismissed the idea of Mr Kennett's having been involved with the girl?

A. No, of his having committed the murder. *(Sensation.)*

Q. But you still thought the entanglement possible?

A. I thought it might account for his state.

Q. Why did the first idea, associating Mr Kennett with the crime, occur to you? *(Witness hesitating, the question was repeated.)*

A. *(In a low voice)* O! just because of something—nothing important—that had happened at the shoot—that, and the extraordinary state I had found him in.

Q. Will you tell the Bench what was this unimportant something that happened at the shoot?

A. *(With emotion)* It was nothing—probably my fancy—and he denied it utterly.

Q. Now, Mr Bickerdike, if you please?

A. I thought that in—in pulling his gun through a particular hedge that morning, he might have done it with less risk to himself, that was all.

Q. You suspected him, in short, of wanting to kill himself under the guise of an accident?

A. I swear he never admitted it. I swear he denied it.

Q. And you accepted his denial so implicitly that you asked him to go home, leaving his gun with the keeper. Is that not so?

A. Yes.

Q. He refused?

A. Yes, he did.

Q. Did not much the same thing occur again, later in the afternoon?

A. Nothing of the sort at all. Shortly before three he came to me, and said he was no good and was going home.

Q. What did he mean by 'no good'? No good in life?

A. No good at shooting.

Q. And again you asked him to leave his gun with you?

A. No, I did not—not directly, at least.

Q. Please explain what you mean by 'not directly'?

A. He may have understood what was in my mind. I can't say. He just laughed, and called out that he wasn't going to shoot himself, and wasn't going to let me make an ass of him; and with that he marched off.

Q. And that is all?

A. All.

Q. He didn't, by chance, in saying 'I'm not going to shoot *myself*', lay any particular emphasis on the last word?

A. Certainly not that I distinguished. The whole suggestion is too impossible to anyone who knows my friend.

Q. Thank you, Mr Bickerdike. That will do.

If witness had entered the box like an oppressed man, he left it like a beaten. His cheeks were flushed, his head bowed; it was observed that he purposely avoided looking his friend in the face as he passed him by on his way to the rear of the Court.

The excitement was now extreme. All attention, in the midst of a profound stillness, was concentrated on a figure come more and more, with each adjustment of the legal spy-glass, into a definite focus. It was felt that the supreme moment was approaching; and, when the expected name was called, a sigh like that of a sleeper turning seemed to sound through the hall. The prisoner in the dock had already long been overlooked—forgotten. He had been put up, it seemed, as a mere medium for this deadlier manifestation, and his purpose served, had ceased to be of interest. He stood pallid with his hands on the rail before him, rolling his one mobile eye, the only apparently mystified man in Court.

As Hugo entered the box, he was seen to be deadly pale, but he held his head high, and stood like a soldier, morally and physically upright, facing his court-martial. He folded his arms, and looked his inquisitor steadily in the eyes. Mr Fyler retorted with an expression of well-assured suavity. He was in no hurry. Having netted his fowl, he could afford to let him flutter awhile. He began by leading his witness, only more briefly, the way he had already conducted him at the Inquest, but with what new menace of pitfalls by the road! The discovery of the body; the incident of the gun (prejudiced now in the light of the possible moral to be drawn from witness's hurry to get rid of it, and his loathing of the weapon); the marked agitation of his aspect when seen by the gardener; the interval in the house, with its suggestion of nervous collapse and desperate rallying to face the inevitable ordeal; that significant outburst of his at the Inquest, when he had exclaimed against an implication of guilt which had never been made; his admission of having bantered the deceased about an assignation—an admission fraught with suspicion of the scene of passion and recrimination which had perhaps more truthfully described their encounter—all these points were retraversed, but in a spirit ominously differing from that in which they had formerly been reviewed. And then at last, in a series of swift stabbing questions and hypotheses, issued the mortal moral of all this sinister exordium:

Q. You chaffed the deceased, you say, sir, with being where she was for an assignation?

A. Something of the sort.

Q. Something of the sort may be nothing of the sort. I suggest that this so-called chaff is better described as a quarrel between you. Will you swear that that was not the case?

A. No, I will not.

Q. Then your statement was a fabrication?

A. I accused her of being there to meet someone.

Q. You accused her. I am your debtor for the word. Will you swear that she was not there to keep an assignation, and that assignation with yourself?

A. I swear it most positively. Our meeting was quite accidental.

Q. On your part?

A. On my part.

Q. But not on hers?

A. I am not here to answer for that.

Q. Pardon me; I think you are. I suggest that, expecting you to return by the Bishop's Walk, she was waiting there to waylay you?

A. She might have been, on the chance.

Q. I suggest you knew that she was?

A. I say I did not know.

Q. Well, you took that way at least, and you met and quarrelled. I suggest that the person you accused her of being there to meet was yourself, and that the dispute between you turned upon the question of her thus importuning you? Is that so?

A. *(After a pause)* Yes.

Q. And I suggest further that the reason for her so importuning you lay in her condition, for which you were responsible?

A. Yes. It is true. *(Sensation.)*

Q. She entreated you, perhaps, to repair the wrong you had done her in the only way possible to an honourable man?

A. *(Witness seeming to stiffen, as if resolved to face the whole music at last)* She had already urged that; she pressed to know, that was all, if I had made up my mind to marry her. I refused to give a definite answer just then, since my whole career was at stake; but I promised her one within twenty-four hours. I was very much bothered over the business, and I dare say a bit impatient with her. She may have upbraided me a little in return, but there was no actual quarrel between us. I went on after a few minutes, leaving her there by herself. And that is the whole truth.

Q. We will judge of that. You say the meeting was none of your seeking?

A. I do say it.

Q. Now, please attend to me. You were on your way back, when you met deceased, from the shooting party which you had abandoned?

A. Yes.

Q. You have heard what the last witness stated as to a certain incident connected with that morning. Was his statement substantially true?

A. I can't deny it. It was a momentary mad impulse.

Q. And, being forestalled, was replaced possibly by an alternative suggestion, pointing to another way out of your difficulties?

A. I don't know what you mean. It was just the culmination, as it were, of a desperate mood, and was regretted by me the next instant.

Q. Was it because of your desperate mood that you refused to be parted from your gun when you finally left the shoot and returned home?

A. No; but because I declined to be made to look a fool.

Q. I put it to you once more that you knew, when you went home, carrying against all persuasion, your gun with you, that the deceased would be waiting for you in the copse?

A. It is utterly false. I knew nothing about it.

Q. Very well. Now, as to the time of your meeting with the deceased. I have it stated on your sworn evidence that that was at three o'clock or thereabouts, and that after spending some ten minutes in conversation with her, you resumed your way to the house, which you reached at about 3.15, appearing then, according to the evidence of a witness, in a very agitated state.

A. I was upset, I own—naturally, under the circumstances.

Q. What circumstances?

A. Having just promised to do or not do what would affect my whole life.

Q. No other reason?

A. No.

Q. Did you hear the sworn statement of the witness Henstridge and another that the report of the shot, which could have been none other than the fatal shot, was heard and fixed by them at a time estimated at a few minutes after three o'clock, that is to say, at a time when, according to your own admission, you were in the deceased's company?

A. It is an absolute lie.

The crisis had come, the long-expected blow fallen; but, even in the shock and echo of it, there were some who found nerve to glance from son to father, and wonder what super-dramatic incident yet remained to them to cap the day's excitement. They were disappointed. Not by one sign or movement did the stiff grey figure on the Bench betray the torture racking it, or concede to their expectations the evidence of an emotion—not even when, as if in response to some outspoken direction, a couple of policemen were seen to move silently forward, and take their stand on either side of the witness box. And then, suddenly, Counsel was speaking again.

He addressed the Bench with an apology for the course imposed upon him, since it must have become apparent, as the case proceeded, that the tendency of the prosecution had been to turn more and more from its nominal objective in the dock. There had been a reason for that, however, and he must state it. The inquiries of the police, and more especially of the distinguished detective officer, Sergeant Ridgway, had latterly, gradually but certainly, led them to the conclusion that the motive for the crime, and the name of its perpetrator, must be looked for in another direction than that originally, and seemingly inevitably, indicated. This change of direction had necessarily exculpated the two men concerned in today's proceedings; but it had been thought best to submit one of them to examination for the purpose of exposing through the evidence affecting him the guilt of the presumptive criminal. That having been done, the police raised no objection to Cleghorn, like the other accused, being discharged.

He then went on to summarize the evidence, as it had come, by gradual degrees, to involve the witness Kennett in its meshes—the scrape into which the young man had got himself, his dread of exposure, the wildness of his talk and behaviour, the incriminating business of the gun, and, finally, the sworn testimony as to the time of the shot—and he ended by drawing a fanciful picture of what had occurred in the copse.

'I ask your worships,' he said, 'to picture to yourselves the probable scene. Here has this young Lothario returned, his heart full of death and desperation since the frustration of his first mad impulse to end his difficulties with his life, knowing, or not knowing—we must form our own conclusions as to that—that his destined victim awaits him at the tryst—if tryst it is—*her* heart burning with bitterness against the seducer who has betrayed her; each resolved on its own way out of the trouble. She upbraids him with her ruin, and threatens in her turn to ruin him, unless he consents to right the wrong he has done her. He refuses, or temporizes; and she turns to leave him. Thinking she is about to put her threat into immediate execution, goaded to desperation, the gun in his hand—only tentatively adhered to at first, perhaps—decides him. He fires at and kills her. The deed perpetrated, he has to consider, after the first shock of horror, how best to conceal the evidences of his guilt. He decides to rest the lethal weapon against a tree (with the intention of asserting—or, at least, not denying, if subsequently questioned—that he had left it with one of its barrels loaded), concocts in his mind a plausible story of a cigarette and an oversight, and hurries on to the house, where, in his private room, he spends such a three-quarters of an hour of horror and remorse as none of us need envy him. His nerve by then somewhat restored, he decides to take the initiative in the necessary discovery, and, affecting a sudden recollection of his oversight, returns to the copse to fetch his gun, with the result we know. All that it is open to us to surmise; what we may not surmise is the depth of depravity in a nature which could so plan to cast the burden of its own guilt upon the shoulders of an innocent man.'

One dumb, white look here did the son turn on the father; who met it steadfastly, as white and unflinching.

'We have heard some loose talk, your worships,' went on Counsel, 'as to the appearance of a mysterious fourth figure in this tragedy. We may dismiss, I think, that individual as purely chimerical—a maggot, if I may so describe it, of the witness Henstridge's brain. There is no need, I think you will agree with me, for looking beyond this Court for a solution of the problem which has been occupying its attention. Painful as the task is to me, I must now do my duty—without fear or favour in the face of any considerations, social or sentimental, whatsoever—by asking you to commit for trial, on the capital charge of murdering Annie Evans, the witness Hugo Staveley Kennett, a warrant for whose arrest the police already hold in their hands.'

Not a sound broke the stillness as Counsel ended—only a muffled rumble, like that of a death-drum, from the wheels of a passing wagon in the street outside. And then the blue-clad janissaries closed in; the Magistrates, without leaving the Bench, put their heads together, and the vote was cast.

'Hugo Staveley Kennett, we have no alternative but to commit you to take your trial on the capital charge.'

A sudden crash and thump broke in upon the verdict. Cleghorn had fainted in the dock.

CHAPTER XV

THE FACE ON THE WALL

THE morning of the inquiry found M. le Baron in Paris, in his old rooms at the Montesquieu. He was in very good spirits, smiling and buoyant, and not at all conscience-smitten over his desertion of his servant in his hour of need. 'It will be a not unwholesome lesson for the little *fanfaron*,' he thought, 'teaching him in the future to keep a guard on his tongue and temper.' He foresaw, be it observed, that certain issue, and felt no anxiety about it. But his face fell somewhat to an added reflection: 'I wonder if they have committed *him* for trial by now. Poor girl!' and he shrugged his shoulders with a tiny sigh.

Having crossed by the night boat from Southampton, one might have looked for a certain staleness in the Baron's aspect. On the contrary, he was as chirpy as a sparrow, having slept well throughout a pretty bad crossing, and since had a refreshing tub and brush-up. He sat down—though very late, with an excellent appetite—to his *petit pain* and rich coffee and *brioche*, and, having consumed them, took snuff at short intervals for half an hour, and then prepared to go out.

M. le Baron's movements seemed carelessly casual, but he had, in fact, a definite objective, and he made for it at his leisure. It lay on the left bank of the river, in or near the district calling itself loosely the Latin or Students' Quarter. He crossed the river by the Pont des Arts, and went straight down the Rue de Seine as far as the Rue de Tournon, where he turned off in the direction of St Sulpice. The great bell up in the high tower was crashing and booming for a funeral, and its enormous reverberations swayed like Atlantic rollers across the fields of air. In all the world St Sulpice bell is *the* death-bell, so solemn, so deep, and so overwhelming it sounds. M. le Baron paused to listen a moment. 'Is it an omen?' thought he, 'and am I going to hear bad news?'

Somewhere at the back of the church, in a little street called the Rue Bourbon-le-Château, he came to the shop of a small dealer in prayer-books and holy pictures and pious images. It was a poor shop in a faded district, and suggestive of scant returns and lean commons for its inmates. A door, as gaunt and attenuated in appearance, stood open to one side of the shop, and by this the visitor entered, with the manner of one who knew the place. A flight of bare wooden stairs rose before him, and up these he went, to the first, to the second floor, where he paused, a little breathless, to knock on a door. '*Que diable!*' cried a hoarse voice from within. 'Who's that?'

For answer the Baron turned the handle and presented himself. It was a ragged, comfortless room he entered, frowzy, chill, without a carpet and with dirty whitewashed walls. A table stood in the dingy window, and at it was seated the solitary figure of a man—emaciated, melancholy eyed—Ribault his name, a designer on the staff of the *Petit Courrier des Dames*. Some of his work lay before him now: he looked up from it with a startled exclamation, and rose to his feet. Those were clad in list slippers: for the rest he wore a rusty frock-coat, and at his neck a weeping black bow.

'M. le Baron!' he exclaimed, in wonder and welcome. 'Who would have thought to see you again!'

'Am I that sort, then?' answered Le Sage with a smile. 'I am sorry I left so poor an impression.'

'Ah, but what an impression!' cried the other fervently. 'An angel of goodness; a Samaritan; a comforter, and a healer in one!'

'Well, well, M. Ribault!' said the Baron. 'You are still at the old toil, I observe?'

'Always at it, Monsieur; but in my plodding, uninspired way—not like my friend's. Ah, he was a great artist was Jean.'

'Truly, he had a wonderful facility. Has he left you?'

'But for the grave, Monsieur. We had not otherwise been parted.'

Tears gathered in the poor creature's eyes; he sighed, with a forlorn, resigned gesture. Hearing his words, a shadow crossed the visitor's face. 'That foreboding bell!' he muttered. He was genuinely concerned, and not for one only reason. 'You will tell me all about it, perhaps, M. Ribault?' he said.

'He was never himself again after that accident,' answered the designer. 'All your tenderness, your care, your disinterested help could do no more than earn for him a little respite from a sentence already pronounced. He was virtually a dying man when you last left him, Monsieur. The light of your healing presence withdrawn, the shadow came out and was visible to me. Ah, but he would talk of you often and often, and of how you had smoothed the bitter way for him. He confided in you much: he told you his little history?'

'Something of it, Ribault.'

'It was the history of a brave man, Monsieur: of patient merit eternally struggling against adversity; of conscious power having to submit itself to necessity. There was that in him could he but have indulged it—ah, if you had only seen!'

'Seen what, my poor friend?'

'Monsieur, he died in June; but before he died, he drew in pastel on that wall, on that bare wall, a face that was like the fine blossom of the aloe, crowning and vindicating with its immortal beauty the harsh and thorny ugliness of those long necessitous years. It was his testament, his swan-song. Less than its perfection would have made a smaller artist; and it was produced by him from memory, as he sat there dying in his chair.'

'From a memory of whom, Ribault?'

'I will tell you. One day, shortly before his death, there had come to see him a step-brother of his, an Englishman, of whom I had never heard nor he spoken. He had a lady with him, this brother, one of the most beautiful you could picture, and her loveliness entered into Jean's heart. He could not forget it; he had no ease from it until his art came to dispossess him of its haunting. I watched him at work; it was marvellous: the wall broke into song and flower under my eyes. That was the man, Monsieur; that was the man; it was his own soul blossoming; and, having done what he must, he grew once more at peace. Two days later he was dead.'

'I see no face on the wall, Ribault.'

'Alas, no, Monsieur! Alas, alas, no! When he returned, this strange relation, this vandal, after his brother's death, to arrange for the funeral and dispose of his effects, he saw the drawing and he denounced it. He did more: in his anger he seized a cloth, and, before I could interpose, that miracle, that dream, was but a featureless smudge upon the wall. And even then he would not be satisfied until the last rainbow tints had vanished.'

The frown on M. le Baron's brow was again darkening its habitual placidity.

'What excuse had the man to offer for an act so outrageous?' he demanded warmly.

The designer shrugged his shoulders. 'What excuse but of the jealous and coarse-grained! He said that the lady's permission should have been asked first; that anyhow the artist being dead it could not matter, and that he had no idea of leaving the portrait there to become the cynosure of common eyes. He was a hard man, Monsieur, and we came to words.'

The visitor grunted. 'M. Ribault, what was the name of this Goth?'

'It was the name of my friend, Monsieur.'

'What! Christian and surname the same?'

'Precisely one, Monsieur. They were *beaux-frères*, no more. With such it may be.'

'Indubitably. And the lady's name?'

'I could show you sooner than pronounce it. It was written by Jean under the portrait.'

'But the portrait is lost!'

'Nevertheless, it is not altogether forgotten. Before it was destroyed I had borrowed a camera from a friend and achieved a reproduction of it. Alas, Monsieur! but a cold shadow of the original—a sadness, a reflection, but, such as it is, a record I would not willingly let perish.'

The Baron's brow was smoother again; his eyes had recovered their good humour.

'But this is interesting, my friend,' he said. 'Might I be permitted to see it?'

'Who sooner!' cried the designer. 'Monsieur has only to command.'

He went to a cupboard, and presently produced from it a photograph mounted on brown paper, which he presented to his visitor.

'You must not judge from it,' he said, 'more than you would from the shadow of an apple tree the colour of its blossom. But is it not a beautiful face, Monsieur?'

'Beautiful, indeed,' answered Le Sage, profoundly preoccupied. 'And did the brother know you had secured this transcript?' he asked presently.

'Of a truth not, Monsieur. Sooner would I have died than tell him.'

'Ah!' For minutes longer the Baron stood absorbed in contemplation of the photograph. Then suddenly he looked up.

'I want you to part with this to me, my friend.'

'Monsieur, it is yours. There is none to whom I would sooner confide it.'

'You have the negative?'

'Truly, yes.'

'Keep it, and print no more from it for the present. Above all, keep the knowledge of your possessing it from the Goth.'

Between wonder and sympathy the Frenchman acquiesced.

'No doubt he would want to destroy that too,' he said.

'Exactly,' answered Le Sage. 'Now, listen, my friend. I have a commission for you.'

It was a very handsome commission, the nature of which need not be specified, since it was in effect merely a delicate acknowledgment of a service rendered. And if the acknowledgment was out of all proportion with the service, that was M. le Baron's way, and one not to be resented by a poor man who was also a reasonably proud man. So the two parted very good friends, and the Baron went back to his hotel, in high good humour with himself and all the world. On the following night he was in London, ensconced in rooms in a private hotel in Bloomsbury, where he learnt from the papers of the latest startling development in what had come to be known as the 'Wildshott Murder Case'. 'So,' he thought, 'it works according to plan.'

He had managed to procure, while in Paris, a personal introduction from a certain eminent official to a corresponding dignitary in the Metropolis; but for the present he kept that in his pocket. There were some smaller fry to be dealt with first: aids to the great approach.

CHAPTER XVI

THE BARON FINDS A CHAMPION

(*From the Bickerdike MS.*)

WHO that was present at that scene could ever forget its anguish and pathos? Its fierce dramatic intensity will remain for all time indelibly seared on my soul. Could I believe in my friend's guilt? Knowing him, it was impossible: and yet that seemingly incontrovertible evidence as to when the shot was fired? If he had done it, if he *had* done it, not his own nature but some fiend temporarily in possession of it must have directed his hand. But I would not believe he had done it. I would not, until I had heard him confess to it with his own lips. However appearances might be against him, he should find an unshakable ally in me. And if the worst were to come to the worst, and the trial confirm his guilt beyond dispute, there would be that yet for me to plead in revision of my former evidence so cruelly surprised from me, to plead in virtue of my intimacy with the unhappy boy—that in the moods to which he was subject he was apt to lose complete control of himself, and to behave on occasions veritably like a madman. It might mitigate, extenuate—who could say? But in the meantime I would not believe—not though the world accused him.

Before he was taken away he and his father met in a room below the Court. Sir Calvin, coming across the floor after the committal, looked like a white figure of Death—Death stark, but in motion. He walked straight on, avoiding nobody; but a little stagger as he passed near me was eloquent of his true state. I was moved impulsively to hold out my arm to him, and he took it blindly, and we descended the stairs together. In a bare vault-like office we found my poor friend. He was in the charge of the two policemen who had arrested him. His deadly pallor was all gone, and succeeded by a vivid flush. He held out his hand with a steadfast smiling look.

'Take it or not, sir,' he said.

It was taken, and hard wrung—just that one moment's understanding—and the two fell apart.

'Thank you, sir,' said the boy simply. 'I did not do it, of course.'

The father laughed; it wrung one to hear him, and to see his face.

'One of your judges, Hughie,' he said, wheezing hilariously—'old Crosson; you know him—told me not to lose heart—that appearances weren't always to be trusted. He ought to know, eh, after three attempts?'

'I wanted you just to hear me say,' said the other hurriedly, 'that I'm glad it's come—not the *way* it has, but the truth. I've behaved like a blackguard, sir, and it's been weighing on me; you don't know how it's been weighing. It's been making my life hell for some little time past. But now you know, and it's the worst of me—bad enough, but not the unutterable brute they'd make me out.' He turned to me. 'So they got at you, Viv,' he said. 'Never mind, old boy; you meant the best.'

'It was an infamous breach of confidence,' I burst out. 'It was that Sergeant led me on.'

'Yes,' said Hugh: 'I supposed he was at the bottom of all this. But I can't help his witnesses. It was the truth I told.'

'He has betrayed the house,' I said hotly, 'he was engaged to serve.'

But to this Sir Calvin, greatly to my surprise and indignation, demurred, in a hoarse broken way: 'If he thought his duty lay this road, it was his business like an honest man to take it. We want no absolution on sufferance—eh, Hughie, my boy?'

'No, sir, no. You will see that I am properly advised as to the best way to go to clear myself. Thank God my mother isn't alive!'

It was said with the first shadow of a break in his voice, and the General could not stand it. He gave a little gasp, and turned away, his fingers working at his moustache.

'She'll see to it, Hughie,' he said indistinctly, 'that—that it's all made right. There was never a more truth-loving woman in the world. But you shall have your advice—for form's sake—the best that can be procured.'

'Thank you, sir.'

It was intimated that the interview must end. The two men just faced one another—in an unforgettable look; and then the father turned, and, rigid as a sleep-walker, passed out of the room without another word. I lingered behind a moment, just to whisper my friend *bonne chance*; then hurried after the retreating figure. We entered the car in silence, and drove off alone together, leaving the household witnesses to follow later. All the way it must have lain in the mind of the stiff figure beside me with what other expectations, in what other company, we had made the outward journey. I thought it best not to disturb him; and we reached the house without a solitary sentence, I believe, having passed between us. Once there, Sir Calvin walked straight into his study, and I saw him no more that day.

What was the true thought in his heart? Faith scornful and triumphant, or some secret misgiving? Who could tell? Perhaps for the first time some doubts as to his own qualifications as a father were beginning to move in him, some tragic self-searching for the seed of what might or might not be in this 'fruit of his blood'. The day stole by on hushed wings; a sense of still fatality brooded over the house. The voiceless, almost unpeopled quiet told upon my nerves, and kept me wandering, aimless and solitary, from room to room. Near evening, Audrey was sent for by her father. I saw her, and saw her for the first time since our return, as she disappeared into his study. What passed between them there one could only surmise, but at least it was marked by no audible sounds of emotion. In that dead oppression I would have welcomed even her company; but she never came near me, and I was left to batten as I would on my own poisonous reflections. They passed and passed in review, with sickening iteration, the same wearisome problems—the evidence, my hateful and unwilling share in it, my friend's dreadful situation. Against the detective I felt a bitter animosity. No wonder that, conscious of his treachery to his employer, as I still persisted in regarding it, his manner had changed of late, and he had held himself aloof from us. Even that cynical official fibre, I supposed, could not be entirely insensitive to the indecency of eating the salt of him he was planning to betray. I was so wrath with him that I could have wished, if for no other reason than his discomfiture, to vindicate my friend's innocence. The thought sent me harking back once more over familiar ground. If Hugh were innocent, who was guilty? If another could be proved guilty, or even reasonably suspect, the whole evidence against the prisoner fell into discredit. Who, then?

Now, this overwhelming business itself had not been enough to dismiss wholly from my mind its haunting suspicions regarding the Baron. So secret, so subtle, so inexplicable, could it still be possible that he was somehow implicated in the affair? If not, was it not at least remarkable that it should have coincided with his coming, involved his servant, been followed by that midnight theft of the paper? And then suddenly there came to me, with a little shock of the blood, a memory of our conversation in the keeper's cottage on the fatal day of the shoot. How curious he had been then on the subject of poachers, of their methods, of their proneness to violence on occasion! He had asked so innocently yet shown such shrewdness in his questions, that even Orsden had laughingly commented on the discrepancy. And that mention of the muffling properties of a mist in the matter of a gunshot! *Why, it was as if he had wished to assure himself of the adequacy of some precaution already calculated and taken to mislead and bewilder in a certain issue!*

The thought came upon me like a thunderclap. Was it, could it be possible that some blackguard poacher had been made the instrument of a diabolical plot—perhaps that fourth shadowy figure that had never materialised; perhaps Henstridge himself, who had volunteered the damning evidence, and whom it would be one's instinct to mistrust? Le Sage and Henstridge in collusion! Was it an inspiration? Did I stand on the threshold of a tremendous discovery? In spite of the feverish excitement which suddenly possessed me, I could still reason against my own theory. The motive? What possible motive in murdering an unoffending servant girl? Again, what time had been the Baron's in which to complot so elaborate a crime?

But, supposing it had all been arranged beforehand, before ever he came? I had not overlooked the mystery attaching to the girl herself. It might cover, for all one knew, a very labyrinthine intrigue of vengeance and spoliation.

And then in a moment my thought swerved, and the memory of Cleghorn returned to me—Cleghorn, white and abject, grasping the rail of the dock. Cleghorn fainting where he stood. What terrific emotion had thus prostrated the man, relieved from an intolerable oppression? Was mere revulsion of feeling enough to account for it, or was it conceivable that he too was, after all, concerned in the business, a third party, and overwhelmed under his sense of unexpected escape from what he had regarded as his certain doom?

I was getting into deep waters. I stood aghast before my own imagination. How was I to deal with its creations?

It was an acute problem, my decision on which was reached only after long deliberation. It was this: I would keep all my suspicions and theories to myself until I could confide them to the ear of the Counsel engaged on Hugo's behalf.

In the meantime some relief from the moral stagnation of Wildshott had become apparent with the opening of the day succeeding the inquiry. That deadly lethargy which had followed the first stunning blow was in part shaken off, and the household, though in hushed vein, began to resume its ordinary duties. Sir Calvin himself reappeared, white and drawn, but showing no disposition to suffer commiseration in any form, or any relaxation from his iron discipline. The events of the next few days I will pass over at short length. They yielded some pathos, embraced some preparations, included a visit. I may mention here a decision of the General's which a little, in one direction, embarrassed my designs. Just or unjust to the man, he would not have Cleghorn back. One could not wonder, perhaps, over his determination; yet I could have preferred for the moment not to lose sight of my suspect. We heard later that the butler, as if anticipating his dismissal, had gone, directly after his release, up to London, where, no doubt, he could be found if wanted. I had to console myself with that reflection. The valet, Louis, we came to learn about the same time, had taken refuge, pending his master's return—he had got to hear somehow of the Baron's absence—with an excellent Roman Catholic lady, who had pitied his case and offered him employment. *He* had no desire, very certainly, to return to a house where he had suffered so much.

Of a visit I was allowed to pay my friend in the prison I do not wish to say a great deal. The interview took place in a room with a grating between us and a warder present. The circumstances were inexpressibly painful, but I think I felt them more than Hugo. He was cheery and optimistic—outspoken too in a way that touched me to the quick.

'I want to tell you everything, Viv,' he said hurriedly, below his breath; 'I want to get it all off my chest. You guessed the truth, of course; but not the whole of it. There was one thing—I'd like you to tell my father, if you will—it makes me out a worse cur than I admitted, but I can't feel clean till I've said it. It began this way. I surprised the girl over some tricky business—God forgive her and me; that's enough said about it!—and I bargained with her for my silence on terms. I'll say for myself that I knew already she was fond of me; but it doesn't excuse my behaving like a damned cad. Anyhow, she fell to it easily enough; and then the fat was in the fire. It blazed up when she discovered—you know. It seemed to turn her mad. She must be made honest—my wife—or she would kill herself, she said. I believe in the end I should have married her, if—Viv, old man, I loved that girl, I loved her God knows with what passion; yet, I tell you, my first emotion on discovering her dead was one of horrible relief. Call me an inhuman beast, if you will. I dare say it's true, but there it is. I was in such a ghastly hole, and my nerves had gone all to pieces over it. If I had done what she wished, it meant the end of everything for her and me. I knew the old man, and that he would never forgive such an alliance—would ruin and beggar us. I had been on a hellish rack, and was suddenly off it, and the momentary sensation was beyond my own control. Does the admission seem to blacken the case against me? I believe I know you better than to think so. I'm only accounting in a way for my behaviour on the night of the—the— Why, all the time, at the bottom of my soul, I was crying on my dead darling to come back to me, that I could not live without her. O, Viv! why is it made so difficult for some men to go straight?'

He paused a moment, his head leaned down on his hands, which held on to the bars. I did not speak. His allusion to the 'tricky business' he had surprised the girl over was haunting my mind. How did it consort with my latent suspicion of a mystery somewhere?

'Hugh,' I said presently, 'you won't tell me what she was doing when you first—?'

'No, I won't,' he interrupted me bluntly. 'Think what she became to me, and allow me a little decency. I've told you all that's necessary—more than I had ever intended to tell you when I promised you my confidence. I'm sorry for that, Viv. God knows if I had spoken to you at first it might have altered things. But I couldn't make up my mind while a chance existed—or I thought it did. She put me out of my last conceit that day, swearing she was going to expose the whole story. It was all true that I said. She may have been waiting there on the chance of my passing: I swear I didn't know it. We had our few words, and I gave my promise and passed on. The evidence about the shot was a black lie. I can say no more than that.'

I give his words, and leave them at that, making no comment and drawing no conclusions. If his admission as to his first emotion on learning of his release might repel some people, I can only plead that one man's psychology, like one man's meat, may be impossible of digestion by another. I found it, I confess, hard to stomach myself; but then I had never been a spoilt and wayward only son.

We talked some little time longer on another matter, which had indeed been the main object of my visit—the nature of, and Counsel for, his defence. I had undertaken, at Sir Calvin's instance, to go to London and interview his lawyers on the subject, thus sparing the father the bitter trial of a preliminary explanation, and I told Hugo of my intention.

'What a good fellow you are, Viv,' he said fondly. 'I don't deserve that you should take all this trouble, about me.'

'If I can only appear to justify my own indecent persistence in remaining on to help,' I said stiffly, 'I shall feel satisfied.'

I could not forbear the little thrust: that wounding remark of his had never ceased to rankle in me.

'Well, I asked for it,' he said, with a flushed smile. 'But don't nurse a grudge any longer. I was hardly accountable for what I said in those days: a man hardly is, you know, when he's on the rack.'

'O! I forgive you,' I answered. 'There's a virtue sometimes in pretending to a thick skin—' and we parted on good terms.

My journey to London was arranged for the morrow after the interview. I had one of my passages with Audrey before going. I don't know what particular prejudice it was the girl cherished against me, but she would never let us be friends. I saw scarcely anything of her in these days, and when we did meet she would hardly speak to me. I could have wished even to propitiate her, because it was plain enough to me how the poor thing was suffering. Her pride and her affections—both of which, I think, were really deep-seated—were cruelly involved in the disgrace befallen them. They found some little compensation, perhaps, in the improved relations established between her father and herself. Circumstances had brought these two into closer and more sympathetic kinship; it was as if they had discovered between them a father and a daughter; and so far poor Hugo's catastrophe had wrought good. But still the girl's loneliness of heart was an evident thing. Pathetically grateful as she might be for the change in her father's attitude towards her, she could never get nearer to that despotic nature than its own limitations would permit.

'You are pining for your Baron, I suppose,' I said on this day, goaded at last to speak by her insufferable manner towards me. The taunt was effective, at least, in opening her mouth.

'You are always hinting unpleasant things about the Baron, Mr Bickerdike,' she answered, turning sharply on me. 'Don't you think it a little mean to be continually slandering him in that underhand way?'

I saw it was still to be battle, and prepared my guard.

'That is your perverse way of looking at it, Audrey,' I answered quietly. 'From my point of view, it is just trying to help my friends.'

'By maligning them to their enemies?' she answered. 'I suppose that was why you confided to Sergeant Ridgway all you knew about Hugh's affairs?'

It gave me a certain shock. I knew that she had read a full report of the proceedings, but not that she, or anyone, had drawn such a cruel conclusion from it.

'Confided, is the word, Audrey,' I answered, with difficulty levelling my voice. 'I can't be held responsible for that breach of trust. Yes, thank you for that smile; but I know what was in my heart, and it was to help Hugh over a difficult place I foresaw for him. My weakness was in thinking other men as honourable as myself. But, anyhow, your stab is rather misplaced, since I wasn't "maligning", as you say, my friends to their enemies, but the other way about, as *I* see it.'

'Well, don't see it,' she said insolently. 'Perhaps—just consider it as possible—I may happen to know more about the Baron than you do.'

'O! I dare say he's been yarning to you,' I answered, 'and quite plausibly enough to a credulous listener. But, if I were you, I wouldn't attach too much importance to what he tells you about himself. I'll say no more as to my own suspicions, though events have not modified them, I can assure you; but I *will* say that regard for your brother should at least incline you to go warily in a matter which may have a very strong bearing on his interests.'

She stood conning me a moment or two in silence.

'Please to be explicit,' she said then. 'Do you mean that you believe the Baron to be the real criminal?'

I positively jumped.

'Good Heavens!' I cried. 'Don't make me responsible for such wild statements. I mean only that, in the face of your brother's awful situation, you should be scrupulously careful to do nothing which might seem to impair the efforts of those who are working to throw new light on it. I don't say the Baron is the guilty one, but it is possible your brother is not.'

'Is that all?' she cried. She stepped right up to me, so that our faces were near touching. 'Mr Vivian Bickerdike,' she said, 'Hugh did not commit that murder. I tell you, in case you do not know.'

'I never said he did,' I answered, involuntarily backing a little, her eyes were so pugnacious. 'How you persist in misreading me! I only want to be prepared against all contingencies.'

'Amongst which, I suppose, is the Baron's wicked attempt to exculpate himself to me, by encouraging my suspicions against Hughie?' She laughed, with a sort of defiant sob in her voice. 'I'll tell you what I truly think: that he is a better friend to my brother than you are; and I hope he'll come back soon; and, when he does, I shall go on listening to and believing in him, as I do think I believe in no one else. And in the meantime I'll tell you this for your comfort: he is really English, and really the Baron Le Sage. He takes his title from an estate in the Cevennes, which was left him by a maternal uncle; and he is very rich, and I dare say very eccentric in wanting to do good with his money; and that is enough for the present.'

'And he plays chess for half-crowns and steals private papers!' I cried to myself scornfully, as she turned and left me.

Poor foolish creature. It was no good my trying to convince her, and I gave up the attempt then and there.

CHAPTER XVII

AND AUDREY

AUDREY had been starting for a walk when detained by the interview recorded in the last chapter. She left it burning with indignation and passionate resentment. That this man could call himself a friend of Hughie, and conceive for one moment the possibility of his guilt! He pretended to be his intimate, and did not even know him. How she hated such Laodicean allies! And that he should dare to try to involve *her* in his doubts and half concessions! It was infamous. It had needed all her sense of the confidence her father placed in him, and of the authority to act for him which he had delegated to him, to stop her from saying something so cuttingly rude that even he could not have consented to swallow the insult and remain on.

She did Mr Bickerdike, as we know, a sad injustice. The truth was, one suspects, that in all this business of his friend's exoneration the unhappy gentleman was flying in the face of his own conscience, and doing it for pure loyalty's sake. He could not quite bring himself to argue against appearances in the Justice's sense; but he *hoped*, and he tried to take a rosy view of his own hopes. It was not to be expected of him, or of his disposition, that he should feel or express that blind and incorrigible staunchness to an ideal natural in a devoted blood-relation; yet it should be counted to him that he was staunch too, and on behalf of a cause which in his heart he mistrusted. Perhaps his suspicions anent the Baron were conceived more in a desperate attempt to discover a way out for his friend, than in any spirit of strong belief in their justification. But Audrey was prejudiced against him, and the prejudices of young people are like their loves, unreasoning and devastating.

She was very miserable, poor girl—proud, friendless, solitary. Essentially companionable by nature, the social restrictions of her state, man-administered, had deprived her of all warm intimacies among her own sex. She was not allowed to know those she would have liked to know; the few selected for her acquaintance she detested. There was none to whom she could appeal for understanding or sympathy. Repellent to them all in her pride, was it likely they would spare her in her humiliation? The very thought made her hold her head high, and filled her heart with a hard defiance. Nobody cared, nobody believed but herself and her father. Poor Hughie, to be so admired and courted in prosperity, so slandered and abandoned in adversity! Never mind; the truth would be known presently, and then the humiliation would be theirs who had unwittingly betrayed their own abject natures.

She crossed the high road, and, entering the thickets beyond, proceeded in a direction almost due west. That way lay the least association with all the squalid events of the past few weeks, and she knew that if she pushed on over the boundaries of Wildshott, she would come presently to a place of quiet woods and streams and easeful solitudes. She wanted to avoid any possibility of Contact with her fellow-creatures, and to be alone. It was a glowing September day, when everything, save her own unquiet heart, seemed resolved into an eternal serenity of peace and happiness never again to be broken. The coney had lain down with the fox and the stoat; the ageing bracken had renewed its youth in a sparkling vesture of diamond-mist; the birds were singing as if a dream-spring had surprised them in the very thought of hibernating. Presently, going among trees, Audrey came out on the lip of a little shelving dingle, at whose foot ran a full bountiful stream watering a wooded valley. And at once she paused, because the figure of a small sturdy boy was visible below her, busy about a spot where a tiny fall plunged frothing and merry-making into a pool which it tried to brim and could not. She paused, watching the figure; and suddenly, driven by some inexplicable impulse, she was going quickly down the slope to speak to it. It was a revulsion of feeling, a sob for a voice in the wilderness, a cry to give herself just one more chance before she flung away the world and took loneliness for her eternal doom.

The boy, hearing her coming, lifted his head, then rose to his feet. He had been engaged over a fly rod, which he held in his hand.

'Mornin', Miss,' he said, grinning and saluting.

'Are you fishing, Jacob?'

'Me and the master, miss. He'll be back in a minute. He'n been whipping the stream up-ways.'

Her lip curled, ever so slightly. There might be better occupation than fishing for a man who cared.

'He's thinking,' said Jake.

'Thinking!' she echoed scornfully.

'Yes'm. He says to me, he says, "Jacob, fishing helps a man to think; and what d'you suppose I've been thinking about, Jacob?"'

'Well?'

'"Why, who it was as killed Annie Evans,"' he says. The boy looked up shyly. 'We knows anyhow as it weren't Master Hugo, Miss.'

'Do you? Did he say that, Jacob?' She spoke softly, with a wonderful new glow about her heart.

'Yes'm,' said the boy. 'He did that. You should ha' heard him yesterday giving Squire Redwood the lie. We was hunting otter, Miss, and was on to his *spraints*, when Squire said something bad about Master Hugo as caught Sir Francis's ear. He went up to him, he did, and he told him he'd lay his good ash-spear across his shoulders unless he withdrew the expression.'

'Redwood! That great powerful bully!' cried Miss Kennett.

'Yes'm. And Squire looked that frit, it might ha' been a boggle had sudden come to life and faced him. But he did what he was told, and saved his shoulders.'

'He did, he did?' She put her hands up to her throat a moment, as if to strangle the emotion that would not be suppressed, and in the act heard his footstep and turned.

He came with wonder and pleasure in his face.

'Audrey!' he exclaimed; 'what good luck has brought you here?'

'I don't know, Frank,' she answered a little wildly; 'but it is good luck, and I thank it. Why do you, who hate hunting, hunt otters, sir?'

'Because they kill my fish,' he replied promptly.

'And so spoil your thinking, I suppose,' she said.

He seemed to understand in a moment, and his face flushed.

'Jake has been t-talking, has he?' he said.' Jake, I'm ashamed of you.'

'And did Redwood save his big shoulders?' she asked.

'Jake!' cried his master reproachfully.

She laughed and sobbed together.

'Frank, will you leave your things here, and come a little way with me, please?'

'O, Audrey! You know—not only a little way, if it could be.'

They walked together along the green bank of the stream, from sunlight into luminous shadow, and forth again, parting the branches sometimes, always with the water, like a merry child, running and talking beside them. Suddenly she stopped, and turned upon him.

'If it could be,' she said, repeating his words: 'that is to say, if I had not a murderer for a brother.'

He cried out: 'Good God! What do you mean? Hugh is not a murderer!'

'You declare it—in spite of all, Frank?'

'All what? I know him, and that's enough.'

'For me, for me, yes, and for you! O, Frank!'—she could not keep them back; they came irresistibly, and rolled down her cheeks—'you don't know what you have done, what you have lifted from my heart! And I said you were not a man—like him. O, forgive me, Frank dear!'

'Hush!' he said. He took her arm and tucked it close and comfortable under his, and led her on. 'I am not, if it comes to that,' he said.

'You don't mean that unkindly? No, you never would, of course. But I can be glad to think it now—glad that you are not. He is not good, Frank. I should hate him for what he has done—I can say it to you now—if he were not suffering so dreadfully for what he has *not* done.'

'I know, Audrey. Poor fellow—for what he has not done. That is the point. How are we going to p-prove it? I have been pushing some private inquiries, for my part, about that mysterious figure seen or not seen by Henstridge on the hill. I can't get it out of my head that there really was such a figure, and that, if we could only t-trace it, we should hold the clue to the riddle.'

'Have you been doing that, Frank? And I thought you had forsaken us like the rest.'

'That was ungenerous of you, Audrey, dear. I should have come and told you, only I was delicate of starting you, perhaps, on a false scent, and thought it better to w-wait till I had something definite to offer.'

'Frank, did you read of the Inquest?'

'I was present at it—in the background.'

'O! Do you remember the master of the poor man who was supposed then—'

'Le Sage? I should think I do. His b-benevolent truthfulness was a thing to wonder over.'

'I think it is. He and I are great friends. He is away for the moment; but when he comes back, I wish you would let me introduce you to him!'

'Why, Audrey, I know him already. Have you forgotten Hanson's cottage and our talk about the poachers? A r-remarkably shrewd old file I thought him.'

'So he is. I have such faith in him somehow. Somehow I feel that all will come right when he returns. I do wish he would. It is all so dreadful waiting. Will you tell him about your theory, when he does?'

'Of course I will. Don't go yet, Audrey.'

She had stopped.

'Yes, Frank, I am going. I feel that every moment taken from your fishing is robbing Hughie of a chance.'

'Audrey—after what you've said—poor Hugh—I'll not be thought a man at his expense—but—are you going to let me hope just a little again?'

'Are you serious, dear? His sister? Think.'

'A m-martyr's sister—the greater honour mine.'

She could not help a little laugh over the picture of Hugh a martyr.

'I love you, Frank,' she said, 'but not quite that way.'

'Well, I love you all ways,' he answered, 'so that any little defect in yours is provided for.'

'How good you are to me!' she sighed. 'If it's to be thought of, it must not be on any consideration till Hugh is cleared.'

'Agreed!' he cried joyously. 'Then we are as g-good as engaged already.'

'You dear!' she said, and jumped at him. 'I will kiss you once for that. No, put your hands down—handy-pandy-sugary-candy, and—there, sir! And now please to go back to your fishing.'

She smiled at him and hurried away, a fine pink on her cheek. After the rain, fine weather; after despair, reassurance. She was not alone; she had these two good staunch friends, Frank and little Jacob, to stand by her. Her heart was singing with the birds, sparkling with the mist. When she reached home she found another comfort to greet her. Mr Bickerdike had already started for London. Then she did a queer, shame-faced thing, in a queer shame-faced way. She got out some old dog's-eared music, long forgotten childish exercises, and sat down to the piano to try if she could remember them. She played very softly in a young stumbling fashion, all stiff fingers and whispering lips. It did not come naturally to her, and she had long arrears of neglect to make good. But she persevered. If it was a question of qualifying herself for the intellectual life, she must not throw up the sponge at the first round. After a strenuous hour she had more or less mastered No.1 Exercise for two hands in Czerny's first course, and had got so far on the road to Audley.

CHAPTER XVIII

THE BARON RETURNS

(*From the Bickerdike MS.*)

I HAD a long and interesting interview with Sir Calvin's lawyers, when I used the occasion to unburden my mind of some of the misgivings which had been disturbing it. I spoke theoretically, of course, and without prejudice, and no doubt considerably impressed my hearers, who were very earnest with me to keep my own counsel in the matter until one of the partners could run down—which he would do in the course of a few days—to examine into all the circumstances of the case on the spot; and, above all, not to let the Baron guess that he was in any way an object of my suspicion. They had, of course, heard of the murder and its sequel, and had been expecting their client's instructions for the defence. They were very sympathetic, but naturally cautious about advancing any opinion one way or the other at this stage of the affair, and the gist of the matter was relegated for discussion *in diem*. I do not, however, describe the interview at greater length for the simple reason that, as things came to turn out, it bore no eventual fruit. But that will appear.

I stayed three nights in town, and returned to Wildshott on the fourth day from my leaving it. Going to Sir Calvin's study straightway, and being bidden to enter, what was my chagrin and astonishment to find the Baron already in the room before me, having anticipated my own return by some twelve hours or so. He was seated talking with his host—on some matter of grave import, I at once assumed, from the serious expression on the faces of the two. Even Le Sage's habitual levity appeared subdued, while as to the General, I thought he looked like a man in process of rallying from some great shock or recent illness. He sat with his head hunched into his shoulders, all the starch gone from him, and with a fixed white stare in his eyes, as if he were battling with some inward torment. What had the man been saying or doing to him? My gorge rose; I was seized with a fierce anger and foreboding. Was I witnessing the effects of that very villain blow so apprehended by me as in course of preparing when that significant journey to London was first announced? My eyes, instinctively hawking for evidence, pounced on the embrasure which contained the safe. The curtain was drawn aside, the door open; and on the table near Sir Calvin stood a packet of papers, the tape which had bound them fallen to the carpet. Had he by chance been learning for the first time of his loss—and too late? I was tired, and my temper, perhaps, was short. In my infinite disgust at discovering how this man had stolen a march on me, I made little attempt to control it. 'What, you back!' I exclaimed, for my only greeting.

'And you!' he responded placidly. 'This is a happy coincidence, Mr Bickerdike.'

I passed him, and went to shake Sir Calvin by the hand. The look of my poor friend as he gave me formal welcome inflamed my anger to that degree that I could contain myself no longer. I felt, too, that the moment had come; that it would be criminal in myself to postpone it longer; that I must give this fellow to understand that his villainy had not passed wholly undetected and unrecorded. Forgetting, I confess, in my exasperation, my promise to the lawyers, I turned on him in an irresistible impulse of passion.

'How, sir,' I said, 'have you succeeded in reducing my friend the General to this state?'

There followed a moment's startled silence, and then Sir Calvin stiffened, and sat up, and cleared his throat.

'Bickerdike,' he said, 'don't be a damned ass!'

'That's as it may be, sir,' I said, now in a towering rage. 'You shall judge of the extent of my folly when you have heard what I insist upon making known to you.'

He sat looking at me in a frowning, wondering sort of way; then shrugged his shoulders.

'Very well—if you insist,' he said.

'I have no alternative,' I answered. 'If I am to do my duty, as I consider it, at this crucial pass, when the life of a dear friend hangs in the balance, all stuff of punctilio must be let go to the winds. If I hold the opinion that an evil influence is at work in this house, operating somehow to sinister but mysterious ends, it would be wickedness on my part to withhold the evidence on which that opinion is founded. I do think such an influence is at work, and I claim the condition in which I now find you as some justification for my belief.'

'You are quite mistaken,' said my host, 'utterly mistaken.'

I bowed. 'Very well, sir; and I only wish I were as mistaken about the character of this gentleman whom you have admitted to your acquaintance and your hospitality.'

Sir Calvin looked at Le Sage, who sat still all this time with a perfectly unruffled countenance. He laughed now good humouredly, and bent forward to take a pinch of snuff.

'Come, come, Mr Bickerdike,' he expostulated, brushing the dust from his waistcoat; 'of what do you accuse me?'

'That is soon said,' I answered, 'and said more easily than one can explain the general impression of underhandedness one receives from you. I intend to be explicit, and I accuse you to your face of having secretly left your room one midnight, when the house was asleep' (I gave the date) 'and stolen a paper from Sir Calvin's desk here.'

He looked at me oddly.

'To be sure,' he said. 'Do you know, Mr Bickerdike, your half-face looking round the post that night reminded me so ludicrously of those divided portraits one sees in picture-restorers' shops that I was near bursting into laughter.'

'You may have eyes in your ears,' I cried, rallying from the shock; 'but that is not an answer to my charge.'

He turned to Sir Calvin: 'The sixty-four Knight move problem: you remember: I told you that, not being able to sleep, I had come down to borrow it from your desk, and work it out in the small hours.'

The General nodded, and looked at me.

'Upon my word, Bickerdike,' he said, 'you mustn't bring these unfounded charges. I don't know what's put this stuff about the Baron into your head; but you must understand that he's my very good friend, and much better known to me than he seems to be to you. Come, if I were you, I'd just apologize and say no more about it.'

It was the collapse of my life. I will own to it fairly, and save my credit at least for a sense of humour. To think that all this time I had been building such a structure on such a foundation! I was bitterly mortified, bitterly humbled; but I trust that I did the gentlemanly thing in at once accepting Sir Calvin's advice. I went straight up to the Baron and apologized.

'It seems I've been making a fool of myself,' I said.

'And I know how that must distress you,' he answered heartily. 'Think no more about it. Your motive has been all through an excellent one—to help your friend at somebody else's expense; and if I've failed you at a pinch, it's not for want of a real good try on your part. And as to my underhand ways—'

'O, they necessarily disappear with the rest,' I interrupted him. 'When one's moon-stricken one sees a bogey in every bush.'

'Well, well,' said Sir Calvin impatiently. 'That's enough said. We hadn't quite done our talk when you came in, Bickerdike. Shut the door when you go out, there's a good fellow.'

The hint was plain to starkness. I slunk away, feeling my tail between my legs. In the hall, to add to my discomfiture, I came upon Audrey. Her face fell on seeing me.

'O, have *you* come back?' she said in a discharmed voice, fairly paying me with my own bad coin.

'Yes,' I said: 'and now I have, everybody seems to love me.'

She looked at me queerly.

'The Baron has returned too: isn't that delightful?' She laughed and moved away, then came again, on a mischievous thought: 'O, by the by! There was another thing I might have told you about him the other day. All the half-crowns he wins at chess he puts into a benevolent fund for poor chess-players. He says a half-crown on a game is like a Benedictine—neither too much nor too little. It is just enough to bring out the brilliancy in a player without intoxicating him.'

I said meekly, 'Yes, Audrey. I expect he is very right; and it is a good thought of his for the poor Professors.'

She stood staring at me a moment, said 'What is the matter with you?' then turned away, moving much more slowly than before.

All the wind seemed knocked out of me by this blow, and I remained in a very depressed mood. It was my greatest mortification to realize on what vain and empty illusions I had been building a case for my friend. I will do myself so much justice. But whatever I planned seemed to go wrong. I had better retire, I thought, and leave it to better heads than mine to grapple with the problem. Nor did my *amour-propre* achieve any particular reinstatement for itself from my interview with Sir Calvin on the subject of my journey, made entirely on his behalf. I found him, when at length he called me to it, very *distrait*, and I thought not particularly interested in what I had to tell him. He seemed to listen attentively, but in fact his answers proved that he had done nothing of the sort. Everything since my return appeared somehow wrong and peculiar. It might have struck one almost as if a cloud had passed away, and a threatened tempest been forgotten. And yet Hugo was in his prison, and nothing new that I could see had happened. I told his father, as he had asked me to do, about the circumstances of his wrong-doing, and even in that failed greatly to interest the General. He did not appear to be particularly shocked. No doubt his principles in such respects were old-fashioned, and took for their text that licentious proverb which, in the name of love and war, exempts a gentleman from those bonds of truth and honour which alone make him one. He was in a strange state altogether, distraught, nervous, excited by turns, and yet always with a look about him which I should have described as exultant pride at high tension. What was the meaning of everything?

During the following day or two I kept myself studiously in the background, proffering no opinions on anything, and only pleading mutely to be put to any use I could reasonably serve. My attitude commended itself to Audrey at last. 'Frank and the Baron,' she once said to me, 'have been meeting and having a long talk together. I wonder if you will disapprove, Mr Bickerdike?'

'Two heads are better than one,' I answered, 'and as good as three when the Baron's is counted in. I'm not sure you weren't right, Audrey, and that I'm not a worse judge of character than I supposed.'

She looked at me in that queer way of hers.

'That's jolly decent of you,' she said; 'and so I'll say the same to you. It's something to be a gentleman, after all.'

Cryptic, but meant to be propitiatory. I forgave her. She had recovered her spirits wonderfully. She knew, or felt, I think, that something was in the air, though she could not tell what, and it made her confident and happy. I fancy it was her dear friend the Baron who kept her on that prick of expectancy, without quite letting her into the secret. Sometimes now she would even condescend to speak with me.

'Do you know,' she said one day, 'that Sergeant Ridgway is coming down again from Scotland Yard to see us?'

'No!' I exclaimed. 'He can't have the atrocious bad taste.'

'O, but he is!' she said. 'The First Commissioner, or the Public Prosecutor, or the Lord High Executioner, or somebody, isn't satisfied with Henstridge's evidence, and he's got to come down and go through all that part of it again. He's to be here tomorrow to see my father at two o'clock.'

'Well,' I said, 'I hope we shan't run across one another, that's all.'

'No,' she answered, in a rather funny way: 'I don't suppose you exactly love him.'

I will say no more, since I have reached the threshold of that extraordinary event which was to falsify at a blow every theory which I, in common with hundreds of others, had built up and elaborated about the Wildshott Murder Case.

CHAPTER XIX

THE DARK HORSE

SERGEANT RIDGWAY, turning up punctually to his appointment, was shown into Sir Calvin's study, where he found, not his former employer, but the Baron Le Sage, seated alone. Characteristically, the detective showed as little surprise at seeing who awaited him as he did embarrassment over his return to a house whose hospitality he had, according to Mr Bickerdike, so cruelly abused. , He could have understood, no doubt, no reason for his feeling any. His commission had been to discover the murderer of Annie Evans, and, according to the best of his lights, he had executed that commission. It was not his fault if it had led him in a direction tragically counter to the expectations of his employer. He had been engaged for a particular purpose, and he had dutifully pursued that purpose—inevitably, if unfortunately, to a regrettable end. But sentiment could not be allowed to affect the detectival philosophy, or the Law became a dead letter. In professional matters he was, and had to be, a simple automaton; wherefore no sign of uneasiness was visible in his expression as he entered the room, nor was there discernible there a trace of animus of any sort. He was quite prepared, if necessary, to own himself in the wrong. His high superiors had expressed themselves as dissatisfied with a certain portion of the evidence. Very well, he would bow to their scruples, and make a thorough re-investigation of that part of the case. He understood that the landlord of the Red Deer inn had been warned, and was to meet him here this afternoon. Personally, he did not hope much from the interview, or attach great importance to a rumour which he understood had got about since the Inquest. But whether that rumour embodied a fact, or proved on examination as unsubstantial as most *canards* of its kind, the finding of the murderer of Annie Evans remained, as it had been, his sole object and purpose in undertaking the case.

All this, or the moral gist of it, the detective took it upon himself to explain to the Baron in the course of the brief conversation which ensued between them. He spoke drily, deliberately, as if measuring out his words, rather with the air of plain-stating a professional viewpoint, and instructing Counsel, than of asking for sympathy. His hearer made a curious study of him the while, wondering and calculating why he was being chosen the recipient of this extra-judicial confidence. Perhaps, after all, there was a thought more embarrassment under the surface than the other cared to admit, perhaps just a hint of a human desire to make a friend in a difficult pass. For the rest, it was the familiar figure of their knowledge which had returned upon them—keen, handsome, dark-eyed, economical of speech, potent in suggestion of a certain inscrutable order of mentality, and exhibiting, as always, that faint discrepancy between mind and material—distinction in the one, a touch of theatricalism and vulgarity in the other.

Le Sage took him up on one point. The Baron, who was looking extraordinarily pink and cheery, had already explained that Sir Calvin was engaged with a visitor in another room, and had asked him to receive and entertain the Sergeant during the short period of his absence.

'Am I to be allowed to opine,' he said with a smile, 'that the rumour to which you refer bears upon your instructions, and is connected somehow with Mr Cleghorn's mysterious double?'

The detective looked at the speaker curiously.

'Meaning?' he said.

'Meaning that supposititious figure on the hill, about which Mr Fyler was so inquisitive at the Inquest, but which he seemed most unaccountably to overlook before the magistrates.'

'Ah!' said the detective drily, 'I expect he'd come to the conclusion, which was my own, that it wasn't really worth another thought.'

'O! so I'm mistaken in fancying any association between that and your particular mission? Well, well, it shall be a lesson to my self-sufficiency. By the by, Sergeant, we've never had our long-deferred game of chess. What do you say to a duel now while we're waiting?'

'No time, sir. Chess takes a lot of thought.'

'So it does. But it can be sampled in a problem. These tests are rather a weakness of mine. Look here,'—he led the way to the window, which, it being a mild warm day, stood wide open, and in which was placed the usual table with the board on it, and half a dozen pieces on the squares—'there's a neat one, I flatter myself. I was at work on it when you came in—black Knight (or dark horse, shall we call it?) to play, and mate in three moves. Take the opposition, and see if you can prevent it.'

He moved the Knight; mechanically the detective put down his hand and responded with a Bishop: at the Baron's third move the other looked up, and looked his adversary full in the face. Le Sage had stepped back. He had a way sometimes of thrusting his hands into the tail pockets of his coat, and bringing them round in front of him. So he stood now, with a curious smile on his lips.

'Dark horse wins,' said he. 'My mate, I think, Sergeant John Ridgway.'

The door opened with the word, spoken pretty loudly, and there came quickly into the room an inspector and two constables of the local police, followed by Sir Calvin and another gentleman.

'I have the pleasure,' said M. le Baron to the newcomers, 'of introducing to you the murderer of Annie Evans, *alias* Ivy Mellor.'

He had hardly spoken when the detective turned and leapt for the open window. The table, which stood between him and escape, went down with a crash: he had his foot on the sill, when a shot slammed out, and he stumbled and fell back into the room. The Baron's bullet had caught him neatly on the heel of his shoe, knocking his leg from under him at the critical moment. Before he could rise the police were on him, and he was handcuffed and helpless.

'A clean shot, though I say it,' said the Baron coolly, as he returned the revolver to his pocket. 'No, he's not hurt, though I may have galled his kibe. Look out for him there!'

They had need to. They had got the man to his feet, and were holding him as if in doubt whether he needed support or not, when he resolved the question for them, and in unmistakable fashion. This way and that, foaming, snarling, tearing with his manacled hands, now diving head-foremost, now nearly free, and caught back again into the human maelstrom—three stout men as they were, they had a hard ado to keep and restrain him. But they got him exhausted and quiet at last, and he stood among then torn and dishevelled, his chest heaving convulsively, dribbling at the mouth, his face like nothing human.

'You, you!' he gasped, glaring at his denouncer, 'if I had only guessed—if I had only known!'

'It would have been short shrift for me, I expect,' said the Baron shrewdly.

'It would,' said the prisoner—'that inn-keeper! It was you contrived the trap, was it? You damned, smiling traitor!'

The mortal vehemence he put into it! 'What I had always suspected, but could never quite unmask,' thought Le Sage. 'The dramatic fire, vicious and dangerous—banked down, but breaking loose now and again and roaring into uncontrollable flame!'

The second gentleman—who was in fact the Chief Constable of the County—put in a reproving word:

'Come, Ridgway, keep a civil tongue in your head, my man.'

The detective laughed like a devil.

'Civility, you old fool! If words could blister him, I'd ransack hell's language for them till he curled and shrivelled up before me.'

'Well,' said the gentleman reasonably, 'you're not improving your case, you know, by all this.'

'My case!' cried the other. 'I've got none. It was always a gamble, and I knew it well enough from the first. But I'd have pulled it through, if it hadn't been for him—I'd have pulled it through and hanged my fine gentleman—his son there—as sure as there's a God of Vengeance in the world.'

He wrenched himself in the hold that gripped him, and, bare-chested, snarling like a dog in a leash, flung forward to denounce the father:

'Curse you, do you hear? I'd have ruined and hanged that whelp of yours as surely as he ruined and murdered the girl that was mine till he debauched and stole her from me. When I put the shot into her, it was as truly his hand that fired it as if his finger had pulled on the trigger. She'd betrayed me, and it was him that led her to it, and by doing so made himself responsible for the consequences.'

The Inspector thought it right here to utter the usual official warning. It was curious to note in his tone, as he did so, a suspicion of deference, almost of apology, such as might characterise a schoolboy forced to bear witness against his headmaster. Ridgway turned on him with a jeering oath:

'You can save your breath, Cully. That devil spoke true. It was I killed Ivy Mellor; and him, that old dog's son, that ought to hang for it.'

M. le Baron spoke up: 'Is it necessary to go further, gentlemen, since he confesses to the double crime?'

'I think not,' said the Chief Constable. 'Remove him, Inspector.'

The three closed about the prisoner, who submitted quietly to being taken away. But he forced a stop a moment as he passed by Sir Calvin—who, greatly overcome, had sunk into a chair, the Baron leaning above him—and spoke, with some faint return to reason and self-control:

'I don't know how much you think you've found out. You've got to prove it, mind. No confession counts to hang a man, unless there's proof to back it.'

'*Par exemple*,' said the Baron, looking up, 'a skeleton key, a coat button, a packet of letters, a false character, a falser impersonation, a proposed disinheritance, and, to end all, a confederate murdered, and the plot to hang an innocent man for the deed!—altogether a very pretty little list, my friend.'

Ridgway, to those who held him, seemed to stagger slightly. He stood gazing with haggard eyes into the face of this deadly jocular Nemesis, who, so utterly unsuspected by him, had all this time, it appeared, while he smiled and smiled, been silently weaving his toils about his feet. He had not a word to answer; but a sort of stupor of horror grew into his expression, as if for the first time a cold mortal fear were beginning to possess him. Then suddenly he stiffened erect, turned, and passed mutely out of the room.

The Chief Constable lingered behind a moment.

'Come, Calvin, old man,' he said: 'pull yourself together. The thing's over, and well over, thanks to your wonderful friend here—by George, as remarkable a shot, sir, as you are a strategist! I don't know which I admired most, the way you stalked your quarry, or the way you brought him down.'

'Really quite simple little matters of deduction and sighting,' answered the Baron, beaming deprecation, 'if you make a practice, as I do, of never loosening your bolt in either case till you're sure of your aim.'

'Ha!' said the gentleman. 'Well, I congratulate you, Calvin, and I congratulate us all, on this happy termination to a very distressing business. I hope now the order of release won't be long in coming, and that your poor unfortunate lad will be restored to you before many hours have passed.'

A pallid, but wondering, face peered round the door.

'May I come in?' said Mr Bickerdike.

CHAPTER XX

THE BARON LAYS HIS CARDS ON THE TABLE

SIR FRANCIS ORSDEN and the Baron Le Sage walked slowly up the kitchen garden together. It was a windless autumn morning, such serene and gracious weather as had prevailed now for some days, and the primroses under the wall were already putting forth a little precocious blossom or two, feeling for the Spring. There was a balm in the air and a softness in the soil which communicated themselves to the human fibre, reawakening it as it were to a sense of new life out of old distress. Such feelings men might have who have landed from perilous seas upon a smiling shore.

The two talked earnestly as they strolled, on a subject necessarily the most prominent in their minds. Said Le Sage:

'Are we not a little apt to judge a man by his business—as that a lawyer must be unfeeling, a butcher cruel, a doctor humane, and a sweep dishonest? But it is not his profession which makes a man what he is, but the man who makes his profession what it appears in him. A lawyer does not appropriate trust funds because he is a lawyer, but because he is a gambler: so, a detective is not impeccable because he is a detective, but because he is an honest man. You wonder that he can be at the same time a detective and a desperate criminal. Well, I don't.'

'Ah! You've got a reason?'

'Just this. What is in that lawyer's mind when he steals? Imagination. It leaps the dark abyss to wing for the golden peaks beyond, where, easy restitution passed, it sees its dreams fulfilled. What was in Ridgway's mind when he planned his tremendous venture? Imagination again. It may be the angel or the devil of a piece, spur a Pegasus or ride a broomstick. The butcher, the baker, the candlestick-maker may any of them have it, and still be the butcher, the baker, and the candlestick-maker. The last thing of which a lawyer, as a lawyer, would be guilty, would be the bringing himself within the grasp of the law: the last thing of which a detective, as a detective, would be guilty, would be the making himself a subject for detection. What induces either of them, then, to sin against the logic of his own profession? Imagination alone and always, the primary impulse to everything that is good and bad in the world. A man may be blessed with it, or he may be cursed; contain it in his being like the seed of beauty or the seed of dipsomania.'

'And Ridgway like the latter?'

'It would seem so. The man is by nature a romantic. I once got a glimpse of the truth in a conversation I had with him. What flashed upon me, in that momentary lifting of the veil, was a revelation of fierce vision, immense passion. It was like taking a stethoscope to a man's heart and surprising its secret.'

'A d-diseased heart, eh?'

'One may say so—diseased with Imagination, which is like an aneurism, often unsuspected and undetectable, until, put to some sudden strain, it bursts in blood.'

'You mean, in this case—?'

'I mean that the murder was not premeditated; that is my sure conviction. It was the result of a sudden frenzied impulse finding the means ready to its hand. The man had plotted, but not that. Why should he, since it meant the ruin of his visions?'

'Ah! You forget, Baron—'

'We will come to that. What I want to impress upon you at the outset is that Ridgway was at soul a gambler. Circumstance, accident, may have made him a detective: if it had made him a bishop it would have been all the same. That fire, that energy, kept under and banked down, would as surely have roared into flame the moment Fate drew out the damper. That moment came, and with it the vision. He saw in it certain hazards, leading to certain ruin or certain fortune; like a gambler he counted the cost and took the odds, since they seemed worth to him. What he failed to count on was a certain contingency which a less imaginative man than he might have foreseen—the possible treachery of a confederate.'

'And such a confederate.'

'Exactly. It was to sin most vilely against all his instinctive code; and worse—it was to stab him with a double-edged dagger.'

'I th-think I can pity him for that.'

'And so can I; and for this reason. Coolness is, or should be, the first quality of a gambler; gamblers, for that reason, do not easily fall in love. But when they do fall they fall hard, they fall headlong, they do not so much fall as plunge, as a gambler plunges, all heaven or all hell the stake. There is no doubt that Ridgway's passion for this girl was a true gambler's passion. To gain or lose her meant heaven or hell to him.'

'I can quite believe it, Baron. But, d-damn it! how much longer are you going to keep me on tenterhooks?'

Le Sage laughed. They had been strolling, and pausing, and strolling again, until they had approached by degrees the upper boundary of the estate, where, amid great bushes of lavender and sweet marjoram, stood a substantial thatched summer-house, cosily convenient for the view. 'Let us go and sit in there,' he said, 'and I will unfold my tale without further preamble.'

As he spoke a figure dodging about among the raspberry canes came into view.

'Hullo!' cried Orsden: 'Bickerdike, What's he doing here?'

'I think I know,' said the Baron. He went over to the elaborately unconscious gentleman—who, pretending to see him for the first time, glanced up with a start and an expression of surprise which would not have deceived a town-idiot—and accosted him genially:

'Looking for anything, Mr Bickerdike?'

'Just the chance of a late raspberry the birds may have left,' was the answer.

'O! I wonder if I can provide any fruit as much to your taste. You haven't a half-hour to spare, I suppose?'

Mr Bickerdike came promptly out from among the canes.

'Certainly,' he said. 'I am quite at your service. What is it?' '

'Only that I am under promise to Sir Francis to unfold for his delectation the story of a certain mystery, and the steps by which I came to arrive at its elucidation. It occurs to me—but, of course, if it would bore you—'

'Not at all. I am all eagerness to hear.'

'Well, it occurs to me that you have a leading title to the information, if you care to claim it, since it was in your company that I found my first clue to the riddle.'

'Was it, indeed, Baron? You excite me immensely. What was that?'

'Let us all go in here, and I will tell you.'

They entered the summer-house, and seated themselves on the semi-hexagonal bench which enclosed a stout rustic table.

'Now,' said Sir Francis, his eyes sparkling, 'out with it every bit, Baron, and give our hungering souls to feed.'

Le Sage took a pinch of snuff, laid the box handy, dusted his plump knees with his handkerchief, and, leaning back and loosely twining his fingers before him, began:

'I have this, my friends, to say to you both before I start. What I have to tell, my story—and not the most creditable part of it—is fundamentally concerned with one about whom, it might be thought, my obligations as his guest should keep me silent. That would be quite true, were it not for a single consideration so vital as to constitute in itself a complete moral justification of my candour. In a few days, or weeks, the whole will be common property, and that figure subjected, I fear, to a Pharisaic criticism, which will be none the more bitter for his friends having anticipated it and rallied about him. Moreover, he himself has bound me to no sort of silence in the matter, but, on the contrary, has rather intimated to me that he leaves to my discretion the choice and manner of his defence—or *apologia*. It may be admitted, perhaps, that he does not see these things quite from our point of view: he derives from another generation and another code of morals: but for what he is, or has been, he has paid a very severe penalty, and we must judge him now by what he has suffered rather than by what he has deserved.

'So much for this confidence; which, I beg you to consider, is still, though unenforced, a confidence, due to you, Sir Francis, through your coming matrimonial connexion with the family'—(Mr Bickerdike, with a start and a positive gape, which lifted his eyebrows, looked across at the young Baronet, who grinned and nodded)—'and to you, my friend, for your unshakable loyalty to a much-tried member of it. And with that I will quit grace and get to the joint.'

The Macuba came once more into action, the box was again laid aside, and the two settled down finally to listen.

'In the following narrative,' said M. le Baron, 'what was and remains conjectural it must be left to events to substantiate. I claim so much, though, for myself, I entertain no doubt as to the truth.'

'My story opens in the Café l'Univers in Paris, where we two, Mr Bickerdike, strangers to one another, were sitting one September afternoon precisely a year ago. We got into talk on the subject of a neighbour, an artist, and an object of interest to us both, who was busily engaged in sketching into a book pencil-memoranda of the more noticeable hats worn by passing ladies. He worked fast and cleverly, and was manifestly an adept at his craft. Presently, after having watched him for some time, I asked you if you had observed anything peculiar about his hands. You had not, it seemed, and no more was said. But there *was* a peculiarity, and it was this: when he lifted his right hand, as artists will do, to measure the perspective value of an object, it was always the second finger of the hand which he interposed before his eye. I watched him do it over and over again, and it was persistently the same. Why, I found myself asking myself? Was the trick due to some malformation of the first finger, or to some congenital impulse? Not to the first, I was presently able to convince myself. To the alternative proposition I was fated to receive an answer both affirmative and illuminating: but it was not to come just yet.

'You remember what followed. The stranger suddenly closed his book, rose, started to cross the road, and was promptly knocked down and run over by a passing cab. I hurried to his assistance, and found that he was pretty badly injured. He was lifted into the cab, and, accompanied by myself and a gendarme, was conveyed to the St Antoine Hospital, in which he remained for some weeks. Both there, and in his own apartments after his discharge, I visited him frequently, and was able to show him some small attentions, such as, in our relative positions, mere humanity demanded of me. He was poor, in his art an enthusiast, and very little sympathy was needed to win his general confidence. His name was John Ridgway.'

The two listeners glanced at one another, in a puzzled, questioning way; but neither would venture to interrupt, and the Baron continued:

'He was John, and Ridgway—pronounced Reedsvay—but for the sake of a necessary distinction I will call him henceforth Jean.

'Jean lived with a friend, Caliste Ribault, in two rooms in the Rue Bourbon-le-Château, a little dull out-of-the-way street in the Latin Quarter. They both worked for a living on the *Petit Courrier des Dames*; but with Jean it was a weariness and a humiliation, and always he had before his eyes the prospect of ultimate manumission and recognition. He was an artist from his soul outwards to his finger-tips. But, alas! his immortality was destined to be of sooner arrival. He never properly overcame the effects of his accident, and last June he succumbed to them and left his friend alone.

'Now, in the course of our conversations, Jean had told me a strange story about himself—a story which I never knew at the time whether to credit, or to part credit, or to attribute entirely to the invention of an imaginative nature. Born ostensibly of humble parentage, he was in reality, he said, the legitimate son of an English officer of wealth and distinction, whose name he could claim, and whose heir he could prove himself to be, contingent on the production of certain documentary evidence which he knew to exist, but which, since it remained in the possession of the putative father, it was impossible to cite. This alleged evidence touched upon the question of a sham marriage, a clerical impost or officiating, which had turned out to be a true marriage; and the names of the contracting parties were recorded, with that of the clergyman in question as witness, on the fly-leaf of a little Roman Catholic *vade-mecum*, which had belonged to Jean's mother but of which her would-be wronger had secured possession, and which he retained to this day.

'So much Jean told me, omitting only the father's name, which he withheld, he queerly stated, from a feeling of jealous pride for the honour of that which was his own honour, but which was presently to be suggested to me in a very singular fashion. You may perhaps recall, Mr Bickerdike, how at dinner on the night of our first arrival here, our host, in answer to some observation of mine about a certain picture hanging on the wall, raised the second finger of his right hand before his eye to test an alleged misproportion in one of the figures of the composition. The action—though, of course, I was already familiar with Sir Calvin's injury—instantly arrested my attention. A vision of the Café l'Univers and of the busy hat-sketcher leapt irresistibly into my mind: I saw again the lifted second finger, and I saw, with astonishment, what, lacking that clue, had never yet so much as occurred or suggested itself to me—the existence of a subtle but definite family likeness between the two men. That sign-manual had solved the problem of paternity, and given some colour, at least, to my friend's romantic tale. Let me put it quite clearly. Before me sat, as I was convinced, the father of the man in Paris calling himself John Ridgway, but who claimed the right, on whatever disputable grounds, to call himself, if he would, John Kennett.

'Judge of my feelings. From that moment I was possessed of a piece of knowledge whose significance I could not then foresee, but which was already half consciously associating itself in my mind with that other curious discovery—that a well-known detective, who bore the very same name as my friend, was operating on a case somewhere in the neighbourhood.

'To return now to Jean's story, and my natural comments thereon. I asked him, assuming for the occasion the truth of his statement, if he had never made an endeavour to assert his rights, and if not why not. His answer did not strike me then as convincing, though I had full reason later to alter my opinion. To attempt and fail, he said, would be merely to disinter a long-buried scandal, and expose to renewed odium the character of a mother whom he fondly loved. Moreover, for himself he had no ambitions save such as centred in his art, to which he was wholly devoted, nor any nerve or desire to take that position in the world to which his birth entitled him. She had told him the story one day, on the occasion of one of his rare visits to England—where she lived—when she was lying very ill, thinking it right that he should know, and leaving it to him to decide for himself what action, in the event of her death, he should take or not take in the matter. She was, I understood, a woman of French origin, in modest circumstances, and many years the widow of a quartermaster-sergeant in the British army. From that necessitous household

Jean himself had early broken away, to follow his bent in Paris, in which city he had remained, working and struggling for a livelihood, ever since the days of his adolescence. He was a man of twenty-eight when I knew him.

'There for the present I will leave Jean's story, turning from it to a subject of more immediate interest to you—namely, the murder of Ivy Mellor, and the methods by which I was enabled to bring the crime home to the actual delinquent. I can claim no particular credit for my part in the business. Destiny, acting blindly or providentially as you will, had woven about me, as a web is woven about a spider, a most extraordinary concatenation of coincidences, from whose central observation-point I was able, as it were, to command all strands of the design. My casual encounter with Mr Bickerdike in Paris; the discovery that he was there to meet Mr Kennett, the son of a gentleman already slightly known to me; the accident witnessed by us; my subsequent visits to the patient, and his confiding to me of his story; my second meeting with Mr Bickerdike in London, and the coincidence of our common invitation to Wildshott; the act which betrayed Jean's father to me, and seemed to confirm the truth of the man's story; the news that a second John Ridgway was at work in the neighbourhood—in all this, considered alone, there lay some grounds, perhaps, for wondering entertainment, but surely none for suspicion. It was only when the murder occurred that any thought of a connexion amongst the parts flashed inevitably into my mind; and since Fate had placed, if in any hands, in mine, what clues might exist to the truth, I was determined from that moment to pursue them to the end. *The key to it I found in a skeleton key.*'

Again the Macuba came into requisition, and again the Baron savoured, over a refreshing pinch, the excitement of his hearers.

'A skeleton key,' he repeated. 'I discovered it before ever Sergeant John Ridgway had had a chance of looking for it, on the very spot where the poor thing's body had lain. It must have been jerked from her hand—she had probably just produced it from her pocket—by the shot which killed her, and had remained there undetected during and after her removal. I was fortunate in securing it only a few minutes before the Sergeant came down to examine the place of the crime.

'Now, what had Annie Evans to do with a skeleton key—she, a modest servant girl of irreproachable character, as the housekeeper had just informed us? I examined the key. It was of the usual burglarious pattern, seemed newly turned, had a slight flaw, or projection, on the barrel end, and was splashed with an ugly Bluebeard red. Had Annie, after all, been quite the impeccable person Mrs Bingley supposed? I wondered. I thought of the manner of her engagement, of her untraceable connexions, and I wondered. I wondered still at the Inquest, when, as it seemed, those same relations were still hopelessly to seek. I wondered no longer when, on the day following the inquiry, I came upon the Sergeant intently examining the ground about the scene of the crime. I came upon him unexpectedly, and surprised him. What was he looking for? He had already overhauled every detail of the girl's belongings. Had he missed something which he had expected to find among them? A skeleton key possibly. But how could he have known she possessed such a thing? Obviously, there was only one answer—because he himself had provided her with it. For what reason—he, John Ridgway? Naturally, my mind flew off at a tangent to the other John Ridgway, my Parisian Jean, and his extraordinary story. A reputedly sham marriage which nevertheless had turned out genuine; documents in proof, and their possessor my host? Was it conceivable that *this* John Ridgway was interested in the recovery of those documents, and had employed a female confederate to steal them for him?

'It was quite conceivable, and quite true, for that, as appeared by degrees, was actually the case. But why was this John Ridgway interested in the recovery of those papers? We shall see.

'In the meanwhile, to what conviction had my reflections led me? That the detective and the girl were in collusion for a certain purpose. But much was to be deduced from that conviction—that the girl was an impostor, that she had secured her situation very possibly by means of a false character written by herself or her confederate, that, quite certainly, her name was not Annie Evans at all. Hence the calculated impossibility of tracing out her connexions.

'So far, then, so good. We come now to the frustrated business of the theft, and the crime which was its terrible consequence. It had inevitably occurred to me that the safe in Sir Calvin's study must be the repository, and known by the confederates to be the repository, of the papers in question; else, if of easier access, they had long ago been abstracted and used to serve their purpose. Probably, as it appeared to me, the girl's first business had been to secure an impression of the keyhole in wax, which she had despatched to Ridgway, receiving back from him in exchange the master-key. I seized an opportunity to examine the safe, and detected about the spot in question certain faint marks or scratches in the paint, which I had once before taken some curious stock of, and which I now perceived might well correspond with that little sharp projection I spoke of at the end of the key. I even once tried the key in the lock myself (that was on the night, Mr Bickerdike, when you stalked me'—poor Vivian looked unutterably foolish—'but without detecting me in my second descent, which occurred after you had returned to your room) and found it easy to manipulate. Then the girl had already been secretly at work there, fumbling her job maybe? But why, in that case, had she not secured the plunder, given notice to leave, and at once cleared out? *Because*—as it was perfectly legitimate to infer from the evidence at the inquest—*she had, in the meantime, fallen desperately in love with our young friend, and had refused to take any further part in a transaction designed to dispossess him of his name and inheritance.*

'Now, that is to anticipate matters a little, perhaps; but grant my deduction sound—as, indeed, it proved to be—and what followed? Necessarily, a breach between the two confederates of a very violent nature. To the detective it meant betrayal and the ruin of his plans. Would that consideration be enough in itself to goad him on to murder? With a man of Ridgway's character and trained cautiousness of disposition I did not think it probable. Assuming, then, that the murder were his act, what more overmastering motive could have driven him to it? What but jealousy, the one passion uncontrollable by even the most self-disciplining nature. He was himself passionately enamoured of his own beautiful decoy, and she had betrayed not only his interests but his love. The crime had been, in the expressive French phrase, and in the fullest sense, a *crime passionel*. I had it.

'To figure the course of events, even, was now no difficult task for the imagination. We will begin with Mrs Bingley's timely advertisement for a housemaid, upon which the confederates happened, and which gave them—perhaps suggested to them—the very opportunity they desired. Once the girl was established in the house, the two corresponded. We know that she received letters, though none could be found after her death. Of course not. She would have taken scrupulous care to destroy all such incriminating evidence, including the fraudulent "character". But they corresponded, and probably, on her part, very early in a tone which gave her accomplice to suspect, with growing uneasiness, that all was not right with her. Accident—it could have been nothing else—brought him down professionally and opportunely into this part of the country. He took the occasion to write and arrange for a secret personal interview with her—we had it from the housekeeper that a letter was received by Annie quite shortly before her death and she answered appointing the Bishop's Walk for their place of meeting. Of that I have no doubt. She was there to keep her engagement with Ridgway, and not to waylay the other. *His* appearance on the scene was quite fortuitous, and, as it turned out, the most fateful *contretemps* that could have happened. He came, and we know from his own confession what passed between them, with what she upbraided him, and with what threatened. Ridgway had overheard it all. He had arrived at the place duly to his appointment, and, on his first entering the copse, had probably heard, or perhaps caught distant sight of, the other male figure coming his way, and had slipped into the thick undergrowth for concealment. His propinquity unsuspected by the girl, she had delivered herself in his hearing of her deadly secret, and he knew at last of her double treachery to him. The lover gone, he came out of his ambush, and damned her with the truth. Likely, even then, it was the presence of the gun, so adversely left to his hand, which compelled him to the deed.

It was the act of a demented moment, unthinking and unpremeditated. It was not until reason had returned to him that the idea of the diabolical vengeance it might be in his power to wreak on the seducer began to form in his mind. To bring the murder home to *him!* What a frenzy of triumph in the very thought! It possessed him devilishly, and verily from that moment it was as if the man had bargained away his soul to the evil one. Everything appeared to favour him—the mood, the motive, the conduct of his hated rival; most of all the fact that to his own hands, by some extraordinary freak of opportunism, had been committed the control of the case. How near he came to success in his inhuman design needs no retelling.

'But meanwhile, there was the murder committed in that instant of madness. Probably he had not much hope at the time of escaping its consequences; probably, in his desperate state, with all his schemes gone to wreck, he did not much care. He had had his bloody revenge for an intolerable wrong, and the rest was indifference to him. He replaced the gun where it had stood, and left the spot. Possibly, as sanity returned to him, some instinct of self-preservation may have induced in him a certain mood of precaution. There is evidence to show, I think, that he lurked for a time in the woods before leaving them for the open hillside. But that he did leave them eventually to make his way up the hill, we have Henstridge's evidence to testify.

'Now, from the first I had never succeeded in convincing myself that that hypothetical figure on the hill was as wholly a figment of the imagination as most people seemed to consider it. The cap pulled over the eyes and the turned-up collar—what butler ever turned up his coat collar?—were strong presumptions in my mind that Mr Cleghorn had not been their wearer. Then the figure had been described as advancing hurriedly; yet it had taken twenty minutes or so to cover a distance of two hundred yards. You may object, possibly, that, in all your experience of Sergeant Ridgway, you have never seen him wear on his head other than a black plush Homburg hat. I answer that on the day of the murder he was wearing a cloth cap, easily, in the distance, to be mistaken for the cap worn by Mr Cleghorn. I know this, because, in the course of one of my drives about the country in the company of a very charming young lady, I had made a point of calling at the Sergeant's one-time lodgings at Antonferry—I had procured the address from Sir Calvin—where, at the cost of a little insinuative word-play, I was able to ascertain that the Sergeant had gone out, *wearing a cloth cap*, fairly early on the day of the murder, and that he had returned late, and seemingly in an exhausted condition, from a long walk. He had, and that hypothetical figure hurrying over the hill—at the moment with little concern for its safety—had been the figure of Sergeant Ridgway, tramping back to his lodgings in Antonferry after the murder. He had passed by the inn, making north by west, and had long turned the bend of the lonely road before Mr Cleghorn, mistaken by Henstridge for the same figure, had arrived at the Red Deer and turned in at the tap.'

The Baron paused for refreshment, while Sir Francis applauded softly, his whole face beaming delight and approval.

'Have I convinced you so far,' continued the narrator, 'of the efficiency of the toils in which I was manoeuvring to entangle my "suspect"? Very well: here was another little *pièce de conviction*. In spying about the scene of the crime I had picked up, in addition to the skeleton key—a button. It was a common horn coat-button, and was lying on the spot whence the gun had been fired—jerked off, probably, by the recoil. Now the Sergeant's overcoat was one of those light covert coats which button under an overlapping hem. I took occasion to examine it one day, when, occupied with Sir Calvin, he had left it in the hall. It had been fitted, I observed, with a set of brand-new buttons, which nevertheless did not correspond with the little buttons on the cuffs. Those exactly matched the button I had found, while the others were of a distinctly different pattern. Obviously he had discovered his loss, had failed again to make it good, and so, for precaution's sake, had renewed the entire set. It was an unpardonable oversight in such a man to have forgotten the sleeves. I made the button over to him—or could it be an exact duplicate of it which I had procured?—telling him in all innocence where I had found it. He took the little blow very well, without a wince, but I could see how it disturbed him. He never suspected me, I think, of more than an amiable curiosity. I have often wondered why.'

'Because he wasn't a fool,' interposed Mr Bickerdike, with a slight groan. Le Sage laughed.

'Or because I am more of a knave than I appear,' said he. 'So let bygones be bygones.' He helped himself to a weighty pinch of rappee, and put down the box with a grave expression. 'I come now,' he said, 'to the supreme crux of all—the apparently damning evidence as to when the fatal shot was fired. If it were fired somewhere about three o'clock, at the time stated by two witnesses, then Hugo Kennett, and none but Hugo Kennett, must be, despite all specious arguments to the contrary, the actual murderer. But it was not fired at three o'clock, as I believe I shall find reason to convince you: it was fired a good twenty or twenty-five minutes later; and this is my justification for saying so. You will remember that, at the magisterial inquiry, the witness Daniel Groome, revising his former evidence, stated that he had heard the clock in his master's study strike the quarter past three—he, by then, having gone round to the back of the house—thereby proving that the report of the gun, which had reached him while he was still at the front, must have occurred during the first quarter of the hour. Now I have taken the pains, since my return, to question Daniel Groome very closely on this matter, and with what result? You will be surprised to hear. The stable clock, to which Daniel is accustomed to listen, strikes the quarters—one for the first, two for the second, and so on. The study clock, to which Daniel is not accustomed to listen, strikes the half-hour only—a single stroke. But the single stroke represented to Daniel the quarter past, and therefore he concluded, when he heard that single stroke sound from his master's study, that it was recording the first quarter, instead of, as it actually was, the second. And on this ingenuous evidence—not realizing in the least what he was doing—was that simple man prepared to tighten the noose about his young master's neck.

'But, if Daniel Groome was wrong, it followed of necessity that Henstridge must be wrong also—as of course he was. He had been simply got at by the detective, and officially bullied and threatened into stating what was wanted of him. As a matter of fact, he had bad no idea of what the time was at all, but had taken any suggestion offered him. The fellow is a blackguard and a coward, and would swear any man's life away for thirty pieces of silver. I did a little persuasion with him on my own account—again during one of those refreshing drives, Sir Francis—and, taking a leaf out of Ridgway's book, had little difficulty in bringing him to his knees. He was abject when I had finished with him. (Parenthetically, I may suggest here—what I am convinced was the case—that our murdering friend had also "got at" Mr Fyler, but in another sense. He had persuaded, I mean, that astute lawyer into believing that there really was nothing worth considering in that hypothetical figure, which we may name the fourth dimension; and that was why, I take it, the point was not taken up again by Counsel before the magistrates.)

'Very well, now: we have got so far as to convict Sergeant Ridgway of murder, following on a plot to disinherit, with the help of a confederate, the very man whom he schemed to charge with the crime. So we arrive necessarily at the question, who was this Annie Evans, whom he had chosen for his accomplice in the business, and whom he had ended by so foully doing to death? To get at the whole truth of the story, it was essential that the mystery of their connexion should be traced to its source.

'To anyone not possessed of the clues which Fortune had placed in my hands, it must have appeared nothing less than astonishing that, with all the wide publicity given to the case, the victim should have remained virtually unidentified and unclaimed. She was beautiful, she was in domestic service—two facts, one might have thought, favourable to an easy solution of the riddle. Still her origin remained a mystery, and so remains, to all but the few instructed, to this day.

'But that very mystery which, to those wanting the master-key, appeared so insolvable, was to me who possessed the key, illuminating. That the girl was in domestic service at the time of her death was no proof that she had ever been in domestic service before. It would be much more in accord with my conception of the astute and far-seeing detective to suppose that he had anticipated that danger of recognition by assigning to his confederate a part through which it would be impracticable, should difficulties arise, to trace her. She had not been in service before, in fact. The business of the photograph confirmed me in that view. You will remember that travesty of Annie's likeness which appeared, enlarged and reproduced from a snap-shot, in the official prints? It was completely unrecognizable, and was intended by Ridgway to be unrecognizable. He knew that no other recent photograph of her existed at all, and for the very good reason that she had not for some time been in a position to be photographed. You will understand why in a moment. It was of paramount importance to him, both first and last, that his accomplice should be and remain unidentifiable. Essential to that condition were her innocence of former service, the absence of any photographic record, and the employment of a false name.

'It was of no use, consequently, my thinking of running Annie Evans, so called, to earth: I must look for her under another title. How was I to ascertain that title?

'It was here again that chance, or Providence, came—I will not say in a totally unforeseen way, but at least in a most obliging way—to my assistance. It occurred to me that at this stage of the proceedings it would be well for me to pay a visit to my Parisian Jean Ridgway, and endeavour to extract from him, if he could be persuaded to part with them, the fullest details possible of the story with whose outline he had already acquainted me. Something, it might be much, I felt, had remained untold which, if revealed, would possibly throw such a light upon the obscure places of my quest as would enable me from that moment to present my case without a flaw. I went—to Paris, Mr Bickerdike; not to London, as you supposed—only to learn from Jean's bosom friend—that Caliste Ribault, of whom I have already spoken—that his loved comrade had departed this life in June of this year. That was a blow, I confess: my hopes seemed baffled, my journey in vain. Yet it was so far from being the case that not the artist's living lips could have more shouted the truth into my soul than did the evidence of his dead hand. I will tell you how:

'One day, shortly before Jean's death, Caliste informed me, there had come to visit him a step-brother, an Englishman, of whom he, Caliste, had never before heard nor Jean spoken. *This step-brother bore the same Christian and surname as Jean*, and he had come accompanied by a girl of such beauty that the dying man could not dismiss the thought of her face from his mind until he had made from memory a coloured drawing of it on the white-washed wall, writing her name beneath. Now, his step-brother being dead, John Ridgway had come once more to arrange about the funeral and the disposition of the deceased's effects, and, perceiving the face on the wall, had been very angry—so angry, that he had immediately seized a cloth and completely effaced the drawing, so that not a vestige of it remained. Why, you ask? You will understand later.

'Thus again Fortune seemed to laugh at me; but it was laughter like that of a mother who dangles over the mouth of her child a cherry—to be his in a moment. And sure enough in such a moment Caliste informed me that, though the picture was destroyed, a copy of it remained in the shape of a photograph which he himself had taken of the original. He showed me the photograph; *and the face I saw was the face of Annie Evans, but Ivy Mellor was the name written underneath*.

'I had found out what I wanted—and more. I had discovered that the two John Ridgways were step-brothers, and light and still light broadened on the path before me. I got Ribault to part with the photograph to me, cautioning him to say nothing about his possessing the negative to anyone, and with my prize I came on the following day to London. Thereafter my task was an easy one. Possessing that face and that name, and associating both with the name of a famous Scotland Yard detective, I had only to place the matter in the hands of a very clever and trustworthy private inquiry agent of my acquaintance to find out all that I needed. His investigations—with the details of which I need not trouble you—yielded the following information:

'Ivy Mellor had been not many months discharged from a reformatory, to which she had been committed for three years for procuring a situation as nursery governess with a forged character, and obtaining goods by false pretences. She was the illegitimate daughter of an actress now dead, and was possessed herself of some decided histrionic ability. Upon her discharge, Ridgway had somehow got hold of her, or had been got hold of by her, with the result that he had fallen a complete slave to her attractions. It was probably she who had been his evil genius from the first; probably she who had planned and perpetrated the "written character" which had procured her an *entrée* to Wildshott. He promised her great things in the event of success, and, in view of those great things, she held him at arms' length; there were to be no questionable relations between them. The man was hopelessly infatuated; he used to visit her under an assumed name; probably "kept her", in the unequivocal sense. I am giving here not only the agent's report, but some of my own conclusions drawn therefrom. Summarized, they showed my case complete, so far as *effect* was concerned. I had only now to penetrate to the *cause*. It could be fathomed, I believed, but fathomed in one direction alone. I determined to go boldly to the fountain-head, and challenge there a decision. In Sir Calvin's hands lay the final verdict. I could hardly doubt what it would be, or that for the sake of the whole truth he would yield at last to daylight the guarded secret of a long-past episode. I judged him rightly, and I need say no more. He told me the story, produced for my examination the written evidence, and left me to deal with the matter as I would.

'But one remark more I have to make before running, as briefly as I can, through the main points of the narrative unfolded to me. While in Paris I had procured from my very good friend, M. Despard, the head of the secret police, an introduction to our own First Commissioner. I saw the latter, confided to his interested, and rather horrified, ears the whole truth of the case, so far as I had then conceived and mastered it, and arranged with him the little trap which was to entice John Ridgway into our midst again—conditional always on my procuring that supplementary evidence which was to prove his guilt beyond any possibility of doubt. The rest you know.

'We come now to the final chapter, which, like the post-script to a lady's letter, contains, in Hazlitt's phrase, the pith of the whole. In relating it I choose my own words, and must not be understood to aim at reproducing the actual terms in which it was revealed to me by Sir Calvin. I wish to give a mere brief or abstract of a painful story, and I wish, moreover, to warn you once more that certain reflections and conclusions of mine, not affecting the main body of the narrative, were and are conjectural, and must so remain unless and until the accused himself shall confirm their accuracy; and that, in my soul I anticipate, will be the case. Here, then, is the story:

'In the early part of the year 1882, Sir Calvin Kennett, then a young cavalry officer of twenty-six, unmarried, and only latterly succeeded to his inheritance, was living in Cairo, attached as military representative to the British legation there. While in that situation he made the acquaintance of a very beautiful young Frenchwoman, Mademoiselle Desilles, the daughter of a tobacconist in a modest way of business, between whom and himself a mutual attachment sprang up, pure and sincere on her part, passionate and unscrupulous on his. Madly enamoured, yet hopeless of prevailing against the virtue of the lady, young Kennett had recourse to the vile and dishonourable strategem of a sham marriage, which he effected through the instrumentality of a worthless acquaintance, one Barry Skelton, who had come abroad in connexion with some Oxford Missionary Society, and who, though not yet in Holy Orders, was supposed to be qualifying himself for the priesthood. With the aid of this scamp the cruel fraud was perpetrated, and Mademoiselle Desilles became the wife, as she supposed, of Sir Calvin. The union, for reasons seeming sufficient as urged by the pseudo-husband, was kept a present secret—even from the girl's father, whose death about this time greatly facilitated the success of the imposture. In July of that year occurred the definite revolt of Arabi Pasha, and the landing at Alexandria of a considerable British force; and Sir Calvin was called upon to rejoin his regiment in view of the operations pending. He went, leaving his wife, as I will call her, in the distant way to become a mother. In a skirmish near Mahmoudieh he lost the first finger of his right hand—a casualty not without its bearing on subsequent events. He was present at Tel-el-Kebir in mid-September, and again, two days later, at the entry of the British troops into Cairo, when he took the occasion—his passion in the interval having burned itself out, as such mere animal transports will—to break the truth to Mademoiselle Desilles of the fraud he had practised on her. I make it no part of my business to comment on his behaviour, then or previously, or to imagine the spirit in which his revelation was received by his unfortunate victim. No doubt each of you can supply the probable text for himself, as his sympathy or his indignation may dictate. It is enough to state the compromise by way of which the deceiver could find the heart to propose to condone his offence. This was no other than that, in order to save her credit and that of her unborn infant, a marriage should be instantly contrived between his unhappy dupe and a certain Quartermaster-Sergeant George Ridgway—a widower with a single young child, a boy—who had been in the secret, yet who, strangely enough, had no more inherent vice in him than was consistent with good nature, a weakness for beauty in distress, and a conscience of the easiest capacity in the matter of hush-money. This man was no doubt a personable fellow; the woman's situation very certainly desperate and deplorable. Anyhow, following whatever distressful scenes, she was brought to consent, the two were married, and shortly afterwards the child was born in London, whither the couple had removed in the interval.

'I am quite prepared to believe that George Ridgway made his wife a good husband during the few years which remained to them in company, for he did not very long survive his marriage. Moreover, Sir Calvin's liberality had placed the two in such comfortable circumstances that no excuse for discontent existed. The Quartermaster-Sergeant adhered honourably to his part of the bargain, and it was not until long after his death that the question arose in the widow's mind as to whether or not she was justified in continuing to mislead her son in the matter of his origin. Of that in a moment.

'In the meantime the two children, step-brothers in fact, were brought up together, and considered themselves as half brothers. They were both christened John—the younger through some unconquerable perversity of the mother in insisting on calling him after her seducer's second name—an anomaly which, however open to curious comment at first, was soon no doubt lost sight of in the inevitable nicknames which affection would come to bestow on the pair. Still, for the purposes of distinction, I will continue to call the one John and the other Jean. Jean was popularly regarded as the Ridgways' child, though in truth no child was born of their union.

'John, though the elder by some three years, was frequently, as time went on, mistaken, by those who did not know, for the younger of the two boys—an error also not without its bearing on subsequent events. Jean from the outset betrayed, if it could have been guessed, an unmistakable sign of his origin in the use of his second for his digit finger—an inherited trick due to the shock caused to his mother by the sight of Sir Calvin's mutilation, associated as it had been with all the agony and despair of that time. He was a dreamy boy, and early developed artistic proclivities. I have no means or intention of tracing the career of either of the children up to and beyond manhood. At some period, as we know, Jean went to Paris; at some period John joined the Metropolitan Police force, with subsequent promotion to a valued position in the Criminal Investigation Department. I pass from these ascertained facts to an estimate of the circumstances which first engendered in the latter's mind a thought of the daring project which has ended by bringing him to his present situation.

'Now I have already told you how Jean, on the occasion of a visit to England, had been at last made acquainted by his mother with the true story of his paternity. She told it him, being herself under the fear of death at the time; and there is no doubt that the poor woman still believed perfectly honestly in the legality of her first marriage, not only before heaven, but on the practical testimony of the little Catholic *vade-mecum* in which the names of the contracting parties, with their clerical witness, had been inscribed. She believed, moreover, on the strength of some muddled innuendo gathered from the Quartermaster-Sergeant, that the creature Barry Skelton had deceived, as much as she herself had been deceived by, Sir Calvin, and that he had actually been an ordained priest at the time of the marriage. It was not true, I think, the ordination having occurred subsequently, as the General took pains to make known to her; for she wrote to him on the subject of the *vade-mecum*, begging him to return it to her hands, whence he had appropriated it when he deserted her. Why, you may ask, had he, after securing possession of, persisted in retaining through all these years that damning witness to his guilt? For the very same reason of the evidence it contained, which to her stood for proof, to him for disproof, of the legality of the marriage. Wherefore he could not make up his mind to destroy it. But he thought it well to pay a visit to his correspondent, to assure her that she was completely mistaken in her surmise, and that the continuance of his support depended upon the utter future abandonment by her of any such attempts on his forbearance.

'Still thinking for her boy, the fond soul was not convinced. So little was she convinced that, when her death came actually to be imminent, she called John to her side and confided to him the whole story, begging him to look after his step-brother's interests, and to vindicate, if possible, his true claim to the name and estates of Kennett, something about which, she told him, Jean already knew. And John promised—she was not his mother, remember; he may have been, for all we are aware to the contrary, a cold and undutiful stepson. But he promised, we know; for he went after her death to Paris, to visit the other, to acquaint him of his mother's end, and to discuss with him the strange story she had committed to his keeping: he went accompanied by a beautiful young creature of his acquaintance—whom he had brought with him probably for no other reason than her pleasure and his own infatuation—only to find Jean himself at the point of death.

'Was it then for the first time that a daring idea began to germinate in his mind? I think so. Whether spontaneously, or at his companion's instance, I believe the conception of the plot dated from that moment. Jean dead, what was to prevent him, John, from personating his step-brother, from claiming himself to be Sir Calvin's son, from profiting by the evidence which was said to prove that son's legitimacy? As to that he had only Mrs Ridgway's word, but it had been uttered with such solemnity and conviction, by a dying woman, as to leave little doubt of its truth. At worst the thing would be a gamble; but there was that in the very romantic hazard of it to appeal to his imagination: at best it would be prosperity beyond his dreams. And what were the odds? To consider them was to find them already curiously in his favour. The similarity of their names; the fact that he himself had always been regarded as the younger; the early death of the Quartermaster-Sergeant, and the consequent long removal of the one most damaging witness to the truth; Jean's prolonged absence from home in a foreign city; his own more apparent devotion to the woman to be claimed as his mother—he could find nothing in it all inimical to the success of the plot. Only the first essential would be to obtain possession of the *vade-mecum*. There was full reason to believe, from what Sir Calvin had told Mrs Ridgway, that the book to this day was jealously retained by him, for the reason stated, in his secure keeping. How to recover it?

'So the conspiracy was hatched. Ivy Mellor was to be the means, the condition of her success the bestowal of her spotless hand upon the rightful heir of Wildshott—a splendid dream, a transpontine melodrama. But John saw at once that a first condition of its success lay in a scrupulous obliteration of all clues pointing to the identity of his confederate: hence his anger on discovering the portrait, and the immediate measures taken by him to wipe it out of existence.

'Well, we know the rest—how the beautiful accomplice betrayed her trust; how she developed a passion for the very man whom she was scheming to disinherit; how, to be sure, she came to recognize that she could much more fully and satisfactorily realize her own ambitions by baulking than by furthering the designs of her fellow-plotter. To be the wife of the problematic heir of Wildshott might be a good thing; to be the wife of the heir of Wildshott *in esse,* a gentleman, a soldier and an Antinous was certainly a better. So, having surrendered to love, she played for the greater stake—and she lost. We can pity her: she was frankly an adventuress. We could pity him, were it not for the thought of that inhuman revenge. Yet he had provocation perhaps beyond a gambler's endurance. To find the very woman, for worship of whom he had been scheming away his position, his reputation, his soul of truth and honour, not only turned traitor to his best interests, but faithless in the worst sense, and for his rival's sake, to her pledge to him—well, one must pause before utterly condemning. And after all it was only a moment's madness served by opportunity. Yes, I can pity him. I have a notion, too, that she told him what was not the truth—that she had already destroyed for her love's sake the evidence of the prayer-book. If she had—it was the last touch. Yes, I can pity him.

'Gentlemen, that is the story.'

M. le Baron ceased speaking, and for a time a silence held among them all. Then presently Mr Bickerdike asked:

'There is only one thing, Baron, which remains to puzzle me a little. Was not Ridgway's employment in the case originally agreed to by Sir Calvin in response to a suggestion of yours?'

'That is quite true.'

'Was Sir Calvin himself, then, never moved to any sort of emotion or curiosity over the association which the detective's name would naturally awaken in his mind?'

'Emotion?—I think not. It would hardly describe a psychology so little superstitious as that of the General. The similarity of the names would have struck him as no more than an inconsiderable coincidence. With all his practical qualities, imagination is the last thing he would care to be accused of. But curiosity?—well, perhaps to a certain extent—though neither deep-seated nor lasting. You have to remember that from first to last, I suppose, he never knew, or troubled to know, what the Sergeant's *Christian* name was; and even had he learned it, it would have conveyed nothing to him, as he knew no better; nor again, probably, had ever troubled to know, by what name his own disowned son was called. And very certainly he had never condescended to note the name of the Quartermaster-Sergeant's individual offspring.'

'I see. And had you yourself, in suggesting the Sergeant for the case, any *arrière pensée* at that time, connecting—?'

'I had merely a curiosity, my friend, to observe the owner of a name—really *ipsissima verba* to me—so oddly associated in my mind with the teller of a certain fantastic story in Paris.'

'Then you did not know—but of course you didn't.' He turned to the Baronet: 'I congratulate you with all my heart, Orsden.'

'Thanks, old fellow,' said Sir Francis. 'It's all due to him there. I'll give his health, in B-Bob Cratchit's words. Here's to M. le Baron, "the Founder of the Feast"!'

CHAPTER XXI

A LAST WORD

Miss Kennett, still in process of qualifying herself for a musician, was at work on Czerny's fifth exercise which, like the *pons asinorum* of an earlier strategist, could present an insuperable problem to an intelligence already painful master of the four preceding. To pick up one note with her was, like the clown with the packages, to drop half a dozen others; to give its proper value to the right hand was to leave the left struggling in a partial paralysis. Still she persevered, lips counting, eyes glued to the page, pretty fingers sprawling, until a sudden laugh at the open door of the room startled her efforts into a shiver of unexpected harmony. She looked up with a shake and a smile that suggested somehow to the observer a bird scattering water from its wings in a sunshiny basin.

'O, Frank!' she exclaimed, and stretched herself with glistening easefulness.

'You p-poor goose,' he answered. 'You'll never play, you know.'

She jumped up with a cry, and ran to him. 'Do you mean it? Are you sure?'

'Absolutely.'

'Would you mind if I didn't?'

'Not half as m-much as I should if you did.'

'But I tried, to please you, you know.'

'But it doesn't please me, you know.'

She looked at him doubtfully. He took her hands, his eyes glowing.

'I love you for trying, you dear,' he said, 'but I shouldn't love you if I let you go on trying—nor, I expect, would anyone else.'

'Pig!' she exclaimed.

'Audrey,' he said, 'you couldn't play when I fell in love with you, so why should I wish you to now? It would never be yourself; and that's what I want of all things. Let everyone develop the best that's in him, and leave affectation to the donkeys. So you'll just come over to Barton's farm with me, to give me your advice about the loveliest litter of bull-pups you ever saw.'

He had something to say to her, and when they were on their way he came out with it soberly.

'I wanted just to tell you—he left a full confession; and—and it showed how the Baron had been right in almost every particular.'

She made no answer for a little; but presently she said softly, 'I think I should like to be the one, Frank, to write and tell him so.'

'Yes, Audrey.'

Again the silence fell between them, and again she broke it in the same tone.

'We heard from Hughie this morning—only a short letter. He wrote from Karachi, where they had just landed. They were going straight on to Rawul Pindi.'

He nodded.

'Now let us talk of something else.'

THE END

Also available

The Black Reaper

Bernard Capes

'And for an hour the Black Reaper mowed and trussed. And before us . . . a fifth of our comrades lay foul, and dead, and sweltering, and all blotched over with the dreadful mark of the pestilence.'

Bernard Capes was celebrated as one of the most prolific authors of the late Victorian period, and his greatest acclaim came from penning some of the most terrifying ghost stories of the era. Yet following his death in 1918 his work all but slipped into oblivion until the 1980s, when veteran anthologist Hugh Lamb first collected Capes's tales of terror as *The Black Reaper*.

Every story bears the stamp of Capes's fertile and deeply pessimistic imagination, from werewolf priests and haunted typewriters to marble hands that come to life and plague-stricken villagers haunted by a scythe-wielding ghost. Now expanded with eleven further stories, a revised introduction and a new foreword by Capes's grandson, Ian Burns, this classic collection will thrill horror fans and restore Capes's reputation as one of the best writers in the horror genre.

Also available

Mr Bowling Buys a Newspaper

Donald Henderson

'I have a book called Mr Bowling Buys a Newspaper *which I have read half a dozen times and have bought right and left to give away. I think it is one of the most fascinating books written in the last ten years and I don't know anybody in my limited circle who doesn't agree with me.'*

RAYMOND CHANDLER

Mr Bowling is getting away with murder. On each occasion he buys a newspaper to see whether anyone suspects him. But there is a war on, and the clues he leaves are going unnoticed. Which is a shame, because Mr Bowling is not a conventional serial killer: he *wants* to get caught so that his torment can end. How many more newspapers must he buy before the police finally catch up with him?

'Henderson pursues a grim little theme with lively perception and ingenuity. His manner is brief, deliberately undertoned, and for the most part curiously effective.'

TIMES LITERARY SUPPLEMENT

Also available

Death at Breakfast

John Rhode

'One always embarks on a John Rhode book with a great feeling of security. One knows that there will be a sound plot, a well-knit process of reasoning and a solidly satisfying solution with no loose ends or careless errors of fact.'

DOROTHY L. SAYERS in *THE SUNDAY TIMES*

Victor Harleston awoke with uncharacteristic optimism. Today he would be rich at last. Half an hour later, he gulped down his breakfast coffee and pitched to the floor, gasping and twitching. When the doctor arrived, he recognised instantly that it was a fatal case of poisoning and called in Scotland Yard.

Despite an almost complete absence of clues, the circumstances were so suspicious that Inspector Hanslet soon referred the evidence to his friend and mentor, Dr Lancelot Priestley, whose deductions revealed a diabolically ingenious murder that would require equally fiendish ingenuity to solve.

'Death at Breakfast *is full of John Rhode's specialties: a new and excellently ingenious method of murder, a good story, and a strong chain of deduction.'*

DAILY TELEGRAPH

Also available

Art in the Blood

Bonnie MacBird

A missing child, a deadly art theft, an unstoppable killer . . .

Sherlock Holmes is languishing and back on cocaine after a disastrous Ripper investigation. Even Dr Watson cannot rouse him, until a strangely encoded letter arrives from Paris. A beautiful French singer writes that her little boy has disappeared, and she's been attacked in the streets.

Racing between London, Paris and the wintry wilds of Lancashire, Holmes and Watson discover the case is linked to the theft of a priceless statue and deaths of several children. The pair must confront a rival detective, Holmes' interfering brother Mycroft and an untouchable suspect if they are to stop a rising tide of murders. The game is afoot!

'Dark, stylish, ingeniously plotted. Holmes and Watson live again.'
HUGH FRASER

Also available

Unquiet Spirits

Bonnie MacBird

An attempted murder, a haunted castle, a terrible discovery . . .

Sherlock Holmes has found himself the target of a deadly vendetta in London, but is distracted when beautiful Scotswoman Isla MacLaren arrives at 221B with a tale of kidnapping, ghosts, and dynamite in her family's Highland estate. To Watson's surprise, however, he walks away in favour of a mission for Mycroft in the South of France.

On the Riviera, a horrific revelation draws Holmes and Watson up to the McLaren castle after all, and Holmes discovers that all three cases have blended into a single, deadly conundrum. To solve the mystery, the ultimate rational thinker must confront a ghost from his own past. But Sherlock Holmes does not believe in ghosts . . . or does he?

'A rollicking tale worthy of Sir Arthur Conan Doyle himself.'
HISTORICAL NOVELS SOCIETY

Also available

Money in the Morgue

Ngaio Marsh & Stella Duffy

Inspector Alleyn just wants to write a letter home to his wife, but his ambitions are thwarted by a daring theft at an isolated hospital on New Zealand's lonely Canterbury Plains. The hospital is crammed with convalescing soldiers – noisy, restless and over-interested in the nurses, who are overtired, underpaid, and desperate for the war to end.

With the electricity lines down, a storm on its way and the nearby river about to burst its banks, the body count in the hospital's morgue begins to rise . . . And Alleyn finds himself stranded with just one night in which to find the thief – and a murderer.

Roderick Alleyn is back in this unique crime novel, begun by Ngaio Marsh during the Second World War and masterfully completed by CWA Dagger winner Stella Duffy.

'Stella Duffy performs a remarkable act of ventriloquism with New Zealand's Queen of Crime. I defy readers to see the join.'

VAL McDERMID